HONEY MINE

HONEY MINE
CAMILLE ROY

Collected Stories

edited by
Lauren Levin *and* Eric Sneathen

Nightboat Books
New York

Printed in the United States
Second Printing, 2022

ISBN: 978-1-64362-074-9

Cover Art: Nicole Eisenman, "Bambi Gregor," 1993.
Courtesy of the artist. Photograph by Los Angeles
Modern Auctions.

Interior Art: Still from ROSEBUD, a film by Cheryl Farthing 1991,
photograph by Della Grace.

Design & Typesetting by Rissa Hochberger
Text set in Fortescue and Avante-Garde

Cataloging-in-publication data is available
from the Library of Congress

Nightboat Books
New York
www.nightboat.org

Contents

"She is the one who inhabits me and who familiarizes me with the universe."

—Nicole Brossard

Dedicated to Angela Romagnoli
(1949–2017)

INTRODUCTION

INTRODUCTION

Hive mind, parlor trick, satchel of dirty love letters turned inside-out: Camille Roy's *Honey Mine* swarms and flexes like a murmur. This is the selected fiction of Camille Roy, a book of urgencies and resistance for queer women and other gender outlaws.

Honey Mine is the most comprehensive selection of Camille Roy's writing to date. This book gathers new and previously unpublished prose alongside hard-to-find publications that capture the intellectual excitement of the 1990's so-called "sex wars," the revolutionary air of ACT UP, and the play of Queer Nation and the growing BDSM scene. Despite the relative scarcity of her early publications, Camille Roy has contributed much to New Narrative's reputation for intelligent, disorienting writing that both addresses real-world political concerns and toys delightfully with pulp techniques and pop culture.

Fans of Camille Roy's writing might know her as a talented and daring playwright, poet, essayist, and prose writer. Her earliest publications were short fictions published in Dodie Bellamy and Kevin Killian's periodical, *Mirage*, and her first published book, *Cold Heaven*, was a collection of plays for Poets Theater. Her genre-bending prose was published in the collections *The Rosy Medallions* and *Swarm* and has been widely anthologized.

In limited edition chapbooks and the magazine she co-edited with Nayland Blake, *Dear World*, Camille Roy participated in the wide-ranging rebuke of the conventional literary establishment, which has continued to overlook the defining contributions of women, queers, and writers of color to the history of literary innovation. For decades, Camille Roy has been pushing and redefining experimental writing, especially (though not exclusively) by and for queer women.

Even so, Camille Roy doesn't offer homilies of queer representation: instead, she gives us queer world-building as a delicious and dangerous secret. Her fictions, with their sexual and gendered awakenings, model (and celebrate!) the liberatory potential of opacity. These stories are populated by characters who have not decided their lives in advance—a position that preserves, even expands, social and political possibility. "As I was folding up my jeans, Isabelle's phone number slipped out of the pocket," the lesbian narrator of "The Faggot" reminsces, "I stared at the tab of white paper, *luscious little thing*. It yanked me somewhere, but I didn't want to go. Why go anywhere? I decided not to call. Then I decided not to decide and slipped the paper back into the pocket." We are brought along, stepping across the threshold of normalcy and into an unexpected new life.

For all its range and wisdom, Camille has described *Honey Mine* as a young book, and it is full of youth's energetic, questioning drive. There are initiations aplenty as protagonists navigate the threats of a hostile, delusional mainstream American life, often finding complicated solace in the various and rich locations of lesbian subculture. The parlor and the bar are their hidden places, promising personal and public revolution.

While this book is not a memoir, it reflects the author's personal history growing up as a "red-diaper baby" on the South Side of Chicago. Migrating from the Midwest to the Bay Area, *Honey Mine* might be read in the American picaresque tradition, as Camille Roy—or an assemblage of avatars—voyages away from sanitized American ideals and into the realities of working-class lives and a vibrant queer demimonde. We anticipate that these stories will now resonate with new readers for their prescient explorations of race, class, gender, and sexuality.

Since her teens, Camille had been attuned to the promise of San Francisco, which she credits to having seen Ntozake Shange's *for colored girls who have considered suicide / when the rainbow is enuf* on Broadway. She made it to San Francisco at last in 1980, and was soon attending the workshops of Gloria Anzaldúa, the first writer she met in the city. Anzaldúa was a mentor who connected the written word with political struggle, and her workshop showcased the writer's witchy charisma, exemplifying her potent blend of poetry, theory, and performance.

Not long after, Camille "wandered off the street," as she puts it, and into the workshops Robert Glück was teaching in the backroom of Small Press Traffic. There, Camille joined a diverse cadre of writers who were playfully experimenting with what would eventually be known as New Narrative. Flagrantly queer, anti-capitalist, and sensitive to intersectional critique, this was a community of writers who sought to record lived experience in all its intensity, complexity, hypocrisy, and glamor. To the workshop table, Camille Roy brought her love for jazz and the early pioneers of experimental lesbian fiction, especially Bertha Harris.

Like her mentors, Camille has also hosted a series of intimate workshops in her own living room, inspiring new generations of writers. Over the months that we met with Camille to discuss her work, we sat with her in the parlor of her Potrero Hill home and were offered delectable foodstuffs, anecdotes of butch-femme revels, and conversation imaginative and analytical. As in the book, there were a lot of good zingers. Camille is a rare combination—a brilliant writer of great confidence and modesty. She was always inquisitive, a fierce truth teller, and deeply kind without any hint of the saccharine.

Thinking of conversations with Camille, we imagine her laughing or making a sharp-edged point; equally, we imagine her listening, poised on the edge of a smile. One feels as though she's eternally eager for the pleasures, interest, or combat to come. That is the atmosphere of this book: wide-eyed without being naive, elegant, and ready for anything. In its specificity, *Honey Mine* is historical in the best sense. It gives us a new vantage on our past and the future on the horizon, and is bound to be a predecessor to so many great queer books as yet unwritten.

And now, we have reached the gateway to Camille Roy's marvelous and perilous world. To everyone reading along with us: *Come on in, honey, the water's fine.*

— LL + ES

AGATHA LETTERS

Dear Agatha,

Is it all point of view? Pleasure, I mean—the surprise in the dark. I suppose it's different for everyone. To Camille it felt empty and fresh, because she was.

She left words out. It wasn't only that she was new at it. *Sex.* It was the business of settling into the body, the one which had arrived with its equipment of muscles and tits and hair about six years earlier. It felt helpless and vivid, but also sensational, a big place accented with childish gestures. A stadium. Was it possible that her body felt like a stadium?

It took getting used to. Which was what she was doing, at her own pace, with minimal use of unfamiliar vocabulary. After dinner on the living room couch, as the roommates swirled in & out, Dusty would say it. For a tease. *Sex*? That word again, slyly reaching into Camille's ear. Camille couldn't stand it. Her fingers butterflied onto Dusty's mouth and pinned those offensive lips together.

Dusty protested with a firm shove, flopping Camille off the couch. Then she fell on top, so the dumb thumbprint of her hipbone prodded Camille in the abdomen. A surge transfixed them both: mutant permission. Girlishly, Camille threw open her legs, clasping Dusty around the shoulders.

Camille felt like a slab of wedded marble, so fucking lavish. The roommates stepped over them, as though ignoring evidence of a slaughter.

Dusty was the whiplash who connected Camille's pieces. Camille was Dusty's little hole through which events streamed. Wordless, in other words. Kisses leapt out of her throat, scribbles leaked from the fingertips. Her hand floated away from her body and covered Dusty's mouth, to prevent any of *those words* from leaking out.

1. What Dusty said was consistent with what Dusty thought.
2. Camille was uptight about just words.
3. Dusty was a woman of action, without regrets.
4. *Irreconcilable differences.*

To get anywhere close to their state of mind I need to empty out the story, so that just the clean gestures of the young are left, brittle and delicious. Their nourishing secrets. . .Then I could claim that nothing mattered to Camille and Dusty except their alert twists through the warm folds of an old pair of sheets, soft as lambskin.

But of course that's not true. Dusty had *legal problems.* After the bust her name had been on the front page of their small town newspaper. Dusty's brother had seen the headlines and called Dusty's mother, who then locked herself in the bathroom and called Dusty.

"I can't believe you've been a. . .you've been a. . .prostitute. . ." she wailed, and broke down into bitter sobs.

As a character, I want Camille to be just a little hole through which events stream. *But she's never little enough.* It's so awkward. Some words flare up from the page. That word whore, case in point. Push it a bit and it opens out into fields of degradation and crime. Which can't be the whole truth. How can a story be true, when it's situated inside distortion?

Camille was an escape artist inside language. *The trick is not getting caught.* This actually works well. The only problem is that you erase your past as you go. I reflected on this the other night as I was driving home, past a long line of dark warehouse doors and tiny, pitted alleys. By the middle of the street I'd drifted into one of those states where this was the only street. The beginning and ending of all streets hung motionless around me as each instant peeled off and fluttered soundlessly into the past. Then I noticed two women standing at the curb. They were sheathed in gleaming body suits, and crimson and yellow boas were piled in snaky coils around their necks. They looked like Vegas showgirls poised to step into a limo, bigger than life, confident in their glittering details. They surprised the darkness. That complexity has always been captivating for me. It's not all the ostrich feathers at once but each separately that charms me, and then my brain starts to fizz. But I was driving. I had to look back at the road.

The feeling had a metallic aftertaste. Otherwise it was just synapses firing according to some schema I'd stored. It didn't add up to either pleasure or pain. Is this melancholy? Or something more inaccessible.

I think of chunks of my past as pieces of brain chemistry. It accounts for how alien they feel, while still being tender. They have moved entirely out of language, into something else—the folds and fissures of this thing I carry around. Luggage between the ears. This story is coming from brain tissue, and that makes it alien and intimate, even to me.

But I'm writing it, and that means I'm taking experience through the fake death which follows artificial life. To me, writing doesn't feel like an act of the imagination. It's more like the sedimentary traces of that act, a kind of cleaning up after the fact. That's all right, at least I can accept it. But then I'm stuck with the question of what gets made when words are piled together. . . This paragraph, for instance. I think it's a dwelling place for a sort of ghost, one who whines, craves visitors, is erotically frustrated. Into this eternal present (which is eternal because it never arrived in the first place), the hapless reader stumbles, turns around in confusion, then crashes through the rear exit. Reading is a kind of crashing through meaning—as the ghost is my witness.

The past sags into ghostliness.

I prefer syllables, on account of what they do to you, Agatha, my dear reader—how they rub your eardrums like tiny rags. All your drums are so clean now. That's how we stay in touch, and I love it, at least in theory.

But I'm getting away from my story. To be honest I'm uneasy with it, especially the hunk of girl love in the middle, steaming and sweet. Camille and Dusty embarrass me. Does the world need more lesbian corn? A writer friend of mine told me, Definitely *not.* I think he was being cruel.

It wasn't a romance. It was this: Camille had risen out of teenage social death like a swamp thing, long hair in knots, her clothes still smelly. As she was still re-learning how to wash, to eat, to talk, she found this girl Dusty. Who had a body like a silky blade. Who was paramilitary when it came to shooting off her mouth. Dusty seemed like a sheriff in an old western, who for obscure personal reasons, had taken up a life of crime. Dusty brought honor to the wrong side of the law. For Camille it was like stumbling into paradise. She had found her flowering shrub.

Yours always,
Camille

Dear Agatha,

Mostly, it's boring to be a girl. You are a prisoner of your girlish appearance. You can't get outside. You are either with all the other girls studying themselves in mirrors as they dream of devouring meat, their own excess flesh, anything to get rid of it permanently, or someone is trying to stuff something weird between your legs. It's one or the other.

I was clear on this. Being a mess gave me a kind of immunity, but it didn't make me stupid. Far from it. In truth, understanding roared inside me as regards to the whole situation of girls, although it didn't quite trouble me, because I ignored trouble even when I was in it. In my characteristically vague but stubborn way, I disregarded the situation of girls. After all, I had never been inside anything, including appearances. I was too skittish.

I never said no, or yes. I trembled constantly, a hungry ghost.

So when I pushed open the pink door of the massage parlor, and found its yellow sateen couch coated with girls and they were wearing bright '70s loungewear and waving cheerfully at me, I leapt over the threshold. I threw myself through the door. As though to the accompaniment of timpani, a drum roll, the cacophony of hormonal triggers. . . It was the summer I turned twenty one.

Some moments are perfectly lurid, but also fresh. That moment rose like a welt from its historical bed and I fell in it.

I was in love with my times, and that meant hate was interesting. Vietnam was over, but it had left residue—the mob in the street, which included everyone I knew. Anyone could join, so we did. Political life was filled with spite, and much of it came from us, or our kind. Each day took place within the margin between the passing hour and imminent collapse, for that was all that many of us believed in. Even the corruptions of the state seemed exhausted. Any small act of rebellion might be the final straw.

It turned private desperation into a kind of festival. I'm digressing now from the specifics of the parlor, but I want to decorate this part of my story with another one, the story of Sara and Sand. Sara was political, in the paranoid style of the times, and Sand was younger, impressionable. Sara became involved in a particularly fierce ideological argument, and when she lost that argument, she claimed the entire revolution for herself. She turned herself into a cause. Sand remained faithful, really she clung to Sara. She became Sara's party of one. For a few months, no meeting or demonstration could occur without Sara and Sand, bitterly silent, striking a pose that conveyed Sara's heroic martyrdom and Sand's abject loyalty. This was widely understood as Sara trying to haunt us with the ghost of her leadership, and it was annoying to everyone. Then, for a few months, they were rarely seen. When Sara surfaced, she announced that she and Sand were going to leave town in a van and travel as gypsy-witch-communists. This was a bit of Sara's trickery, an example of her inclination towards subterfuge, for instead of leaving town, they wrapped themselves in toilet paper and lit it on fire.

Sara went up like a torch and died. Sand lost her nerve at the last instant, and rolled frantically around on the wall-to-wall shag. Still, her ear burned off, as well as the skin on one arm. She lay in a burn bath for a month, then she was shipped home to be cared for by her alcoholic parents.

The war at home. It was luxurious, all that anger. It sprang forth everywhere like the weeds of a wet hot summer in Mississippi dirt. I still miss it. I believed in that anger, in its promises. I got through everything, any grueling adventure, because I was waiting for that anger to finally and completely arrive—a moment when the daily world would shimmer and crack into pieces, a broken mirror, and we would all run into the street, barking like dogs. *Free at last.*

I couldn't separate my ideas from my bad dreams. What was a good idea? A bright skeleton gleaming through burning flesh—but that was Sara. She had ideas. Once I dreamed that she came to my bedside, surrounded by dogs who were baying and leaping and quivering with excitement. I can't remember if she said anything, or just looked into my sleeping face. Then they all ran off, flowing down the stairs in a pack, and out into the silent street. Gone. My eyelids slid up as I felt the pressure of her image.

If it weren't for loneliness I wouldn't have fucked anyone. I didn't want to participate in anything. I wanted to just watch.

I mean, Camille wanted that. And the parlor was the best place for that, for her. . .because, in the parlor, the mouth of the world and the mouths of girls were pressed unusually close together, so the girls got to trick out something precious, something which the world didn't want girls to have: information. *This is how the world works*, baby. Camille wanted her life illuminated by the information which the world told her she couldn't have. And whoring was perfect because it was like life, but more blunt.

The world takes off its pants for every teenage whore. Is that real enough? Camille thought blunt meant no secrets, but she was wrong. There were plenty of secrets in the parlor, just different ones.

I have one photo from those days. It's a headshot of Spark, Timmy, and myself. Looking at the those three heads, grinning mischievous young women, you'd never guess where it was taken. That's why I saved it. I'm always covering my tracks, then going back and uncovering them, whatever that takes. I don't know why. The backdrop in the photo is the burnt orange drapes, tightly drawn, as they always were. Their color seeped into the air, which I breathed over slow afternoons until I felt their burnt orange dusk had filled my lungs. I had long hair then, no particular color, just dark. Its strands spread messily across my face. In the shot I don't look at the camera. My neck is bent awkwardly to the side. It's the same pose I struck in the group photo of the field hockey team in the high school yearbook. Just being visible embarrassed me.

Spark is in the middle. The photo was cropped just where her chest began its steady and inevitable rise. Her breasts were like mountains of good health, perfectly formed, capped with perky nipples. They made her, as we used to say, "popular." That, and her calm. Her style epitomized a Midwestern version of eternal Mom, and it worked on everyone, not just the clientele. Her nasal twang would be ringing with irritation and yet girls would still come up and nudge her, like needy puppies. Timmy was one such girl, tiny and Black, and in the photo her chin is pressing up against Spark's shoulder. Timmy's eyes are closed. She's been snapped mid-giggle. Someone was making us laugh.

We laughed a lot. I remember that. We laughed the way a cat sprays. And it was the same idea: marking territory. I wish I could remember the joke. Who told it. How it fit into all the other pieces of that particular day. Was it winter or summer that afternoon? Was I really there, if I don't remember these things?

Camille. The name feels like an accident repeating itself through this story, even as the girl attached to me through that name remains somehow indecipherable. She won't turn to look at me. She has urgency, but not in relation to me—her future. That feels unfair. I want to tell her she's just stuck in the past. But I sense she chooses to be indifferent, and that wounds me. Why would it be otherwise? What would attach her to me, now that her suffering has gone off, who knows where, like a flock of birds. I can't believe this has happened: I'm too old for her. Yet my investigation disturbs something—a body, vacated. Its nerves are tender but stupid, its silky exposed organs radiate a thing like pain. Perhaps it's just information.

Camille sprouted everywhere, like weeds. She was the product of too many accidents. It's true that I erase and embellish and even lie in everything I write about her, but I don't think she would mind.

Sincerely,
Camille

Dear Agatha,

I learned: to feel comfortable. To wash regularly. To come for Dusty every single time.

You have to give happiness its due, the moments when you were on top of everything, quivering. Even if that was a mistake! You won't believe me, of course. But I thought all the elements of my life were wholly contained by the imagination of God. I had a terrific feeling of being inside that, and outside everything else. I guess that's one way of saying that my sense of belonging was ecstatic.

Is paradise just being protected by the right idea? My stubborn happiness ignored every crisis & required only Dusty. The strangest thing I had for her, the one new quality I'd never given anyone before, was loyalty. Inexhaustible, dumb, & sexy.

Our difficulties continued. After the parlor bust, the incest secret blew up. Incredible destruction. One night, after a movie, her mother asked her about the stepfather, and Dusty told the truth. That was the beginning of the disclosures—Dusty had six siblings, and she told them one by one.

I was there when she told Clarence, her second youngest brother. We were in Spark's yard, sitting around her flimsy card table. My silence was complete, almost breathless. The day was hot and moist. Clarence sagged when he heard. Shock revealed the terrible forward momentum of normality; losing it was like dying. I watched him become estranged from himself the moment he realized: *My father is a child molester.* Blood drained from his face as he peered down at his plate and teacup.

Mostly her siblings tolerated the news, swallowed it whole, without visible disturbance. The strongest reaction was the sob, *Let go of the past and stop disturbing our family.* Dusty said this was normal, even though the stepfather was a real predator, cornering Dusty every week when Mom was at bridge club & raping girls in the neighborhood.

One night, Dusty's mom called and wailed into the phone.

"Oh Dusty I couldn't say anything to him. I tried and I couldn't. I'm going to poison him. I'll get a book out of the library on poisoning, that's what I'm going to do. I swear it to you, Dusty."

Afterwards, Dusty sat there on the bed, expressionless. Then she toppled over. The sobs that barreled out of her mouth sounded like nothing I had ever heard. . . blasts of wind. I lay down next to her and put my hand where her rib cage throbbed. A calm entered me which felt like love, but also resembled neutrality. I sunk into it with relief. Eventually Dusty's sobs became shudders, which slowly faded away.

Dusty sat up and grabbed the phone.

"He should give me money. I want to call him. I'm going to ask for money."

"Blackmail him. It's a public service announcement. Tell him if he doesn't pay you off you'll leaflet the school where he teaches. Leaflet the neighbors. Put up a billboard. Everybody should know he's a child molester."

"I can't do that. What a fucking lot of work. And my family will hate me."

"They hate you already."

Dusty handed me the second receiver and then dialed. She wanted a witness I guess, or just support. I felt a guilty interest. I was going to listen to the perp talk. I'd be secretly observing him in his monster life.

"Hi Dad."

He grunted. I pictured an overweight white dude in a recliner, probably in boxer shorts, relaxing out on the screened-in porch. I'd never met him but I'd seen a photo in which his sour face floated above a roomful of lively kids. His tiny eyes sucked up all the light. He didn't like kids but he sabotaged Dusty's mom's birth control, so she'd had five with him, plus there were two from her first marriage: Dusty and her brother Seth. Dusty he had molested and Seth was the punching bag. From Dusty's brief and reluctant descriptions, I imagined the stepfather as sullenness in a wad, until he crashed down and silenced everyone: *Shut up or I'll give you something to cry about.*

"Dusty? What do you want?"

"I want money."

"What are you talking about?"

"I'm going to need lots of therapy after what you did to me."

"I don't know what you're talking about."

"Yes you do. You molested me, what was it—hundreds of times? When mom went to bridge club. When she went to bingo. Every chance you got."

"That was years ago. I've moved on. You should move on."

His voice was nasal. The only emotion it conveyed was resentment. What kind of person was this, drenched with sullenness—*drip, drip.* He didn't deny anything. Was it not even important enough to lie about?

"Money."

"Anything I give you comes right out of your mother's pocketbook. You want to deprive your mother of her basics, just because you haven't been able to let go of your miserable childhood? I'm not giving you a cent."

Your miserable childhood. Dusty was silent. Her face had

emptied out. Then she took a deep breath.

"I've told everyone."

"What do you mean?"

"I've told Mom and all the kids exactly what you did to me and the girl down the street too."

He was silent. When Dusty was a kid he'd threatened more than once to kill her mother if she told anyone.

"You're sick and now everybody knows it," Dusty said.

Then she hung up.

"Well you did it," I said. "You told him."

"Yeah. The asshole won't kill anybody. He's too old. I'm out of the house. And everybody knows."

"Right."

My love was so selfish and perfect that I could handle anything. Dusty's grief streamed into it. She became strange in her eating habits, restricting herself to boiled spinach and boiled eggs and seeds. She got thinner. I remained serene.

There were books on love in the parlor which had been left by a retired lawyer named Albert. He'd leave them behind, like droppings. It was Albert's higher calling, spreading the message of his love guru, Leo Buscaglia.

Once I flicked through the pages.

Real love always creates, it never destroys.

. . .

Love is open arms. If you close your arms about love you will find that you are left holding only yourself.

. . .

Love is a warm and wonderful encounter. . .with Leo Buscaglia.

What I had was so good I felt cruel. A little room opened in my brain & started showing movies, which I could almost ignore or turn off, but not quite. Mostly the images were of a knife stabbing a soft white belly sprinkled with hair. No face, no sound. I wanted to do it.

I told Dusty what was going through my head.

"Life goes on, even for psychos. My problem is not your problem," Dusty said.

"But if anyone could kill him, I could. I'm the one."

"Listen," said Dusty, "I have a sense of justice. So shut up."

It was true. Dusty preferred justice like some people prefer the color yellow. It seemed arbitrary but there it was.

I walked around just doing my business and sometimes the movies played and sometimes they didn't. It made me feel like a somewhat abstract personality. Still, my love thickened its root. It stunned me. I was so happy. Love, love, love.

Sincerely,
Camille

Dear Agatha,

Mostly I remember the people. Brandy for instance. Brandy was the one who led everyone right into trouble, when it was festive, like discovering money. She had a parched thinness that was underneath gender, deeper than that split, eviscerated & sexy. She was Peter Fonda incarnated as an elongated girl.

Her band used to play on Friday nights. I picture her as I write this: Brandy on the bass guitar in a dark corner of the stage wearing a pair of mirrored aviator shades that she swore were vintage sixties.

Karen was the one who taught me about information. That it was there; all I had to do was ask. I was shocked, and weirdly honored, and giddy at that brink. She nailed capitalism; union organizing; the correct political line on sex work. She told me who was blowing who and for what. She gave me a copy of *Pedagogy of the Oppressed.*

Karen was a fiend for organizing, really a genius. She didn't get caught up in the parlor bust because she was at a meeting to organize a transit workers union. But she planned the whole defense.

In her schoolgirl white blouses and wool skirts, Karen didn't look anything like what she was: prostitute, communist, queer. She had that helpless genius incongruity with her own body. Towards the end of her life she began wearing knee-high boots with her skirts. On Karen, stacked heels and stubby toes looked like an odd racy flowering of femininity, a bit of a shock. It seemed she was edging towards something new. But she always drove herself with such urgency and then one day there was an accident on an icy road.

The one political cause Karen never mentioned was animal rights. It may have been the most important. I found out about this when I went to her farm, for some organizing meeting. I'm not sure why I went. I was only a body at various events, I never organized a thing. But I piled into the pickup with Dusty and Brandy.

On the way, Brandy told me that Karen's dad had a slaughterhouse. He forced his kids to work in it.

"Blood flowing in the gutters. Body parts swinging from the rafters. So now she's got fifteen rescue cats and six rescue dogs. A 500 pound rescue pig, a pony, a cow. She feeds their tumors," Brandy said, with relish.

Dusty gazed soberly ahead. This whole campaign was mostly to get her off and today she was serious about that. I felt her thigh solid & warm against mine.

As soon as we walked in the kitchen, Karen handed Dusty a paper. At the top scrawled and underlined was the heading *Three Pronged Resistance.* And there were three columns drawn, with subheadings: Provocations, Events, Celebrities.

Then she noticed me. I thought her eyes scrambled. I was such a nobody I guess. Politically I mean. I hadn't done anything, I didn't register.

"I have a pony. Her name is Sparkle. Not that it matters, Sparkle doesn't come to Sparkle, if you know what I mean. You can ride her if you want."

I went out to the barn to meet my new pony friend. I felt fine-tuned and fatalistic and full of deadly curiosity, but no one else seemed to notice this. Bitterness of youth! Stuck with nature for conversation!

But this is more true: *so happy to be there.* After a month of awkwardness, Dusty had become a sturdy sexual partner, so believable that I sunk deeper into my love-state, pliant and yet grounded: muddy. Sweaty and unclean, or not, I woke up feeling nude. Smooth.

It was brilliant outside. The morning rain clouds had scattered and sun shone down upon the clover underfoot. The breeze was soft as lotion, almost sickening. I kicked at the mud rivulets which scored the road down to the barn. My boots, lifting up, slurped.

The barn door was a pocket door, the kind that disappears into the wall. I pushed and the door slid smoothly away, releasing manure and animal sweat. There was rustling inside. When I got used to the darkness, I walked around. The pig was in a stall that bore a nametag: Tony. He was nearly as big as a bull. Tony's eyes were tiny but he regarded me with a skeptical intelligence. He stood with a kind of nobility, a whole pig country, midway between a pile of clean straw and a puddle of manure. The cat mewing at my feet had no eyes at all.

The pony was drowsing in her stall, ears askew and eyes half closed.

"You're coming with me," I told her.

I didn't notice the tumor until I'd gotten her tied up in the hall. A dark knotted growth, bigger than a grapefruit, distended from her stomach. Was this alarming thing going to flop around? I squatted to stare at it. Black mane-like hairs sprouted from among the wrinkled folds. It appeared to be firmly attached. The pony ignored me, dozing, her tail lazily slapping a fly now and then.

If it jiggled during the ride I couldn't feel it. Bareback we went through the meadows which were lush and deep. Grasses stroked the bottom of my boots. There were clouds in big white piles and biting flies fell from the sky. Sparkle and I went off down a tractor trail that eventually led through a glade of cottonwoods to the Pontiac River. There the diseased pony drank the muddy water while I warbled an old Beatles song: *Love is all there is, love is all there is,* or something.

After the ice storm the following January, when Karen's Toyota landed upside down in a glade of leafless birch, breaking her neck, the hardest part of wrapping things up was Tony. The other creatures were placed, including Sparkle, who got to be a companion pony. All Sparkle had to do to earn her keep was to plod around and eat grass in the pasture of a valuable and nervous thoroughbred. Poor, smart Tony. He went to the slaughterhouse. Who can take on a 500 pound pig?

Agatha. I picture you laying this letter flat upon the plank table in your screened-in porch. It's destined for the pile at the back of a desk drawer. But you will read it thoughtfully, as you sip tea from a steaming little cup. To your right is a stone teapot—flecked black and white granite from the quarry near Northgate. What awed quarryman was moved to make that for you? You flavor your smoky tea with dried elk berries and garden mint, which you particularly savor during a fast. Don't tell me I'm wrong. Our tastes differ; I've taken that into account. You rest on the verdict of your experiences and have chosen restraint. Whereas I walk around on mine like a fly on the screen, dazed by the heat.

You see, Agatha, our livelihoods were more lively than substantial. Being a criminal is hard work (so I've been told).

I can love that time only in retrospect. I have a photograph of Camille in which she leans against a brick wall, her eyes closed. She's wearing a knit cap in summer. I know she's got a strange image of herself—flooded with disrespect. But it barely matters, because she's got the coating of youth, that impervious rubber blanket. Do you think she's as beautiful as you were? I would say—almost. True, she's a little thin, but that gives her a bony charm, oddly spacious, as though she's been gently pulled apart. That's something you might understand.

Sincerely,
Camille

THE FAGGOT

Pearl put down the knife she was using to slice carrots, then picked up the cigarette balanced on the rim of the sink. She took a drag and sighed, eying me carefully.

—Start packing, kiddo. This summer you're going to be staying with the Budds.

Oh Mom. . .A whine went off in my brain, but I kept it zipped. For a moment we both watched her smoke drift under the kitchen light. Then I chose a wry tone and one of Pearl's own favorite expressions.

—So, this is the cutty sark. . .

She jabbed the cigarette at me.

—It'll be great. They've got stuff. Horses. Peacocks. Kids your age. I dunno, livestock. . . A lizard! Willie spent three years in prison for draft resistance during the Korean War.

She said that with pride. Most of Pearl's closest friends had spent time in prison, usually for something political.

—Anyhow, they live in an old mining town, high in the Rocky Mountains. Ruby Ridge it's called. Derelict—she grinned at me—but cultural. Mina Loy just moved there. The poet Mina. I hope you get a chance to meet her.

Pearl paused, suddenly wet-eyed, moved by my opportunity.

I felt a broad and pointless caution. I shuffled to my room and began to pack, stuffing all my blue jeans into a pillowcase. Then I took a bath. Through the steam I stared at the Mina Loy poems Pearl had thumbtacked over the patches of mildew on the bathroom wall. What if I met her. Would I tell her that my mother had covered her poems in saran wrap so we could read them in the bathtub? Mina, the lost poetess, beloved by Pearl. I attributed this love to Mina's life, which went up in a bohemian blaze whenever Pearl talked about it. Fiery truths. I couldn't like the poems, but I was attached to their difficult sounds, which made them seem to glint from under their coating of steamy saran wrap.

A tempered tool
of an exclusive finishing-school
her velvet larynx
slushes

Pearl drove fast, grim with the task of moving my body over one thousand miles, across the inland sea of parched grass and shimmering heat. But she looked smart, in an orange cotton shift with black marks like paw prints; it was Finnish. At night she rinsed it out in the motel sink. By morning it was as dry as a bone and hung stiffly over her tanned & slender knees.

I licked my arm when we left Nebraska. The hot wind had replaced sweat with tiny crystals of salt. I was being dumped. *What a late blooming baby.* Soon I would be in a place where the air was so pure it sparkled. How was it possible? I felt a melancholy nostalgia for Chicago's dismal intimacy of block by block racial tension. Vacant lots soaked with lead and streets of abandoned warehouses.

Gray blue hills rose at the horizon. White streams tumbled in a blur. When the Mustang lurched up for the long climb, Pearl began telling stories about the town. About the Budds. Her stories were for the eye, like movies, and that reliable. I never listened so much as watched. But this time I closed my eyes, dozing as she spoke.

It was familiar, at first: Industrial ruin. Towering gray skeletons next to heaps of slag. The mines had been abandoned for fifty years and the dumps were feathered with grass clumps. Pearl had wandered there by herself, looking for silver nuggets. Surely the tens of thousands of miners who came and went like a flash flood must have left a few pieces of silver behind. She'd found bullets. In the meadow below her, the Budds were picking wildflowers. Newlyweds, they gave bouquets to each other. They were happy because Willie Budd had just gotten out of prison and they'd scraped together the cash to buy a lodge in town. It cost next to nothing—after all, the town was almost abandoned. It was falling apart. You could have bought half the houses for a couple hundred in back taxes, and that would include a small opera house, and a mansion whose wide staircase was built with Virginia oak.

I woke up when a damp wave entered my nostrils. It was the sweat of gardens. Pearl drove slowly as our stares swiveled from one side of the road to the other. We were in town, and it was not what we expected. Each house had porches and neatly whitewashed gingerbread trim, and all the lawns were thick. We passed a park with a gazebo and an American flag snapping in the wind, over beds of marigolds and daisies.

—It's changed, Pearl said.

The Budd Lodge faced a dusty pine thicket. I left Pearl at the car and walked under the trees, past cages of birds and scattered old mining spools to a red sprawling building. I followed the steep flagstone steps down to a dim basement kitchen. A girl stood by the table, humming along to the worst song of the summer, Alice Cooper's "Only Women Bleed." I grimaced some sort of smile, and the girl's soft eyes turned to me. Her lower lids were rimmed with tears. If she put her hand in mine, I suspected it would be wet.

—Hello, you must be Camille, she mumbled.

That was Willa Budd. We bonded as though we'd been Krazy Glued. It happened instantly, although it was new to me, the deep and sticky bonds of girls, leaking fluids. It's easy to get the wrong idea. Gloom gives a girl plenty of room and we didn't talk much. Mostly, I extracted the local gossip from Willa's weary mumbles. And Shane was there—from the beginning he was part of our cloud. That morning in the kitchen, he'd eyed me silently from the couch, although I hadn't seen him. He didn't bother to greet me because Willa was doing that. They were twins. Shane was older by a breath.

Whatever you have the nerve to do, I will also do. Things happened and swallowed me up. I wiggled up waterfalls after Willa and Shane, to find blasted valleys and cliffs crumbling to dust under our feet. If a few tiny trees hung to a cliff, we would stop scrambling and eat our sandwiches there. I grazed on tiny blueberries and strawberries and mushrooms, drank from creeks that tasted like mineral snow. Mountains hung over us like relatives, the ones who hate you, their gray craggy faces threaded with ice. Big silences, with clouds.

It suited me somehow, but Willa especially, because she loved rocks. Just loved them, incomprehensibly. She knew a lot of geology, but it was deeper than that. This love was in her big feet and her tawny yellow eyes and the slump in her shoulders. At fifteen, she was already almost six feet tall and she would stoop to pick up any ugly pebble we passed. Then she'd tell us a story about it, talking so slowly and for so long that I'd use the chance to throw myself on the ground and gasp for breath. I got used to altitude eventually. I even learned a thing or two about rocks.

I'm getting ahead of myself. I need to start at my spot, which was the couch in the kitchen. That's where I slept, restlessly, due to the babbling fish tank and the slurping hot water pipes under the floor. The whole Budd apartment was a snaky linoleum lined tunnel under the Budd Lodge, and it ran into interference from plumbing and wiring. That first night, as I was dozing off, an iguana crept into the blue flickering light of the fish tank and eyed me, pumping up and down a few times. Then he crawled behind a pile of magazines, his tail still visible. I stared sleepily at the lizard tail, a bright green snake except for the gray stub at the tip, where it had been broken. Fish shadows drifted across the heated yellow floor, dreamy disturbances from the animal world.

Mrs. Marian Budd's "Good Morning" chirp yanked me out of my sleep. It was just after dawn when she hustled to a corner of the kitchen table and began throwing things together. Baking. I sat up to watch, pulling my blanket around my shoulders. A woman of great height, she could cook without moving her feet. Cupboard doors all around her were opening and slamming. Ingredients flew together. She had a soft mouth and thick arching eyebrows, and even when she smacked the bread dough it was with an awkward tenderness.

—It's only bread, she said, as if I were worrying about it.

Mrs. Marian Budd plucked handfuls of dough and dropped them in boiling oil. She called these scones; they were breakfast. Their dreamy odor called forth every family member. Willa, in an orange quilted bathrobe and fluffy slippers, shuffled up into the kitchen from her bedroom in the cellar, which she shared with hundreds of jars of home canned apricots, peaches, jams. She huddled at the breakfast table. Shane walked through, grabbed a handful, and left.

I got my scone and a cup of coffee and retreated to my couch. Willie came in, swinging his arms with gregarious pleasure. His voice boomed but his body was small. He was talking about his newest horse, a black thoroughbred mare with floppy ears. She was progressing nicely. He'd found her by a road wrapped up in barbed wire and bleeding to death, and bought her on the spot for forty bucks. Next spring, he was going to breed her to an Appaloosa stud and train the foal for the tracks.

All the magazines piled on the floor next to my couch were about horse racing. Not the regular kind—Appaloosa. I paged through *Appaloosa Stud* and stopped at a full-page, full-color ad for a spotted little stallion with a well-muscled rump. Stud service? Try This Sleek Little Jackrabbit.

Who would have guessed? Appaloosas were bounding all over the county tracks of Montana, Wyoming, and Colorado. I learned there was such a thing as Appaloosa Racehorse of the Year, and it came with a thousand dollar prize and a trip to Vegas. It turned out Willie had even bred a winner, a fast and vicious mare named Sparkle Plenty. She swung her head like a club, teeth bared, whenever anyone got near her. He sold her before she won the prize.

Horse racing, on the cheap. I was fascinated. One night after dinner, as I sat hunched on my couch, sketching the family tree of last year's Appaloosa Racehorse of the Year, Shane walked over to me.

—Hey faggot, he said, his big boned face and body leaning over me. I looked up at him, mystified. His hair was the color of sand.

—Faggot, he repeated. We're going out to the bar tonight. Are you coming?

There was a silence during which Willa examined a ring on her finger and didn't look up. Finally, she said softly,

—They let us in if we go up the backstairs.

I went. The faggot went to her first bar. It was called Mountain Fish Joint. A huge rainbow trout was mounted on the wall, so old its scales had peeled back and glistened like cellophane fur. Men in beards and flannel shirts loomed in the smoke. Their faces were red and they laughed furiously. I turned around and around, one moment after another sprinkled with the lemon pepper of dread and adrenaline. Willa and Shane were walking stealthily as panthers, their shoulders slumped. That's what I imagined, anyway. Willa stopped next to a guy and the color drained out of her face. Their shoulders touched. His big black framed glasses hung crooked on his face and he had those lean muscles that looked like they'd popped up overnight and grabbed him, causing him pain. He scowled and shoved his glasses back up his nose.

Then Shane grasped the tender point above my elbow with his thumb and forefinger.

—Faggot, he whispered, it's a good time for you to learn how to play pool.

He steered me to the back, to the pool table which looked soft as pasture under the layer of smoke.

Sullenness rose like a wad across my face. I pointed myself at this task like any girl of the street. I got good enough at it to beat him after a few games. I guess that bored Shane, for he retired, and I started playing various drunks. Mostly, I won. I only stopped because my last opponent, a guy with a cowboy hat and a Texas drawl, sprayed something bright pink onto the green felt. We all stared, amazed, as it foamed up, even the Texan who'd produced whatever-it-was, bubbling with stomach acid. Tequila, possibly. Then Shane bought me a beer.

The reaction happened later. After we'd all gotten home, and I locked the bathroom door. Most of the time my brain is a sealed chamber but then something happens, the tiniest pinprick, and it leaks in, flooding everything, like, uhh, puffs of squid ink. Dread and horror tumble, tiny twins, down every rung of my spine. *Fag, no way,* I told myself. *What does that mean anyhow, for a girl?* I stared at my face, brows floating up across a pointlessly high forehead, a long skein of greasy hair down my back. It was braided, the loose strands tucked behind my ear and kept back with a rolled-up kerchief. My headband. I was very attached to it. I'd started with it back home after a neighborhood boy declared his love on the wall outside my bedroom window. They were just kids I ran the streets with: Paul, a foster child, so light-skinned I think he was mixed, and Shaquille, who tried to walk like he was street—a lope and a roll of the shoulders and a lope and a roll and a lope. . .They were standing on the wall below my window, sweet as pecan pie. When Shaquille got to the *Would ya be my girl* stuff, Paul crumbled in giggles and fell off into the bushes. That's when I hit the bed, flattered and terrified. I was so deeply not interested.

Today I don't think it's so different. Being a dyke. It helps you get over being a girl, but so does whoring, or professional sports. Back then I thought I was smelling my own death, and what do you do with that? Perhaps, during that moment in the mirror, I realized that I was in fact a lucky girl, to have lived in a neighborhood so rough and distracted by racial tensions that there was more room than usual for junior homosexuals. But I doubt it. I was too distracted by my new situation. The headband that no one noticed at home drew reactions here. Like Shane's first words to me: *Welcome home, Pocahontas.*

Cloud Boy

Spooky as I was, I loved the mescaline. It came from Cloud Boy.

I met him at Callie's, where the door was always open. All day, Callie tipped elegantly in her spike heels back and forth from the bed, with its view of the television, to the window of her tiny manager's unit in the Budds' new motel. Over the fistfuls of pansies stuck in the window box, she exchanged guest money for keys. She always wore black. It sent a message: formerly of the Hells Angels. She was open about this. It had intrigued Willie Budd. He'd hired her on the spot, without references.

The place had been a worn-out motel called The Skunk. The Budds hammered up white wooden icicles and window boxes, planted a few spruce trees out front, and then reopened under the name Tyrolean Villas. Willa, as the Budds' only daughter, was obliged to be the motel maid. Every morning in a fury she'd head to the Tyrolean Villas, rip the sheets off the beds, and collect the tips that were spending money for the day. Then she'd stop off at Callie's unit. Shane would already be there, sprawling out over most of the floor. Willa would flick on the tube and lay next to him as they watched the day's episode of their horror soap opera, *Dark Shadows.*

By the time I showed up, Willa was too absorbed to acknowledge me. She was eyeballing a television screen washed with spooky fog and a gleaming black river. There were moans off-screen, then the camera moved in on a terrified actor. Splash. Willa loved this stuff. *Dark Shadows* was her daily horror pulse.

Callie came in, jiggling keys. As soon as she sat on the bed, Shane jumped up next to her and lay his head down in her lap. Absentmindedly, she stroked his hair and his grin was full of joy.

—Whatta puppy you are, said Callie. He stuck his tongue out and panted, then pulled Callie's head down, her long black wavy hair covering everything but his fingers.

Her skin was pale and tender as the underbelly of something wild, not to be touched. I couldn't stop watching her. Maybe she was on the run from a nasty biker boyfriend, but she seemed too cool for that. Cool as the devil. She was the witchiest woman I'd ever met and not because she believed in the earth goddess. Callie was at least fifteen years older than Shane and twelve years older than her other boyfriend, Cloud Boy.

Dark Shadows was getting really good. A stabbing. Shane slid off the bed and hit the floor next to me as the camera closed in on a big ghoulish face that opened out into screams every time the knife entered his chest. His teeth shone like gray pearls. Eyeshadow ran down the gutters in his cheeks. We huddled around the screen as Callie folded up some bills and put them in a box on her dresser. That was when the door swung open and Cloud Boy came in.

He strode up behind Callie and gave her a teddy bear hug, a smacking kiss on the neck.

—Sweetie PIE, said Cloud Boy. How's my girl?

In his big hands, she was as still as a tiny porcelain figurine. But soft, unimaginably relaxed. He nodded in my direction; his eyebrows bobbed.

—Howdy. The name's Cloud Boy.

—Cloud Boy, I said slowly, remembering. Willa told me about your, uh, group therapy?

—Yeah. Our group leader was trained by Werner Erhard himself.

—That means no bathroom breaks. They're not allowed to pee during group, Willa said. Her eyes didn't stray from the screen.

—You can't leave the room. It's resistance. Nothing works if you resist. That's something we learned.

Cloud Boy was bright in a dumb way, a boy light bulb. Willa had told me he was supposed to inherit a million in six months, when he turned twenty-one, but there would be nothing left. Mom was on a spree. She had been for years. So, Cloud Boy sold drugs for pocket money. Drugs were the patch of ice under the lumbering Volvo of the town class structure; anyone could skid up, or down, or slide all around. People were either flipping burgers for tourists, or in this other group. Trust funds. Mostly it was the burger flippers who were selling drugs to the people with high class cash. But Cloud Boy's tracks were greased, and he could go anywhere.

—Look what I've got for you kids, he'd say, tenderly.

Then he would chop and divvy up his line of good earthy mescaline, which oozed over hours and hours.

Late one night, tripping, Willa and I followed Shane into an Aspen grove. The trees were white stems and the leaves shivered, sounding like music that had broken into tiny pieces. Shane was jumpy. He insisted that all these trees had Aspen Rot. That, he said, was a black succubus which attached to the white papery bark of the trunk and then slowly rotted out the inside of the tree. He pointed out the black circles that were dotted everywhere on the slivery trunks. Dead branches stuck out from their centers like arrows in a target. He broke one off and gave the tree a hard push. It tore through the canopy and crashed to the ground. We all started pushing trees. They fell with a soft sickening rip of roots through soil. We pushed over a whole rotten forest.

Party

After *Dark Shadows*, Willa and I went down to the pasture and jumped on the backs of a couple of the Budds' scrappy Appaloosas. Beating their sides with our heels, with sticks, we got the old quarter milers to race. It felt like one big throb. Maybe it's always like that, when you're on an ex-racehorse and he knows you're asking for speed. My shadow drifted along like the shadow of a plane, but my body was caught in the roar of takeoff, with the thud of hooves and wind and rocks thrown up and to the side, as one leaping stride after another ended in hard dirt.

One day, for a change, Willa hopped up on the old swayback mare, Maxine. I got on behind her, and then we galloped bareback up and down the meadow, the old horse wheezing. After a while Maxine got fed up and bucked us off. We sailed through the air and hit the ground with my hands still around Willa's waist. The mare yanked at some tall grasses and eyed us evilly. Willa sat up and dusted herself off.

—There's a party tonight up on Red Hill, Willa said.

We walked up to the party. It was a cool blue evening and the crickets were out. The view was so big you could fall through it, the whole valley gaping and shadow-streaked at our feet, dark in its cracks, under a haze of orange dust. Strings of barbed wire sagged at the edges. Laid down carefully in the red dirt was an asphalt road, oily and smooth. It fed driveways to hidden houses, built to suck in the million-dollar view.

—That's the lot Elton John bought.

Willa pointed out a slope of broken rock, tipped with a cloud of Indian paintbrushes, weedy tufts of red and coral and pink and orange, poking up between the stones.

—After he bought it, he sued his neighbors for having a cow.

She snapped a grass stalk, chewed it.

We found the driveway and walked down it towards a building made of heavy cedar logs. The door opened soundlessly, and Willa and I slipped in, to smoke and the smell of tequila. The young crowd flowed nervously over low couches and Indian rugs.

—That's the hostess, Willa said under her breath.

There was a chair carved with gargoyles and Gothic crosses, all black, fifteen feet high. The woman sitting in it was waving at me. Actually, she was waving dreamily at the crowd, like a beauty queen in a car. Her smile was stretched so tight she could have been wearing a nylon over her face, like a bank robber. Face lifts?

—She's incredibly old, I whispered to Willa.

Was that why everyone seemed grabby? Half full drinks were everywhere, as were glasses overflowing with butts. Willa didn't hear me; she'd found someone and his hand was on her shoulder. Snag. She slowed down, distracted, that awkward drag across her face, creamy and horrible.

I went off to look for Shane. I found him telling a story to some girls. His eyes were blurry as his big hands sliced through the air.

—Dude was wearing a monster Navajo belt buckle; the biggest one I ever saw. He's a belt buckle collector. He told me he's a Republican. A law-n-order man, anti-taxes. This guy is the biggest coke dealer in the state, and he has two miniature poodles, he calls them Spunk and Junk.

The girls tittered. I fled to the yard. Party sounds sagged in the crystal-clear air.

—Rod Stewart fucking kills me, I muttered.

—What?

It was a girl's voice. I took a suck off my beer and wiped my mouth and continued,

—I can't stand it. Spunk and Junk. Poodles?

—You're too sensitive.

—My mom told me this town used to be artistic. . .

—Hey I'm a musician. A violinist. I'm at the summer music school.

The girl had a head of rolling black hair and was wearing something orange, like a dress. I guess it was a dress, but the filminess was confusing. She was looking at me with one eyebrow raised, mockingly.

—Music school. What's that like?

—Oh. . .kinda boring. I practice violin all night and my roommate practices bassoon. It's so loud I think we're confusing the furniture. Then I go to bed. Then a couple of hours later I wake up cause my roommate is fucking whoever he picked up that night in the fag bar.

—Wow, I said.

—Fucking noises, she said, every night.

—That's. . .intense. For you, I mean.

She laughed, then touched her lip with her finger. Then she looked at me coldly.

—So, I told him he had to take me to that bar. And he wouldn't.

—Why?

—He said it was a bore. So small town the men don't even dance with each other. They just sit and drink and stare.

She stroked one hand with the other and sighed, deeply and with disgust.

—Let's go, I said. Maybe we'll run into your roommate.

We left that party and surfaced at a table with a round of sweet drinks, the kind that make the back of your throat close up. Fuzzy wuzzies. How is it that drinking age was never an issue? No one in town noticed. I vaguely remember dodging some tourists as they flopped around the dance floor, so perhaps we came in through the back. The interesting part was all the men crowded in the front and along the sides. No one was talking. They reminded me of animals in a dark barn, stamping, shifting their weight, letting out long sighs. There was that thickness, almost a chewiness, of animals being present. The human element was a strong feeling of paranoia.

It made me focus on the girl across from me, on her hands as they wandered around the table and across her lap. Her silences, which I felt I was supposed to fill up. She crossed her legs and scratched the corner of her lip.

—So, I said, listen to what happened last week. Willa and Shane and I, we went up into the high country and everything was fine for the first three days but then we wandered completely off our maps. So, what do we do. . .

It's always safe to walk down, right? We do that, walk down, and eventually we come into this enormous valley, wide, forested. We crash though the woods, through cowboy camps, nude girls carved into the pines and rusted cans. After a couple more hours we get to a road. We have no idea where we are. We wait for an hour. The first car that comes by, stops. We all climb in the back, the three of us. A pair of skinny old cowboys are in the front. They start telling stories.

I sighed. It's hard to capture the important details, to peer through the haplessness of every person, especially myself. And when I do get to the point, I feel lost.

—What's your name? I asked.

—Isabelle.

—OK, Isabelle, so what was amazing was their stories. They had been ranch kids. They'd each run away from home at fourteen. Home was Wyoming, the flat part, land of antelopes and future steak. That's so far away from any place I've ever been, I couldn't even visit. Do you know what I mean?

—Uhh, yeah. . .

—So, they joined the rodeo circuit. That's what they did, that plus running drugs from Mexico, racing across the border in a pickup. They'd done twenty years of horses, bulls, and speed. Anyhow, they drove us all the way home. It took hours. And we drank the whole way. Cheap whiskey from a paper bag. Around and around that car went the paper bag, and we got so deeply drunk, like sliding into warm dirt. Shane passed out, then he woke up and couldn't stop giggling. I kept looking out the window and thinking, at this moment there's no fear. It's gone, disappeared, and that feels like forever. Maybe it was because the guy driving had been thrown so much. He'd hit the ground hard so many times, every joint in his body was loose. That's the opposite of fear, dontcha think?

—I don't know, she said.

We looked at each other. She was such a girl—delicate, highly trained. What kind of person plays the violin?

—At least you're not bored, Isabelle said.

—There's that, I agreed.

—Maybe we could do something sometime?

She wrote her phone number down on a piece of paper. I bent my head humbly and accepted the paper, rolling it into a tube and slipping it into the pocket of my jeans. Then the Rod Stewart song came on, the same one that had been playing at the party, and Isabelle stood up furiously.

—It's that song you hate, she said, as though it were an affront to my dignity.

Actually, I loved the song. I couldn't stand it, but I loved it. It's about a teenage boy involved with an old woman named Maggie.

At night you take me to bed
In the morning you kick me in the head.
Oh, Maggie I couldn't keep trying, anymore. . .

I followed Isabelle out of the bar and stood by her in the doorway as she ran her fingers through the long black wool that sprang from her head. She was talking about rehearsals, concerts. It sounded worrying. Sympathy for her troubled life. . . My neck wobbled and my head dropped, plunging through all of her hairs. Push, then kiss. Her lips felt cool, so I tried it again. A streaky dazzle dropped from my ribcage into my pelvis, distant but piercing. . .that part that shoots like a star. Her tongue was warm. I could smell her hair.

—That was nice, I said, and I touched the gauze of her dress. Did you like that?

—Of course.

She meant it. But she sounded irritated too and that edge dragged through my gut. It thrilled me; I couldn't tell you why.

—You have my number, she said.

Then she walked away down the dark street. I watched her get smaller. It was like watching someone I would never know, any girl in an orange dress.

Later that night, I held up my long stringy hair and studied it in the bathroom mirror. The door was locked. I was naked, except for steam, and the long hair which I held up like a crown of wires. My tits stared back at me, small sunny faces. It was absurd, the cheeriness of my own body. . . Was there something faggoty about that?

As I was folding up my jeans, Isabelle's phone number slipped out of the pocket. I stared at the tab of white paper, *luscious little thing*. It yanked me somewhere, but I didn't want to go. Why go anywhere? I decided not to call. Then I decided not to decide and slipped the paper back into the pocket.

Mina

Days passed. Willa and I hung together, loosely, twins of gloom. We hardly talked, but that didn't matter. Budd family life flowed around me. I was absorbed and startled by it at the same time, especially by Mrs. Marian Budd. She had a sincere earthy sweetness that everyone ran over, took for granted, ignored. It was their dirt. I don't mean that in a bad way.

One morning over breakfast, Willie set down his coffee cup and made an announcement.

—Pussy is having a lawn party. We are invited.

Pussy? I looked to Willa for help, but she was mouthing her scone slowly and with distaste, as if it were some foreign object. In my neighborhood, that word appeared on the back wall of the supermarket, the playground, the school. . . Gang tags alternated according to turf, but *Pussy* was everywhere. No one actually said it, though.

—I love Pussy's lawn parties, piped in Marian. Last time there were violinists, and what were those drinks?

—Gin fizzes.

—Yummy.

—Pussy is our landlady, Willie said dryly. That means everybody goes. Except Camille. You can do whatever you want.

—It's the horse barn that we rent from Pussy, Marian explained. She lives in that lovely house that overlooks it, the dark one.

Anyone would notice that house—at the end of Willie's pasture was a tiny lake, and on the other side, at the top of a rise and surrounded by tall pines, a Victorian mansion. A spire rose between the trees, its windvane shining with gold paint. Otherwise the house was painted black and seemed to disappear with all its bulk into the gloomy shroud of surrounding pines. I chewed thoughtfully. So that was the chilling *house of Pussy*.

—Maybe Mina Loy will be there, Marian added.

—Of course, she'll go. Pussy gives her money. How else could Mina afford to keep a room in the Hotel Jerome? Especially when she mostly stays with Pussy. They are some weird old people.

Shane gave me a look drenched with significance.

—Shame on you! Marian's words reverberated through every helpless family member, like some sort of *call of the normal*. She continued,

—Camille don't pay attention to Shane. Mina is elegant and intelligent. And Pussy! Well, she built the ski runs, financed the music school. She's a fine lady too.

The Budds dressed in powder blue for that party. Probably Marian sewed all those clothes. They drifted in a cloud down the street, easy and relaxed, the sweet airs of summer sliding around their bare arms and legs. I watched them go in my baggy shorts which sagged from the prongs of my hips. I was too comfortable in my grunge to go somewhere nice. On the other hand, Pussy's house was a draw. I'd seen its stained-glass windows gleaming dully in the pine thicket like the scales of a dark lizard. Its general atmosphere of obscurity and elegance made something sprout in the back of my throat. Something like appetite. I wanted to attach myself to that like a tick, and suck.

I tailed the Budds sheepishly. When they disappeared into a swarm of people on a lawn, I took a deep breath and followed. What can I say? It was a lawn party. The sun sparkled on the beds of pink impatiens and the alto knock of croquet mallets against balls sounded sweet. True, gloomy pines towered overhead. But everyone was circulating and pressing hands and making a kind of love which even then I thought had to do with money, specifically real estate money.

It was coming to town. That released a zest, like shaving the rind off a lemon.

The Budds were nowhere to be seen. Instead women with frosted pink lips and heavy turquoise necklaces struck poses on the grass. They were tall & very thin, trophy wives, mostly from Texas. Cowboy hats were perched on their gleaming blond hair helmets, decorated with clever feather hat brim ornaments. As new arrivals made their way up the lawn, the women rotated their lovely heads gracefully, and all at once, like a team of synchronized swimmers.

Wealth could seep out of the dirt. I hadn't known that. Here, the local ranchers were land rich. They'd lucked out and they were beaming, in their nylon blend boot flare jeans and western shirts snapped over their spreading bellies.

I was learning so much. Just this morning, Willa had taught me about ticks. She had stretched out her woolly sheep dog so we could peer into the soft nook between his foreleg and chest. A mommy tick had taken up residence there. Once hard as flint, she had swollen up into a gray and puckered balloon, and all around her head, baby ticks were nursing on dog blood. They looked like little brown petals.

I strolled along, thinking of ticks. How could something so hard get that soft? She had snapped her tiny jaws shut and sucked and sucked and then blew up into a purse of blood. . .

—Watch it, barked a waiter.

His tanned and muscled chest heaved through his open shirt. I backed off, apologizing.

I noticed a pair of purple shoes in the grass. The heels were wide at the bottom, like Turkish coffee pots, and a nubbin of suede decorated each toe.

—Excellent shoes, I said.

—Do you think so? bubbled from a wide coral mouth, a shapely mouth, although it belonged to an old woman with a big mat of gray hair.

—Peggy bought them for me in Venice when I showed up at her doorstep, shoeless. It happens, dear.

I stared at the woman, waiting for a moment of recognition. Then I remembered I'd never seen a photograph.

—Are you, by any chance. . .*Mina Loy*. . .?

She stood there, looking like a fairy godmother, until I interpreted her silence as yes. Then I blurted out,

—I know your poems. My mother is. . .uh, a fan. . .

Mina swiped a glass of champagne off a passing tray and took a swig, rolling it from one cheek to the other, surveying the crowd.

—I suppose I should be appreciative. . .I try, Lord knows. Do you like this. . .place?

—Sure. Why not.

—Well I wouldn't be anywhere near this town if it weren't for Pussy. Do you know they've hammered decorative icicles to my window at the Hotel Jerome? It's summer, for heaven's sake. . . There she is. Pussy, come here—

A blue-eyed woman in a black skirt and squarish loafers approached us. Her gray hair was pulled back in a stubby ponytail.

Mina grabbed my hand and placed it in Pussy's.

—She's the culprit. The root of it all, our accidental mother. . .

Pussy smiled at me dryly as Mina held our hands together.

—Pussy came here before anyone. The town was a wasteland, in every way. When Glenn Gould came out to visit, she had to open up the Hotel Jerome and have the only piano in town dragged out of the basement, so Glenn could give a concert in the lobby. Twelve people showed up. They stood around the piano afterward, gossiping and drinking sherry. Glenn said, Pussy, why don't you start a summer music school? That's how it started. It should be called Pussy's Music School.

I took back my hand and smiled awkwardly. Pussy looked bemused. Then Mina's expression slid disconcertingly towards the tragic. She indicated me with a flick of her wrist.

—The girl says her mother is a fan of my work.

—Mina, Pussy said patiently, That's nice. We're happy about that.

She gave me a wide smile, one with teeth.

What could I say? Mina's poems decorated our bathroom—they were wall upholstery. On the other hand, I knew them well. I knew them by heart. So. . .

The human cylinders
Revolving in the enervating dust
That wraps each closer in the mystery
Of singularity
Among the litter of a sunless afternoon
Having eaten without tasting
Talked without communion
And at least two of us
Loved a very little
Without seeking
To know if our two miseries
In the lucid rush-together of automatons
Could form one opulent well-being. . .

—Marvelous, crooned Pussy.

Even Mina lit up with a smile, tender as a baby's, and then she slipped her hand into the crook of Pussy's forearm. A sparkle hit the air; it was Pussy's eyes, glittering. She put her arm firmly across my shoulders and quietly said,

—You must come over. We'll entertain you. We'll have tea, or something. Say next Tuesday, at 5?

—Sure, I said.

—Very good, she said, and released me.

I sprang away from them as though I'd been pushed, and when I looked back, Pussy was already extending her slender hand to someone else. You don't know my name, I wanted to cry out.

Instead I found Shane and Willa. They were sprawled on the green velvet of a Victorian couch. It was the living room, and all the furniture had claws. Vases of tall, slender throated Calla lilies were everywhere.

—Did ya see them? Shane said. The friends of Mina Loy. They hang together like I don't know what.

—Oh Shane, Willa sighed. He has worries that roaming packs of ancient bohemians will spoil. . .

—Shut up. Lemme show you.

—. . .the little town of Ruby Ridge, Colorado, she continued, and snickered.

Shane led me past the finger food, through the French doors and onto the patio, where three violinists were skewering their instruments. Then he stopped.

—There they are.

He pointed at a group of ancient hipsters perched on lawn chairs. They were slim and small and wore black. The man had a shaved head, paved with freckles and tiny wrinkles, and the women wore muscular silver jewelry with large dark stones. They were intent on eating. Occasionally they would stop and chew, surveying the party with total indifference.

—What's the big deal, Shane?

He gave me a hard look.

—Faggot, he snorted, you haven't got a clue.

Whatever. As I walked home with Shane and Willa, it struck me. An instant of clarity sparkling like morning dew: I could invite Isabelle to this tea. I ran into the house and called her. She seemed unsettled at the idea. What? Where? Why? The questions came out like slow complaints, reflective bottoms under every word—that was Isabelle. Basically solemn. Finally, with reluctance, she agreed.

Tea

Mina met us at the door and walked us into the living room, where Isabelle and I sat together on the claw-footed velvet couch. Pussy was standing next to the grand piano, her black slacks crisply pressed. She sipped something green. Absinthe? Mina was wearing an ostrichey dress, the color of old film, with tatters or feathers hanging from it. It gave her a vagueness, like Big Bird, as she stumbled across the living room floor with our tray of jasmine tea and ginger snaps.

—It's remarkable. . .I can't believe it. . .someone in this town knows my WORK, she said.

—You know Mina's work, Pussy repeated softly.

What would I say about it now? I don't like it. It's a fish bone in my throat. It grates on my ear. With deliberate awkwardness, it occupies lyricism like an enemy territory. But that makes me return to it and savor it. It's my crush. Back then I was too passive and suspicious to formulate an intelligent question, but there were lines I'd always wondered about:

Your drifting hands
faint as exotic snow
spread silver silence
as a fondant nun

What the fuck did she mean by fondant nun? But I didn't ask that, instead I mumbled how much I liked the *work*. I had never used the term the *work* before, and it was followed by a risky silence, in which the ladies looked at me like disturbed cats. Isabelle's cheeks were turning a tender red. The party was stranger than she had expected. This gave me a pang, which turned to nerve, and I splattered our gathering with another Mina Loy poem:

Your chiffon voice
tears with soft mystery
a lily loaded with a sucrose dew
of vigil carnival. . .

—I love that, I lied, my voice cracking.

It didn't matter. Isabelle turned to me with a smile, all the fierce little prongs of her teeth displayed.

—I love it too, she said.

Mina settled herself on the couch next to me and ran her cool fingers across my wrist.

—You're not from here, are you dear?

—Oh no, I said.

She gave my ear lobe a hard squeeze.

—It's excellent for the ear. Memorize as many poems as you can. That's my only advice.

Then Pussy stalked to the turntable and put on something very old and sexy, Louie Armstrong's "Mack the Knife." Mina raised her big head, with its clean, broad cheekbones and strong brows, a beautiful face even near the end of her life. She stood up, held out an arm, and they began to dance, the feathered tatters of Mina's dress swaying against Pussy's black pants.

We watched them. It seemed there was plenty of time. Sometimes it opens and sucks your eye down like a well. Time, I mean, and at the bottom are watery faces, like your own but cold and probably more elegant. It was like that, watching the two old women spinning across their love puddle, back and forth, in a sort of silent film loop.

They seemed to forget we were there. Finally, Pussy told us to run along.

—Go prowl, girls. . . Explore. Anywhere you'd like.

Mina half-opened her eyes and whispered,

—Upstairs is better.

We walked stiffly through the hall. We began to run as soon as we were out of sight. The whole house. We had it. There was a moment of excitement when something may just as well have yanked me up by the armpits and through the ceiling, plaster cracking and falling everywhere. Of course, that didn't happen. I saw a white flash of Isabelle's underwear and then we were at the top of the stairs, breathing hard, where four large bedrooms were laid out in a square. What were they like, Pussy's bedrooms—people have asked me that. But people, get a clue. They were about as sexy as a 19th century bank. The bedspreads were white, with nubs like towels, stitched in a pattern of turkeys and Indians. Lace doilies sat on top of stout, heavily carved dressers. Isabelle and I walked down the hall, peering into each room. Was this all there was? The beds were four poster and sat in the middle of their territories like forts.

Then Isabelle found the door to the attic. It opened with a creak and a soft push of new smells: dust and abandoned furniture. Heat. Nervously we climbed the narrow stair. It was dim at the top. The only light bled past the rim of a window shade, pulled all the way down, but it was enough to make the white porcelain doorknobs gleam. There were twelve porcelain doorknobs on twelve small doors.

We opened each one. Each room held an iron bedstand and a dusty table.

Only one of the beds had a mattress and it was stained. The threads were worn in the dark places, as though someone had lain on it for a long time, barely moving.

Isabelle sat on the mattress and traced the outline of the stain with her finger.

—Whaddya think this is?

—It looks like a body shadow. Someone died here. . . Or was an invalid? Maybe an insane aunt. . .

—Look at my arm, she said.

I sat down next to her. I could smell the sweat under her armpits and a slight sweetness coming off her hair. Hair rinse, probably. I rubbed the spot she had pointed to gently with my thumb. It looked like it might hurt. A rash of tiny bumps had spread across her skin. She pulled at the hem of her dress where there was another red patch.

—Look, there's another one. . .

—You're getting rashes, I said.

Stating the obvious. I wanted to put off doing anything, just for a moment. It's that feeling of being about to tremble under a coat of fresh paint. I leaned over and pressed my palms into my eyes, flooding myself with reds and oranges—eyelids are a sheet of bloody laundry. Inside, something to count on.

When I raised my head again, she said,

—You scratch it.

So, I ran my fingers around the perimeter of the red mark on her thigh. Then I dug in with my fingernail.

—What does it feel like. . .

—A hot spot. It happens to me. Don't worry about it.

She was looking down at it, frowning.

—Do you want to leave?

—No.

We sat for a while next to one another, on top of that disintegrating stain. She said she liked the way it smelled up there, like dry roasted dust. She laughed and I looked at her and it seemed that her face had gone soft, or had just gone somewhere, leaving behind two eyes and a pouch of skin. . . I tried kissing it. Her breath deepened; a sigh emptied out.

I climbed on her hips, up on her white panties and I sat there for a moment, looking. It was so unfamiliar, a girl rolling between my legs and the little blast offs in my blood. She gripped the mattress with both hands, arched her back, and it hit me: I could be anyone. What a blast, what a fucking relief. Curious all of a sudden, I reached my hand down, along my back and ass, and reached for what was there. Whatever it was, under the girlish white underwear, the fine black hairs. Her impossible sour and wet surfaces.

We were up there awhile. Years, possibly. When we came down, Mina had left, and Pussy was reading the Wall Street Journal at the dinner table. The dinner dishes had been pushed aside. When she heard us she took off her reading glasses.

—Hullo, girls, she said. Welcome to the ground floor.

We stared at her stupidly.

Pussy nodded at a book on the table.

—This is Mina's *Lunar Baedeker*, the 1923 edition. A treasure, really. Someday it will be valuable. It's even autographed.

She nudged the book towards me.

—Camille, Mina wants you to have it. Now tell me, how did you come to know the work?

The question slid in like a fishhook. I understood perfectly, or thought I did. It was another variation of the question *How did you ever live*? How how how, and now. I picked up the book slowly. I felt its spine with my fingertips. Suddenly I was almost too tired to stand up. The truth sagged out of me.

—Pearl—that's my mom—she covered our bathroom walls with these poems.

—I see.

Pussy knit her fingers together.

—Well, we loved having you. It's delightful having girls prowling around, and so unusual, around here. . .

She cleared her throat. We watched as red points formed on the tips of her cheek bones and when she finally spoke it was the driest thing I'd ever heard. Water without water in it, a dry spring bubbling out of dry earth. She said,

—We want you to come back. Mina insists. It would give her great pleasure. Next week?

We stared at her again, but this time it was work. It's a grind discovering anything, even when you are a spy. You have to adjust. Finally, Isabelle answered, almost sadly,

—We will.

Tuesdays

Isabelle was a dressy girl. It was like she wore herself, and then slipped some simple dress over that. Always dresses. On Tuesday evenings, they were the only spot of color in the room. I remember one which was lime green with a blue hem, sleeveless and short, that she wore with sandals. I ran into Isabelle one evening out on the street, when she was wearing the green dress. We looked at one another and the air seemed to twist up. I'd just learned to make her come but I hadn't used that word yet.

Because I snubbed her, Willa and Shane never saw her. We all walked by, headed to some stupid bar or party. In my world no one knew her name but me, and I kept it that way. It'd be easy to twist that into something filmy and reticent, but in fact it was just her eyes on my turned back and I didn't feel a thing.

She had those rashes. She'd sit on the edge of the mattress and we'd watch it grow outward from one tiny spot, stopping when it got to be about the size of a quarter. Sometimes it crept down her thigh like a brush stroke, and I'd follow, with my finger or tongue. It was boredom, scraping from the inside against her skin, trying to get out. She liked to kiss hard. Maybe that was the same thing—boredom. She'd pull me towards her by the throat.

Isabelle was the kind of girl who'd lay back, throw her arms over her head, and she'd be there. It was like asking someone for a quarter and they fill your hands with so much change it spills out from between your knuckles. It got to me, but it wasn't me, if you know what I mean. That's a load of bullshit. Usually I made the first move. Why not? Every move was a plunge. It drove me nuts. I'd spin into that world and she'd be there, inside it, waiting on the mattress in one of those dresses, with her rash spots. Somehow, she was the girl and I was the big mess. But the rashes went away as soon as she came.

Answer this question: What's the difference between desire and slither?

Strange stuff began coming out of my mouth.

—All your pubic hairs are citizens of my country, I told her, and we both cracked up. I started calling her Pussy. Pussy this, Pussy that. She didn't seem to respond one way or the other. Then one night with a quick jab snapped my jaw shut on my tongue.

—Ow, I yelped, blotting my tongue on my hand and looking for blood.

—What's the matter... Cat got your tongue?

—Don't do that, Pussy.

—Quit calling me that.

—Oh, all right... I drummed my fingers in the soft spot that stretched between her hip bones, just under her belly button. I loved it there. Happy Trails...

—You won't believe what Shane calls me... I said, plugging for sympathy. *Faggot.*

—That dipshit. You don't even look like a boy. Why does he call you that?

—I dunno.

—I can't believe you don't just deck him.

—It paralyzes me, or something.

—I'd deck him, she said. You're the pussy.

—Yeah right, I sputtered. I don't think so. . .

—Why not?

—Well for one thing, you have such little hands.

She held them up and we both studied them, as if they were her puppies. They were lean and strong, but very delicate. Whippet hands.

—What should I do with these? she said and thought about it a few moments. I'm gonna be a jazz musician.

—But you play the violin.

—My dad is a jazz musician.

Then she named someone famous. A trumpeter, Italian, sort of Hollywood—Dion with swing. One of his tunes had infected the radio waves for at least six months. I'd heard it a lot, simply because I was among the living. So, what if it sounded like shiny ripples beamed at the masses from a celebrity golf tournament?

—Wow, I said, impressed.

Isabelle looked at me with scorn.

—It's not what you think. I grew up in Santa Monica.

I buried my head in my hands. Clueless again, what the fuck was Santa Monica? I mumbled that question and it seemed to loosen her sympathy, finally. She took my hand and nibbled on my fingertips. Between nibbles she explained,

—It's a California beach town. There are hippies everywhere, even on our lawn. Actually, I'm not allowed to talk to them. I run from the door to the curb, and practice violin. That's my life. Christ, my dad is such a control freak. Last winter for two months we had only nuts and fruits in the house. That was his detox diet. But he's still a pothead. Our house stinks.

She put my hand down and stared at me glumly.

—I'm going home soon. What a crashing bore.

The day Isabelle left I came back to the Budd house and there were five Birds of Paradise in a vase on the kitchen table, and a note which read,

For a bird of paradise xxx Isabelle.

I was so stunned I thought a quick shit was going to run out of me. When I staggered to a chair Marian came to me and gently put her arm around my shoulders.

—We can't always control the kinds of attention we get, dear. It's not your fault.

Then she took the flowers, broke their stems, and stuffed them headfirst into the trash.

Secret

When the next Tuesday rolled around and I was reading a comic book, my body got it: she was gone. On Wednesday, also, she was gone. Then she became one of the miscellaneous cravings to which I seem to be susceptible. It could happen anywhere. I'd be chugging a beer next to the pool table in the cowboy bar and by the time I put the bottle down I was in the middle of an Isabelle flash. Then I'd peer out at the bleary crowd of beards and flannel shirts from inside my little room, the one in my brain.

I felt sort of special. My secret was my message, and it came back at me in the haywire sunshine sparkling on the crystals under my boots, reflecting off bits of ground-up mica in the dirt. I found a chunk of watery blue turquoise on a trail and gave it to Willa. It was poor quality but pretty, and I felt generous.

Willa and I did the rodeo. During my event, the barrel race, my horse fell over and crunched my foot. He was pigeon toed, unfortunately. Afterward I discovered I liked limping around. It made me feel bigger and bloodier. Wounded. Shane had gotten thrown from a bull, dislocating his shoulder, so Willa was the only one who brought home a shiny plastic trophy (in Pole Bending), three inches of gold cup on top of a podium of imitation wood.

The trophy was sitting on the kitchen table the morning Shane opened the newspaper to a shot of serial killer Ted Bundy, taken at a press conference after he had been captured by the Ruby Ridge police. He wore a big happy-to-be-in-your-town smile, so that the handcuffs seemed incidental. We passed the paper around. His face was a bundle of even features, high cheekbones and brown hair, so generically handsome he resembled no one in particular. The cops were grinning too. It looked like a party celebrating law enforcement: *from concept to action*. The press peppered him with questions. Who are you? Why do you kill for thrills? Instead of answering, Bundy went around the room and gave each journalist a satanic fortune cookie. That's how it seemed. Actually, he just answered the questions.

—Each of us is as unique as a snowflake might be. But that's not to say that I'm so special that no one can understand me, or nobody has the capacity to understand me. . . I'm not unique. . . although obviously special.

The richest part, what really killed us, was that only hours later, before press-time of that same day, Bundy escaped. Apparently, he'd wriggled out of his cell through the air conditioner tubes.

The presence of a serial killer frog-kicking through City Hall's ventilation system somehow made Willa want to go swimming. She offered to buy the beer. The parties wounded in the rodeo, Shane and I, could sit on the bank and drink while she jumped in and out of the river. I liked the spot: sun on the wildflowers, the river bouncing over massive brown boulders and tossing cold spray. A moldy abandoned cabin at the site had been the location of an infamous party, which Willa and Shane had described to me in loving detail. A friend of Willa's had found a sack of cocaine while he was hiking right outside of town, and he'd thrown a party for everyone he knew. I was mystified.

—How big was that sack?

—Really, really big, Willa answered vaguely.

It suited my mood to be there, after it was over. That feeling of missing it. Being in the right place at the wrong time. The whole crew had been at that party, waiters, bartenders, maids, the crowd that had streamed into town to nourish the tourists. They were abnormally muscular and sleek, that was a requirement. It was a brilliant afternoon. People sat by the river, drinking beer and strumming guitars, or they waited in a line outside the cabin. No one was allowed to stay in there for more than fifteen minutes, but you could go back as many times as you wanted. Inside the cabin there were rows of bent backs and haunches in gleaming bike shorts.

I never got to the river to swim with Shane and Willa. They left before me and I was supposed to hitch a ride and get there later. I did climb into a tan Buick, where I sagged into the bucket seat and closed my eyes. I was meditating. I did that for a long time, and it was a good thing, to tumble in the dead space, with ghosts. When I opened my eyes, I saw I'd gotten a ride with a demon.

It's all in the past, which means it's here now and also in the future. That's why stories don't work; there's no real sequence. It's always breathing and dying and spitting resemblances up. Try it: grab one. It'll squirm like jellyfish and carry a mean sting. It'll make your hands sticky, and if you're lucky, it won't be blood. I'm talking about the past.

—Do you carry life insurance?

That's what the demon asked me. I told him I was only fifteen and life insurance wasn't a big issue yet.

—I sell it, I know. Everyone should carry life insurance.

—Yup, he said.

He kept saying that. His cock looked like a big frog.

—Yup, yup, I wanna fuck you.

I can spot the gruesome a mile away and normally I react. But this stuff just floated into my empty head. Whatever was in there to begin with had completely cleared out. *You got in the wrong car this time, kid.*

—Hey, I said carefully, and then I added a tinge: annoyance. This won't work cause I'm a dyke.

That's a fucking big word. Dyke. I hadn't known that. I discovered it that day. A swerve and a shove and then I was getting to my feet, my hands and knees all scraped up.

I carried a switchblade for years after that. It was a kind of marriage. On that day my pockets were empty. I turned and watched the Buick pull away. It had a big trunk; it wouldn't have been a tight fit.

Writing a story is a little like dragging a tree out of a dark wood and then wrapping it with strings of starry lights. I'm partial to the flashing green jalapeño peppers, even the little spotted jersey cows that twinkle on and off. Why is it that no one makes clowns? Whatever. I have a couple more strings and then I'm done.

I hitched a ride back to town. The driver didn't even come to a complete stop. After skipping along for a while, I managed to hop in, he hit the gas, and we were rocking to the Grateful Dead. *Driving that train, high on cocaine, Casey Jones you better watch your speed. . .* Swirls of psycho colors radiated from Dead posters. The van smelled like dog. The driver looked too stoned to live.

As I was sitting cross-legged on a purple cushion with orange tassels, thoughts fell out of my brain like hisses from a snake. *I've never fucked a guy and now, I still haven't.* For the most part I don't remember these thoughts, which is a good thing, probably, because I also had the feeling that my brain was shrinking and hardening into some sort of turd.

That was just another mystery, and I didn't question it. I felt unbearably agile, lucky, and bitter, but all that was the past. In the future, I was going to call Isabelle. What would I say? The word dyke, of course. Dyke dyke dyke. Perhaps I'd mention the hot and friendly feeling which was spiking my chest. It was about weaponry.

She hadn't left me her number. When I got to a phone, my fingers were shaking so bad I could barely dial Santa Monica information. It took several tries and attempted spellings of her father's last name. Finally, I got something. The phone rang for a long time, and then a loud rasping voice splattered my ear.

—Where are you! it screamed, I'm waiting and waiting!

The accent was heavy Italian. All I said was Isabelle, but her name was Gina. After hearing about diabetes and bad teeth, I finally understood she thought I was a home care nurse, sent by the county.

—I'm sorry, Ma'am, but I'm not a nurse. I'm just looking for a girl named Isabelle.

—No Isabelle here! She hung up the phone.

After that it goes blank. I don't think there was that much summer left. I'm sure I got back to the Budd house just fine. I probably lay around on my couch reading copies of *Appaloosa Stud* magazine for the rest of the afternoon. I still like that idea: spotted horses with barely any tail. Someone should string them up, fasten little plastic horseshoes to their pink hooves, and make them twinkle. I'd decorate my living room with something like that.

Now I longed to get back home, to the streets of sturdy brick apartments and familiar drunks. I even missed Tina, the girl with mismatched eyeballs who hung out on my block night and day. Her eyes bulged out and pointed in opposite directions, and she had one kid after another, losing them all to foster care. She always wore something flowery, even when it was cold.

One day the scrape in the gravel outside the Budd house was Pearl in the blue Mustang. When she came in the kitchen door, there was a fierce moment of recognition and relief. Of course, all I could do was mumble *Hi* and *Okay*. My head was a blur of monster words: faggot-pussy-dyke. They had a shimmer and a slickness as I held them back in my throat. It felt better than a secret.

I gave Pearl the autographed copy of Mina's book. *The Lunar Baedeker*, 1923 edition. She practically pinched my cheeks off.

I did hear from Isabelle again. I got a postcard a few months later. From what I remember, it went something like this:

> "dear Camille.
> I still like you, believe it or not. But, silence is golden. . ."

It had no return address, so I burned it.

ISHER HOUSE

It was a weird moment to grow up in a historical district. For us, the past existed—there were its buildings, after all, ruined mansions with marble entrances and broken-down elevators. They were solidly constructed of red brick, as if 'red brick' signaled the emphatic end of something better, and it gave them durability, after the roofs collapsed, even after the windows had blown out. One mansion was filled with dog shit.

The present, where we played and ate and fought and went to school, stretched across the scene like a yellow police line. We were living in the aftermath, a time of wearing down, so palpable it was almost a physical sensation, like grinding. The shops on our streets stayed the same, or closed. When windows broke in our school, it got colder. We felt innocent in our actions, but knew that our surroundings entered us, and made us wicked. We got to live in big houses, and the houses that weren't lived in, we could plunder and explore.

A crime is an intimate form of knowledge. It breaks you, then remains present, like the water running in the sewers. When I'm lonely, the faint background gurgling seems to turn into a whisper—*Your history is unbearable.* But whose history, I want to know.

Amy Brooks lived next door to the mansion filled with dog shit. Her house was small and normal—perhaps it was built to be the carriage house. Red brick, of course, two story, with elms in the front. The elms were going to die soon but we didn't know that. The rest of the block was taken up by the grounds, which were surrounded by a fourteen-foot-high brick wall topped with rusted cast iron spikes. Behind this fortification, a rotting and craggy mansion rose, looking weirdly Scottish according to the affectations of turn-of-the-century money. It even had a name: Isher House. It seemed outraged by its own neglect.

Amy Brooks went to sleep every night to the howling of the guard dog in Isher House. For fifty years only dogs slept there. The owners had left decades before white flight had hit the neighborhood. Not because they were prescient but because their son had been murdered. A couple of rich young men, sharing an idle moment while being chauffeured somewhere, dreamed up what they thought was the perfect crime—a kidnapping and ransom. Things went awry, and the little boy they snatched never went home. The parents of the boy surprised everyone by refusing to sell the house. They moved away, and kept it empty, except for the guard dog. Generations of guard dogs lived their entire lives in that house.

One day in the schoolyard, Amy ran towards me, breathless, the baby fat around her belly jiggling. From a squat, I rocked back on my heels.

—The dog quit howling. I think he's gone or dead or something.

—So, was Doggy run over or did Doggy get shot?

Carol popped questions as though they were quips. Amy bubbled over with details: Two cars had pulled into the circular driveway, two, two cars, she repeated solemnly. That had never happened before. The usual pattern was that the caretaker, a gloomy and squat Polish dude, came in a black Cutlass twice a month. Always alone, carrying a paper bag. This time, no caretaker and no bag. The dog must be dead! Maybe they buried him on the grounds somewhere. . .

—You want to dig up the dog? Carol asked.

Amy looked crushed. She smelled great, like baby powder.

—Amy, I said, let's break into Isher House.

—Oh. Her face relaxed.

—We'll sleep over at your house on Saturday night. After your parents are asleep, we'll go over the wall. . .

We all got excited. What was the necessary equipment? The only thing we could come up with was flashlights. Carol pointed out to Amy the drainage pipes that snaked up the walls of our school.

—You should be prepared to climb up pipes like those, she gravely intoned.

Carol and I had gotten to the roof that way, more than once, and the thrill of being on top of that detested institution was indescribable. John D. Flynn School loomed over the neighborhood like a Victorian mental institution. It was a misery of a school, charged, among other things, with enforcing a form of racial separation known as tracking. It was an exercise in bad faith, in which students were separated into different classrooms supposedly based on ability but really the criterion was race. We heard the teachers of the lower tracks howling through the doors and walls.

Amy gazed up the drain pipes in wonder. For a moment, I loved her open face, flat and a little dumbass-looking.

Maybe we all looked that way. *I grew to manhood in an era of dumbass.* I'm not a man, not a transsexual, but manhood sounds so much more succinct than adulthood. And womanhood, what is that? There was a sloppiness everywhere then. It was the style. Carol and Amy and I had identical long brown hair, all waving the same raggedy flag. My mother was forever irritably scraping her fingers down my cheeks to pull the long hairs from my mouth, to no avail. Nothing my mother did could impact my sense of my own cool.

Pause. Rewind the story. Carol was the center of something, which I need to summon up.

Amy raced towards us across the blacktop because she wanted something. . .the avenue of our secret life. Carol and I did have one, even though it consisted of nothing more than creeping about our neighborhood like twin versions of Harriet The Spy. We escaped serious harm because the conflict in our streets was too real to be wasted on us. We dressed to be invisible girls, which meant grubby sweatshirts and jeans. But we lived within the terror and power of place. That is the word I prefer but the one more often used for such fiercely contested urban territory is turf. My word is better, because its slight degree of abstraction resists the histrionics. Once I was telling a white woman from the suburbs about my neighborhood, its racially separate gangs and deadpan, even ironic, criminality. She gasped all over me, "That's so Hard Copy." I feel drenched, even now, by her little seizure, her relish.

Carol was my steady companion. We had things in common, and I believed in the significance of those things. Commonality equals solidity, amidst all the fluid perils. That's why people join gangs. I've always had a little gang in my life, and Carol was the beginning of that. That's why I was so startled when it came to me one day, years later and out of the blue: I'd been to Carol's house only once.

I thought we were always together, but I guess that was outside, or at my house.

On the day of my visit, Carol had forgotten her house key. She ran into her house for it, and I followed, uninvited.

Bertha, her mother, stood at the kitchen sink. Bertha watched me with mild curiosity. I don't think she spoke but something warm came from her, blurry but sincere. A glass next to her on the counter contained brown-tinged orange juice. Meaty flecks of orange stuck to the ice cubes. Her hair was a frizzy auburn puff with a yellow kerchief awkwardly placed on it.

I scampered out. Carol followed, jiggling her keys on their ring, not saying anything.

Bertha was / was not a problem. Like a dead end road, she never left the property. Whereas Carol's father was a public figure, of sorts. He was facing down the HUAC, not only by refusing to testify when they called him up, but by filing one of the lawsuits that challenged their legal right to exist. The House Un-American Activities Committee. It really did exist. Fighting it made him a hero in our leftie neighborhood. In fact, having a heroic father was another bond Carol and I had. Although Carol might not have been aware that I felt this way, because her father was the big hero and mine was a little one.

The memory of my father's heroics arouses a tenderness in me, which I suspect is partly nostalgia. He had a stubborn, yet oddly flirtatious, struggle going on with his employer over a loyalty oath. As a card-carrying communist, he couldn't sign, and after he left the Party, he wouldn't. It didn't reach the lawsuit stage, because all the hospital did was hire him on one temporary contract after another. Maybe Helen Chute, his boss, manipulated him to get this result, because he retired without a penny of pension. But he loved their game. And Helen Chute did come to his memorial service, even giving a brief tribute in her thrilling voice.

—That Helen is one smart cookie.

That's what Dad said, whenever the temporary contract was up and Helen called him into her office to offer him something permanent. Over dinner Dad would replay to my mother and me what enticements had been added to the contract to manipulate him to sign, and then he would sternly rehearse his resistance.

It's odd that we were resisting Helen, the smart cookie. She was breathtakingly butch. She entered a room with a startling Amazonian stride. Helen wore suits with gold cufflinks and her Italian shoes were so shiny they looked mean. No one commented on this, because the social movements that would generate that vocabulary hadn't happened yet.

There was real power in her position, but her voice was what held us. Held the neighborhood, even. It was honeyed and deep. We were clasped in the arms of that mellifluous voice. It was a relief to believe in her ability to steer the biggest employer in the neighborhood through the dangerous shoals of white flight, economic decline, and racial tension. DePaul Public Hospital was a beleaguered institution, running low on public money at the same time it was running out of patients who could pay. Its weirdly gothic flying buttresses seemed to be clawing the ground. Helen ran DePaul as well as it could be run, I suppose. It survived the era.

I grew up believing the social body was rotten and powerful, but also endangered. Helen was a mysterious example of this. Dad would come home and report on what Helen had said, and we'd laugh helplessly. One night at dinner, taking on Helen's voice and body language, he gave us the announcement of the day.

—DePaul Public Hospital will become the first hospital

in the country to have its own mobile and armed police force. The unique mission of our police force will be signaled by white cruise cars painted with red crosses.

We got hysterical. It's what we did as a family. Crack up until we cried. We weren't done until we were all like damp rags at the bottom of a bucket.

On the other hand. To poke back at Carol's dad. Something vexed me, that was hard to put my finger on. His name was Jack Dahl. He was one of those people who walk without swinging their arms. I was passing by once when he was giving a speech, the crowd was gathered in the concrete lot in front of John D. Flynn School. Everybody was watching Jack. Was it a joke? He cried out *HUAC* repeatedly and jabbed a finger skyward. His eyes were eerily oversized under a broad forehead and sprightly black hair. He quivered with authority. Someone once told me he was a crusader who needed no followers, only lawyers. But the crowd was respectful.

We lived off of resistance. Resistance deepened my intelligence. Perhaps I'm flattering myself.

Amy, Carol, and I did try to break into Isher House. After Amy's parents went to sleep, we crept down to the kitchen. Amy got us steak knives, in case the dog wasn't dead after all. We rolled them in newspaper tubes and stuck them in our back pockets. This made us feel serious, though the knives kept tilting backwards as if to fall out. We put the flashlights in a backpack.

Around 2 a.m. we slipped out the back door and pushed through a line of bushes. There it was: an abandoned world. The broad drive was tufted with weeds but neatly laid with brownish red brick. Isher House was the same scabby color. Whorls and medallions of brick in the walls looked undecayed but spiteful. The windows were blanked by large wooden sheets.

I felt breathless, looking up at Isher House. I imagined chandeliers, whose curves we could trace with our flash-light beams, draped in spider webs. Maybe this house had a library, filled with volumes, instead of books. I yearned for volumes.

We went up the wall where it connected to the house near the door. Carol scrambled up first. I saw her butt heave up and over, then thud.

—Are you okay? There was a silence, then,

—Fine. Come on.

I gave Amy a leg up, then a hipbone, then a shoulder. I had to push her up by the soles of her feet. With a mournful yelp she hit the ground on the other side.

I went up in one deep breath, scraping my knuckles, then grasping for the rusting spikes at the top. They looked like medieval spears, as though a line of soldiers had been bricked into the wall. Once up, balanced perilously on my knees, I paused. The moon faces of my companions were turned towards me, my nearsightedness rendering them expressionless. Two creamy white blanks. What shocked me was that there was no lawn. What did I expect—croquet? Amy and Carol were waist deep in what looked like a cloud of dust. It was weeds. There were a few random, forlorn trees on the lot, which took up most of the block, and then the black rim of the surrounding wall.

I didn't feel nervous anymore. I'd blasted into one of those time-stopped nuggets, giddy and criminal, yet loaded with the luxury of the pause.

I crumpled to the hard ground. When I stood up, Amy's fearful eyes were locked on me.

—Everything's fine, I told her, in a normal voice.

I felt so relaxed, I thought I could give relaxation to anyone.

—How am I going to get out of here? Amy whispered hoarsely.

—We'll call the fire department.

—No, Carol said. We'll tell the butler to call the fire department.

The laugh loosened us up. The nerve Carol and I shared was wiggling with pleasure, thrilled to be here. The two of us struck out alongside of the house, as Amy scuffled behind, whimpering whenever she stumbled over a rock.

—Guys, can we take out our flashlights yet?

—Alright, alright.

I stopped and pulled them out of the backpack. Three weak beams played upon the wall. Graffiti that vanished with a stroke. Then we started strobing Amy with the lights. Her t-shirt slid up and her belly button caught the beam.

—Hey guys, don't, don't, please, you guys!

Carol's laugh wobbled into a shriek.

We continued plodding around the house, looking for a way up or in. Finally, around the other side, we found it. The way in. It was terrifically wrong.

—Freaky, Amy squealed.

It was the payoff moment. Amy made little steps and twisted her hips as if she had to pee.

A huge bite had been taken out of the Isher House wall. Cautiously our flashlights traced the ragged outlines of the hole. One brick after another slid under our beams, stubby and broken and dusted with gray powder, as if the connective cement was dissolving. Our flashlight beams wavered over the central darkness. Then Carol was up at it, her hands grasping the lower edge.

I scrambled up there, joining Carol astride the crumbling wall. I remember her breathing next to me, that steady sound.

—Wow. . .wow, she said.

A staircase was attached to the cement wall of the basement, but the stairs only went halfway down. The last step was askew, and the rest had fallen away. Our flashlights followed the deep cracks that marked the missing steps down into the basement. Down there, at the heart of it, the wainscoting and floors had collapsed into a mess of decaying beams. Here and there were the black gleams from stagnant pools of water. Greenish shards looked like they might be pieces of roof. There were drifts of white stuff which was probably decaying dog shit, but it didn't smell. Isher House didn't look like anything, except scoured. The deepest vacancy, the ruination of the familiar.

—I can't believe they even kept a dog here. Stupid for us to go down there, Carol said, gesturing dismissively towards the basement.

I nodded, too disappointed to speak. It felt weirdly like being abandoned by the past.

Within a few months, the house was demolished as a hazard. The surrounding wall came down too, which meant that everyone I knew swarmed the weedy grounds and inspected the scrapings of rubble which were all that was left of the famous House. I went again, but this time I was by myself. Carol had stopped returning my calls.

I knew I'd been dumped when I walked into our ninth grade class and Carol had moved from the chair next to mine to a seat on the edge of a cluster across the room. She moved, in other words, from me to an empty spot next to the Black girls, who looked at her doubtfully. She was wearing a sideways-draped baseball cap. It went with a new attitude and slang: talking "Black," which for Carol meant barely moving her lips, while slurring her words ironically. It was beyond embarrassing. That first day a thud of astonishment went through my classmates, but after a week everyone seemed to accept it. It was weirdly amusing, this version of Carol, even to me.

It was also excruciating. She quit saying "Hello" to me, and started saying "Yo" to everyone else.

Carol didn't make new friends. She'd dumped me for a zone with no one in it. There wasn't a word for where she was, or an idea that related. It was against the way things worked, which was quite specific: kids played with anyone. But teens travelled in racially separate packets. If you'd asked us, I'm sure everyone would have said the same thing: we're just more comfortable this way. But what does comfort mean, when everything is uncomfortable? It was the history we were stuck in, and there's no boundary. It just seeps in.

I sat in class and watched our teacher, Miss Adele, stunned. She had been the teacher we had loved together, on the basis of her warm good looks. Miss Adele was a little woman, with tiny hands, but big cushiony breasts and springy hips.

—Like a baby with equipment, Carol had once whispered.

Before Miss Adele, we hadn't believed an adult could be adorable. Then we heard the sensational report that she had been held up at gunpoint, but refused to give the robber any money, and her reward was to live in the fuzzball of our incredulous love. She had kids too. What a badass. We wrote her fan notes during class, which we stuffed in our pockets and burned up later with matches. More little secrets. Now Carol wouldn't look at me. What was it all about?

I glided into a funk that lasted until the following year. In the middle of it, Carol was yanked from our class into something special—an academy downtown for students so gifted they needed to be rescued from failing schools. I didn't have time to be jealous, she just disappeared.

I hear news, once in awhile, even after twenty years. I ran into someone who reported that Carol's head was shaved, barely fuzzy, and purplish red. How does that work, having no hair and dyed hair, on the same scalp?

—Did you know Carol was a doctor? my informant asked.

No, I didn't know that.

—Remember Helen Chute? She's living with her. As in, they're dykes. Helen Chute, who used to run DePaul Hospital. And they've adopted three little boys from South America. There's Pablo from Peru, Henry from Columbia, and another one from Brazil.

But Helen Chute must be pushing seventy!

—The paper ran an article about them.

I admit, it bugged me. News of divorces, mental illness, addictions, the legal problems—it's easier to take. When I heard about Helen Chute and Carol's boys and Carol's lesbian hair, I experienced a deeper pang. Perhaps I sensed yet another thing I should have done—become a lesbian? What an embarrassing thought.

She had a new lesbian name too, flowery but assertive. An appalling name, actually, one that stuck out like a little sign which said, *I am not my father's daughter.* Which is what she said, I heard, to someone from our school.

But you are your father's daughter. That's the truth.

And I'm here, pacing the floor, in my little truth shack. Welcome, Carol. It's cramped, and it annoys me, but it's what I have. It rents by the month, sort of. I didn't know this was going to turn into a letter, but writing has its own logic and I need to let myself follow that (according to my drug counselor).

DEAR CAROL. . .

It's been a long time. Hope you are well, et cetera. It's winter and I'm holed up in the small coastal town of Two Creeks, Oregon. I came here for fog, cold beaches, and wholesome companions. Have you ever needed to chill out? I have tried it before, and to tell the truth, the boredom became so stifling I was willing to crawl out through the air conditioning ducts. This time I'm trying something different: every sick thought gets flushed to the page. *The writing cure.*

Do you remember the intersection of 47th and Jennet? Crossing from north to south would get your ass kicked if you were white and vice-versa if you were Black. Fuck was life, at least in our part of Chicago.

So I left. And I discovered a fucking big country. You must have noticed how dumb this country is. I'm still not used to how many white people there are. How did you deal with the stress of hauling your ass across the map? How did you arrive in the visible world?

A year or so ago I ran into Amy Brooks. She's thin now and has wrinkly eyes. She couldn't remember the night we tried to break into the Isher House. I asked what she did remember from the old neighborhood, and she admitted she had no memories at all. Just an emotion: fear.

I remember everything. It's a distraction, like being haunted.

But I liked the streets after a rain. All the airborne soot drained down the gutters and the cobblestones were shiny.

It's been two weeks so I'm allowed day passes to get out of the house. Today I walked down the main street of this little town. It was lined with ornamental fruit trees and the branches were dripping—black shiny branches, no buds yet. They looked like the writing on this page, all jumbled up. The street took me right down to the ocean and then stopped in a cluster of concrete cubes. I sat on one and felt the wind-blown sand scratch my face, erasing it. I don't know what I want. Whatever comes after this blot of time they call rehab, the thought of a new lover or job, it just exhausts me. Is there something else, an empty space, that I can go into and touch? With my instrument: a liquid spade, and my heart: a fear radiator.

Do write back.

Sincerely,
Camille

MY X STORY

MY X STORY

X and I travel south through a county
          of big white cars
                                        & sweet plums—
                              there's funk on the radio.
          I wear a low brimmed hat with a feather.
X has on stockings and heels, there's a jaunty cut to her coat.
          She says   *With you I felt no guilt.*
                                        I was willing to do almost anything for that.

Her cigarette makes a red spot in the dark.

I look out at the lights of Bakersfield, Rosedale, Oildale.
The industrial rim marks a boundary
between the city and the desert.   *I'm shy about death.*
Before the factories shut down I could see fires
from my window at night.

HONEY MINE

Car wheels churn gravel up a steep driveway. Ocean, clouds.
I meet Alfred. The ex-husband has a moist tan.
He gives me a room alone
a sky blue window ledge
comfort at being enclosed.
In the afternoon X
presents herself,
looking smart
in a black dress
and little red hat.
I've put on my grey silk tie.
We're compatible in a way,
says X. *I like you, and you*
like my looks.
I have a slip.
White rags
spread with a butter spoon
soft spotting under
my skin—
it's so easy, at first—
my tongue laps her cheekbones
thin as rails
something I lean against while looking out
on a ship,
a tanker,
spidered with helicopters.
Distant line of fire.

Later, we watch one another
as indifferent Alfred smooths the sheets.

When I was small the world started at my stomach and melted outward in waves. My sisters ate at the same table. The three boys were farther and measured in their distance, moving like a clump at sunset along a cord stretched between two women. One snipped the flowing butt off a firefly and put it on my finger.

That was Sam. When I was fourteen he did a slide show, a week after he got his discharge. Pictures of dead people taken by someone I was related to was the closest I'd ever been to death. The bodies were lying in tall grass and were hard to see. Sam had smooth eyebrows over brown eyes and a sloppy jaw, jerky with amphetamines. He'd enlisted because he loved Goldwater and when he got out he was a drug addict. But at least he learned a trade.

Sam was the cousin who leaned down into the window of the sandwich shop, grinning. He'd landed the helicopter in my parents' front yard and hitched into town to see me. Around that time there were rumors he would fly for anyone—running guns or drugs for the wrong side in small countries. It's not impossible. Sam worked whenever he wanted, otherwise lived in a trailer with a woman named Sara.

Composition is like a new car, or kitchenettes.

It creates a frame around disconnected events.

So after Sara left him for nobody, leaving no note,

Sam wrote a spy novel. That's the story.

MY X STORY

For X, sex is a combo of string and
past tense. It covers her yards of mouth.

I lick the flesh like an envelope. (Bondage.) Says X,
How bad were you today

baby**.** Her knees press my temples,
there's a curly fence near my mouth.

(Imploded recognition.) When I learned
about gender I was very surprised.
The proceedings slid from a folder,

there were loose papers all over the floor.
Before that, I had only

experienced animals. *It's not impossible*,
I thought,

Anyone who likes to be fucked is a
girl,
anyone who only likes to be fucked is a
woman.

The soft light over the Los Angeles hills seemed rubbed with an eraser. I was 16. I felt like I was hitchhiking, since I hardly knew the cousin who was driving. His name was Jim.

His pickup had beer in the back. We drove up a canyon to his place, an apartment in a weathered turquoise building next to a stand of eucalyptus. It was June, and the eucalyptus

had dropped dry skinny leaves all over the parking lot. We walked up the stairs; inside were Sam, Mike, my sisters. Jim's apartment was a one-bedroom with a kitchenette.

Mike pulled open the back door to show me what a fucked place it was: the back stairs had been torn down so the door opened on empty space. Mike was the family golden boy,

he turned in the light like a fish, sluggish. He left the door open and settled back on the couch, next to Sam, who drew his long legs up. It was twilight and through the open door

the sky was turning a deep blue streaked with smoke. There was an odor of beer. Then the cousins made a show of picking up and flipping through some porn magazines.

My sisters went for it, arguing like their own sincerity was forever. It was hard to take. My grandmother was new in the dirt, buried that day and no one could shut up (except me).

MY X STORY

My sister said I shouldn't have sex until my nipples turned
brown, which I figured she thought would never happen.
She was older, and kept her drugs and screwing

in the basement the same way she kept her jewelry there. Her
lovers were thin white men whose trouble was drug-related.
When Paul left Cook County Jail he carried an odor of rape

he had large nerve spots in his eyes. Fear moving like a breeze
in a prison yard, I could feel that in my stomach when he was
around; otherwise I didn't care. I thought about Monica.

Her sharp teeth and brown cheeks. The way her greed
slid across my hips could be scary but her palms were
narrow as slots, that made it okay to have sex with her.

Monica was Black in a segregated city; so the closer we got

the more transparent I became, my longing vicious

as wavering lights of association. Relation—the spot where

we're the same, or at least rolling downhill on a boulevard

lined with palm trees and novelty shops.

So when Sam said, *Any real man would rape a 14-year-old*

if he saw her naked,

it shut me up.

Pressure doesn't yield a true statement but softens
underfoot,
like nylons in a wad. It's more than gymnastics.
Doors and windows of the body squeak, light as paper.
This carpet I'm eyeing glints back
an acrylic mat, fishy browns.

Next on my list

Thrusting
my hand through
the ribs of X
Warm slimy blood
on my fingers,
bits of bone
What a mess.
I want to do
something
for you,
I say
to X, staring
at my hand.
I wrap it
in my shirttail;
now it looks like a bandage
thought the gesture
was sexy & fun.

One day after school Monica brought me home.

I sat on a yellow chair and we listened to the radio: *WVON, Otis Spann The Blues Man,* coming from the kitchen. A plaid couch was covered with sisters with white teeth and dark skin, laughing at me I thought. The rooms were hot, or just full of the weather and leaning out over the window sills I saw white stone pots of geraniums at the door. We watched the street—a tall drunk wobbled after a woman in a flowered house dress whose crooked eyes bulged out in two directions. She turned and hacked out a laugh. Monica said her stomach split every year with a new kid.

<u>Or was that my block?</u>

I liked the closed-in feeling—relation defined through position and abandonment, the meaning of **fix**. *So the streets were deserted after dark and any stranger carried death!*

It's one a.m., and the snow is falling through a web of fine black particles, soot from the mills. Monica's shielding her cigarette from the wind while I try to remember where I am; on a block that slides uneasily from white to Black. She's wearing a red T-shirt under the black jacket. We've just come out of the basement. We started out watching each other, lips back, drinking beer. Where our skin slides together along the damp basement wall, there's a streak of feeling like a welt. I open another beer, to sink this awful strangeness. Then her palms are warm and under my jaw, sliding back around my head. That's okay, so I peel off her t-shirt. it is very interesting how dark her nipples are. I touch them with my fingers then my lips then I lean back, feeling thin as a sheet. I'm washed out, ripped. She kisses me clear to the back of the throat, where the tongue splits. I figure I don't

She tells me her mama said *You're old enough to know to keep your pocketbook closed*, and we laugh about that.

Monica walks into school
her fingers loosely rolled
a snap to her stride.
It's September.
Still summer
there's that other kind of light.
Weeds line the crack, there are gardens in vacant lots.

Between classes we're kept in formation, think lines of skittish kids on opposite sides of the hall. Green iron bars cover the windows. Gang wars edge in over the grey pavement of the school yard. Monica is light on her feet, quick by necessity. I want to please—I don't know why—I follow and give her books from the library. *I'm sorry they're stolen*, I say. She says, *Sorry didn't do it, you did*, and laughs. Like she does when she tells me about the death. Even I know that's wrong, to laugh at her daddy, dragged out of a taxicab, dead of a heart attack at 44. It's late in the day. We're standing by the window in an empty classroom, the sky behind her shoulder is a dull blue. When I tell her to quit laughing, she wipes a smile on and runs out of the building.

She got poorer after that. She had to move out of the district.

X spreads gleaming

micas across her eyelids

& clips her hair. The

blond ends fall on a

glass-topped vanity table.

Her relatives cut their

hair off before they split

up

she's heard that. She strokes her lips
red. *I'm the private glamour in a dead*
public, she thinks. After each orgasm
she's happy for hours, it makes her want
to change course and slip

under what she wanted before. Pursing her lips for the mirror, *I should hang cool sight lines next to the bed, a thin frame containing light footsteps across the water. If I were certain of finding what I want*, she wonders, *would I become smaller.*

X and I are driving through a warehouse district after getting out of a movie. I'm morose; my mood is bruised. X stubs out her Camel filter and asks *What's the matter, babe. Too much wild, wild life?*

I'm thinking about the moment when Freddy Krueger jumped out of thin air. *Horror movies seem so familiar*, I say. *It's like waiting grimly for some lunatic thing to pop out of a family's member's mouth; then it happens and you want to slide under the table. But I like to go to them; they're so repetitious. It's like my own private joke.*

X says *You feel vindicated when something horrible happens.*

I'm thinking it's true, it's the only thing that makes the inexplicable burst like a bubble. I look out the window at the warehouses.

Nah, I say, finally. *It's just that something always pops out that reveals the essential nature. And you're either waiting for it, or you've been set up, and which is better.*

X laughs, sort of cautiously.

It's that climate of expectation, I say. *Like when I was a kid and it would get so fucking hot even the Lake*

was hot but you had to go swimming
even though the Lake had pee in it.
I mean a lot of pee
and dead fish. It was that hot
I was with my sister
before she was a beatnik
she was wearing a yellow bathing suit
with a white belt and cat eye glasses.
She was sitting on the beach
eating a hot dog with pickle relish
and reading her theatrical magazines.
I ran in diving and splashing
coming up inside a bunch
of grinning kids whose teeth gleamed
like an ad for toothpaste.
The biggest pushed my head under
once, twice. I surfaced gasping
knees scraped.
The horizontals were dazzling
those stacked grins like ladder rungs
I couldn't climb.
A glimpse of a withered grey pier
then a Black finger in my eye
and the shining water smacked my chin.
I was under again.
I started to kick.
I must've made some noise

because my sister ran into the water,
waving her hot dog.
My tormentors scattered at the sight
of her adult-size thighs, laughing.
That was it.

I'd thought skin color was decorative.

I found it was territorial.

And I stayed out of the water, walking up and down the beach picking up pieces of worn glass bottles, mostly green some red and blue. Blue was the rarest.

X says, *You mark time backwards to the moment of damage.*

She threatens but she won't leave me. I'm already missing something. If there's a window in the room I'm looking out of it, leaning against the wall, hands stuffed into my pockets. I frown a lot, my face has acne scars.

Now Christmas eve is on with strings of big colored bulbs in the living room, and Eartha Kitt is drawling *Santa, baby*. . . on the radio. I pick up the *Sporting News* while X finishes her dressing, fastening a brooch with red and green paste jewels to her wool crepe jacket, then pulling on little Xmas boots, spike white heels under red felt. I have a weird yearning to get fucked up. Lately my mind sort of plops from one to the other of all the drugs I've got in the house. *I've got heroin in the basement*, I think, while reading about baseball contracts.

X likes hallucinogens and I like opiates—one of our differences.

HONEY MINE

X's chopped hair is cut like a cap.
She leans toward the mirror
gently pulls one lower eyelid down
then draws the short stub
under her lashes, making a thick black line.
When done with both eyes
she tosses the pencil into the trash.
Another girlfriend gone.

MY X STORY

X gave me the word this morning, but
I can't think about it

. . . those perfect pouty lips. . . It was really a bad sign when
she painted them red before 9:30 in the morning. . .

I stare at those lips. An impossible disruption. Breach, that's
what this is. My mind foams, *Am I on the other side?*

It's my way or the highway, babe, says X.

An elastic grin surfaces under my feet. If we could
just shut up when we get close to one another—
then I'd be action NO PLOT, while X marks
the beginning of the story. I eroticize dread.
It's beginning again. Is our aggression a manner of speaking,
conversation taking shape?

HONEY MINE

More wishes:
A white car or a wide receiver.

Driving in the narrative of shadow.

X tells me I'm too much for her aching stomach.

I say, *If I left you I could steal anything*.

MY X STORY

Afternoon sun flattens the beige shingles of the apartment building where I used to live. There's something unexpectedly cool about the reflected yellow light. In one window a FOR RENT sign hangs. That apartment has two radiators in it, I happen to remember. My taste for accuracy is like gleaming chrome window knobs on an abandoned car. The apartment is roomy, there's room for two. X worked as a bookkeeper and I was a thief. Once I stole a whole Xerox machine and stripped it for parts. It was there when Camille, a neighbor, bought a stereo and speakers from me for 75 bucks. X gave her attitude, eyeing her disdainfully while painting her toenails on the couch. I think Camille liked that. She's the kind that likes a bruise. Anyhow she seemed pretty interested when she was casing our stuff. There's not much of a market for hot copiers. I piled what I couldn't sell in the middle of the living-room floor when we left town.

I knew those two. Frank, the building manager, told me they left an answering machine behind when they split, with a bunch of messages on it from *your husband, Alfred*. Frank ran into them when they were packing up their car, a white '67 Plymouth Valiant with decorative turn signals on the hood and a dark red interior. They said they'd be going south down Interstate 5 to Bakersfield, then cutting east to Las Vegas. He was surprised that they were all paid up on their rent, but I wasn't. It was the honest bookkeeper girlfriend, settling accounts. She had the soft round eyes of a calf and a smudged pout. When I bought a stereo from them she eyed me like I was one of her girlfriend's vices. I figure the thief was the kind who ignored bills. She had long skinny thighs and a weird bob in her walk, like her joints were too loose. She was secretive but could flash a warm smile on and off, at least for me.

That got me razzed; I don't know why. I want to peel that smile off and put it in my pocket.

CRAQUER: An Essay on Class Struggle

1. Lydia & Pearl

My cousin Sam called me and asked if a spur of the moment visit was okay—sure, but why, I wondered, after so long? We hadn't seen one another in such a long time that this was the first time I'd met Sam's twelve year old son, Darryl. Mostly Darryl roamed around the house as Sam and I had ginger-lemon tea in the kitchen. Sam and Darryl were in the middle of an exhausting drive from Los Angeles to Eureka. He told me his mother (my aunt) had given him a copy of my first book. He didn't elaborate but I understood what he was referring to—the passage about his speed addiction and rumors that he ran guns and drugs for the wrong side in small countries. My cousin is a helicopter pilot, a skill he learned in Vietnam. He shopped that skill around after he got back.

Then Sam told me what he'd been doing for the last decade. In retrospect it seems like he performed a polite, thorough, even quasi-official registration of a "change in character." Helicopter rescue—that's his job. It turns out my cousin is a leading innovator in this specialty, being the only pilot in the country who can do it without any assistants. This makes him very popular with strapped rural county fire, flood, and mountain rescue departments. He works wherever a disaster breaks out in Northern California. The work comes in keen adrenalin surges. Bobbing free lines over choppy water. Scooping chilled corpses from the ocean. Raising children up out of the flames.

I guess Sam didn't like what I'd written about him. He said, "I tried writing, and I found I just couldn't do *that* to other people."

I objected but mildly. I sipped my tea. After he left, I found myself stewing, then I began a strenuous argument in my head. It boiled down to this—if I'm the only one with the appetite to tell a story, it must belong to me. I do the work. It comes down to my appetite, which in turn comes down to whatever grips my powers of recognition. That's what makes my little engine purr. I take the facts and expand along lines of thrill, aiming for unreliability, its quivering heart.

Of course, here I am assuming my cousin was referring to my writing. But he'd just been talking about his mother, Lydia, telling me various sordid difficulties. He was trying out the thing one tries at one time or another: "naming the experience." That followed by a dazzled look, as his features relaxed and fell away from one another. Why do those loaded difficult words feel empty? The ones used to label childhood traumas. Whatever. Maybe Sam gave up on writing because he couldn't write about his mother, or around her. This I can understand. Our moms are sisters, daughters of the stalwart Mabel Margaret. My mother, Pearl, is the blond one, the milkmaid, but built for the fifties. All sleekly muscular curves. Lydia, Sam's mother, was built the same way but tawny in coloring, brown irises surprisingly dark. She has a widow's peak. Raymond, their dad, was a wayward gambler-prospector with a gift for abandonment. Dumping his family during the Depression, he ran off for high times with a couple of seriously odd women. More about that later.

My mother, Pearl, was born babbling in the nascent Los Angeles of the 1920s. Her accent was dubbed "American West" by an Italian linguist, who studied her in astonishment. I imagine she probably told him she was born in

Winnemucca, Nevada—it sounds more appealingly Western than LA, the hard desert sun boiling everything down versus coastal haze. When I mentioned Pearl's birth in Winnemucca to Lydia, her brown eyes glared at me in outrage—Pearl once again pulling a fast one. Lydia ran off for the birth certificates. They verified her story: Pearl was born in Los Angeles, and Lydia was born in Winnemucca.

They had different personal styles: Lydia took the truth hostage, guarding it jealously. Pearl abandoned it on a daily basis. What was at stake?

Family reunions were rare but intense. I recall one reunion where our moment of collision gave way to a rolling obscure fight which lasted three days, wet and smothering with too much booze: Lydia's four boys versus Pearl's three girls—a strange proliferation, all charged up. We didn't argue, we fought. Lots of politics, especially relating to sex. Still I loved them fiercely, each strange male cousin. Once Sam snipped the butt off a firefly and put it on my finger. Bitterness inside a sexual fog—that was the surface. Underneath was the grudge we inherited, Pearl and Lydia's inscrutable calculus of betrayal and loyalty.

Lydia didn't remember Raymond, she was a baby when he left. Pearl was older—probably around seven—but didn't remember anything before the age of sixteen. Pearl's lack of memory was terrifically odd, itself a thing of great plasticity. It was as though out of pure will she'd substituted imagination for memory.

At fifteen, I was a rapt audience for Pearl's nightly performances, my attention made out of hard particles of dread and identification. Families are nuclear, and nuclei are smashed together. Do you know the difference between the weak and the strong forces? The strong one is the massive force of the universe, binding quarks of opposite charge. It's only exercised across tiny distances, such as families. Everything else is weakness. I loved the dazzle: Pearl's career as a high diver at the Depression-era fairs (aborted by an exhibition high dive belly flop that left her sinking to the bottom of the pool in a coma), the swim to glory and medals, making the Olympic team the year the games were cancelled, Pearl's socialist Jewish father, Raymond, and his movie star friends (who even had movie star animal pals), the opium dens of Winnemucca. History made of such sparkles. The father in this tale even had a violin. (Lydia would later insist it was only a guitar.) The stories disappeared into one poignant pang after another. I couldn't notice how they didn't add up. I was too pleased with being part Jewish, and striped with Olympic muscles. It helped me in the neighborhood.

Sam remembers Raymond. At least, he thinks he might remember him. Twenty five years after dumping Lydia, Pearl, and my Christian Science grandmother, Mabel Margaret, Raymond rang Lydia's doorbell. Sam was three, banging a spoon in his highchair. Lydia had invited Raymond to come. It was oddly like dating: mutual friends had introduced father and daughter to one another. *Life is strange on the frontier.*

Raymond arrived wearing a big Stetson and black lizard skin cowboy boots. His shirt had that swirly piping on it, I imagine it as yellow piping on soft cream colored rayon, a cowboy shirt with iridescent snaps. Very fifties, Hank Williams Senior—love that dude, don't you? Anyway, when Lydia told me about this she handed me a postcard. *The Silver Dollar, Winnemucca, Nevada* was written in thick toothpaste script on the photo of a cowboy bar interior—saddles on the wall, spurs. That's Raymond behind the bar, she told me. He looked tall but old, gazing down at the beer he was pulling.

Lydia had been a baby when Raymond left. There wasn't money to feed two children, so Mabel Margaret sent Pearl to relatives. Mean ones, of course, a chilly farming couple who were unhappy to have to share their bread and garden peas with a boisterous little girl whose nickname was Butch. Filled with high-spirited declarations, Pearl always insisted that she refused to see Raymond ever again. She was good at leaving, we all have that survival skill. So, of course, I believed her, in fact I adopted her attitude—*Nasty Pops, you may be dead but I'm never going to speak to you.* Actually, Lydia admitted to me that she had kept Raymond's visit to herself. She hadn't told Pearl that she knew where Raymond lived, or even that he was alive. Three months later he was dead.

Winnemucca, that's where the family's sense of itself is somehow concentrated. As a place, unbelievable. It doesn't cohere. I think I've actually been there but I don't remember it. After the highway signs—hasn't everyone seen them?—347 miles to Winnemucca! 213 miles to Winnemucca! 24 miles to Winnemucca!—I got there, drove through, and nothing stuck. I want to go back, but it has to be the 1930s. I want to see the top half of Raymond's face. Fleshy, grinning. Holding the squirming laughing baby that resembles my mother. This is the only photograph remaining of Raymond and it shows only his jaw. The rest were destroyed. But in the one remaining you can see his reddish skin, a fringe of white blond hair. He doesn't look Jewish. My mother's eyes are the color of aquamarine.

Hopscotching all over the west in his helicopter, Sam ended up spending time in Winnemucca, where he nosed out the old gamblers who had known Raymond. *Oh yeah, Raymond, dirty bastard. Died owing me three thousand dollars.*

Sam's legs under the table tilt and amble with the autonomy of length. Sam is a *long drink of water.* His head droops languidly onto his upraised hand as he leans forward, his voice husky with a secret. Have you heard the one about Raymond and Aimee?

Of course I had. But I had put it in the magic box along with so many of Pearl's stories—like the one about Pearl hurling herself over ski jumps for cash prizes. The repeating theme, with endless variations: *poor girl but plucky, poor girl but so lucky*. The ski jump story particularly puzzled me, it just didn't square with the character of Pearl, who was not at all relaxed about falling. I didn't exactly not believe it, either—I didn't disbelieve any of Pearl's stories. I was incapable of such concrete, restrained opinions. There was some essence shared by every fable told by Pearl, and I believed in that spacious combination of style and unreliability. The narrative gesture—that's what I believed in. It swayed me. I believed in anything that swayed me.

Pearl landing in a powdery snow puff, having fallen or flown through hundreds of feet of sparkling air. . . This image in a repeating loop, with her face appearing, gathering gravity, creamy pink and blond and yet, with the square jaw, oddly butch. Her milkmaid skin, etched with a dazzling smile, becoming in that white fog—becoming what? I was caught in many such puzzles. Of these, Raymond and Aimee was possibly the least significant.

I'm talking now about Aimee Semple McPherson, the first Pentecostal monster of the twentieth century, and female. The first woman to cross the United States in an automobile (something she did fourteen times, with her mother and young son). It was a 1912 Packard touring car with 'Jesus is coming soon, get ready!' painted on the side in gold.

Not an ascetic. A minx, a woman made for *worldly love.* She drew crowds everywhere, preaching her words of fire in a low silky voice.

There are four major charismata (or gifts of the spirit) defined by the Pentecostalists: glossolalia (speaking in tongues), prophecy, interpretation of tongues, and the gift of healing. In the last, Aimee was prodigiously talented. She became a healer of such documented genius that a major church would be built upon it, a church which still stands. Invalids, cripples, the blind and deaf filled the streets by the thousands when she preached. Her ascent began in the early days of Hollywood and her temple was built there in 1924. She strode the pulpit like a star in robes, her hair pressed to her scalp in rolling blond waves, her voice palpitating the crowd. On August 7, 1925, she took up in her palm a field stone and called out in a booming voice,

> *A new heart also will I give you, and a new spirit will I put within you: and I will take away the stony heart out of your flesh, and I will give you a heart of flesh.*

She was too sexy for God. Rumors swirled around her. She disappeared for weeks, and would later cover for these absences by claiming to have been mysteriously kidnapped.

Lacerated in court and in the press about these stories, she would only say, "That's my story, boys, and I'm sticking to it."

For me, the only odd thing about the story of Raymond and Aimee was Pearl's troubled gaze as she told it, as though she herself found it almost unbelievable. What kind of story would Pearl find unbelievable? That question I could barely pose, let alone answer. It didn't invite inquiry. But that day in my kitchen, Sam told me he had investigated it in Winnemucca. The old gambling buddies of Raymond once again came through with the details. Apparently Raymond claimed Aimee had beach boys stashed in towns up and down the coast of California. Of all these men, Raymond used to brag, *I was the one Aimee loved for his mind.*

A joke rumbled along my synapses, tickled my tongue. *Sam, we come from a long line of sluts of both sexes.* But that's pushing it, and it's not even what I meant. I wanted to point to the heart of the story, a quality of perishing, or making another perish, for a romantic idea. Those painful yet pleasing sacrifices. . . A family pattern. Then, by the same gesture, we live perpetually in the melancholy aftermath, the empty house. Five years after Raymond left, Lydia and Pearl stood near as Mabel Margaret sat heavily down at the kitchen table, holding Raymond's first letter. It would contain the divorce papers.

Meanwhile, excuse me, this word, *ruthless*, keeps flickering as I write this. . .a scorching little flame. Where did it come from? Sam, I want to say right now, You are wrong about me. I'm not ruthless! At least not today. I had to go back to my diary to discover he'd actually called me that. Well, sort of. What I wrote above is a misquote. Sam actually said, *I could never be a writer. I'm not ruthless enough.*

My cousin Sam: *Floats like a butterfly, stings like a bee.* Perhaps his words wouldn't sting if they weren't in some part true. Still it pisses me off. And I'm the writer, so vengeance is mine. Listen to this: Sam, in the midst of his speed addiction, used to claim he'd been invaded by alien space worms. To prove it, he took a match to one of his arm hairs—and before it burnt to the skin, it straightened, pointing up to the heavens. *See,* Sam would hiss, *they're alive.*

Sigh. A petty gesture, making Sam look ridiculous. Is that what you're thinking? You weren't at the table, you weren't floating suspended in my peculiar family history. I remind myself of an oil slick, over deep and choppy waters. Comfortable it isn't. Anyway, it occurs to me that by repeating malicious gossip I'm only spoiling my own case—in this manner discovering that I have a case, and that I want to present it to you, dear reader. Who knew! A little self-sabotage can go a long way.

But what could my case possibly be, given that the prospect of verifying any of these family stories is unbearable, as well as irritating? I've given up. That's my "case." I don't care what the truth is—not enough to pursue it, anyway. I'm registering something more vague—a sort of cloud at the center of the story, which is where I've spent most of my life. That's the first principle.

Then there's the second, which is the net cast over my flowing perceptions, a.k.a. "aesthetics." At one time, I envied and loathed the access gay men had into that word/world. Whereas lesbians seemed to occupy cultural space which was aesthetically null and void. I'm not sure how it changed, socially or personally. But now it seems that I just can't get out. The urge to aestheticize, to edit and invent, is my urge to think. There's inescapable falsity in my condition. *If you believe what I write, watch your back.* I can't stand behind my stories because I don't think that way. The power is in the filter—whatever my brain dishes up as the next thought, well, it feels like me, but it's not.

Who hasn't been lied to, constantly? Viewed from another angle, it's a gift. I remember Pearl, eyeing me after a few vodkas with the closest thing that she possessed to wickedness, *You*, she snapped, *can write. You're like your father. I just can't.* Then stalking off into the remainder of her mysterious evening.

Pearl's stories pulsed with desire, fantasy, and dread. They became me. Then they blurred, disappeared. I live in the aftermath. The snag, its lingering disturbance, feels muscular. It resides there, as I shove one foot ahead of the other, in all the sites of pleasure and aggression, intact as my confidence.

Still, realization is difficult. I mentioned something about this to Sam. Jewish, or not? Olympic, non-Olympic. . . He grinned in his loopy way (his lips are thin but his mouth is wide and stretchy) and told me this story about an Indian, whose name was also Sam. Sam met Sam during a forest fire, in the little town of Union Hill in the northeastern corner of California. The ridges were ablaze, and Sam was doing what he does, dropping fire-fighting chemicals possibly, or rescuing ranch hands. In between shifts, Sam holed up in the only hotel in town. You'd think that since he was rescuing people and livelihoods, the townsfolk might have been a little friendly. But not so. This was a High Sierra town which held on where the roads ended, and it had a particular psychology. To the east, hard granite ridges propped up the rim of the sky. The mountains were so rugged there were no passes over for hundreds of miles—and to the west, there was nowhere to go but down.

There were three vegetables in the Union Hill grocery store: a small pile of hard tomatoes, some withered carrots, and a single head of iceberg lettuce. This was distressing because Sam is a vegetarian. Everyone looked at him with hatred, except the other Sam, who wouldn't stop talking. With every breath, he told my cousin the legends of himself, and they were spectacular, if you appreciate rodeo. This Sam had been a champion many times over. There were stories of bulls and broncos, silver spurs, money that flowed. He was also a terrible drunk. Sam practically told these stories from the floor, or the gutter. Knee level at the highest. It all gushed unbelievably, the stories and the booze. Still, after the fires had worn themselves out, while the air was still smoky, Sam stopped at the local library and looked up the dates and stories in newspaper archives. Everything, it turned out, was true. Sam was so famous, his horse was famous too. Sam's nickname had the word *diamond* in it.

2. Blur

Remember the class struggle? I do. The adults in my household were commies. When I was a kid, class struggle was a thing bigger, and more vivid. Bigger than what? *Like Iron Mike, like Tyson.* It's what this essay is supposed to be about. In truth, I am slouching, ever so slowly, into that conversation. We're in the post-communist era now. All that was reddish has fallen into a pit of silence—which is not particularly new or different. Pretty much everything falls in there.

But back to the story of Pearl. How do we get from Nevada to anywhere else, ideologically speaking? It must come down to character. Picture this: Pearl, radiant & shining (but in a dumb way), as she stumbles down the center of a deserted road. Pale cracks at the horizon light the scene for sacrifice. Each pair of oncoming headlights flattens and drains a little more from her rosy charms. She's fifty miles out in the desert with only a thermos of Bloody Marys. It doesn't look good. But Pearl is too subtle for this particular disaster. I can guess from an assortment of possible scenarios: She'll hitch a ride with a local Spanish speaking priest or, alternatively, with a chivalrous dyke mechanic who goes by the name Eddie, or perhaps the mild-mannered man pulling over in the burgundy Buick will turn out to be a Nobel prize-winning physicist driving to a conference in Taos. Whoever her companion happens to be, Pearl will persuade him or her to stop at a vista point to watch the sun rise over the desert and talk politics (Pearl will do most of the talking), while they slurp what's left from the thermos. And Pearl will arrive home spouting a joyful music about decency, reliability, solidarity, community, etcetera.

Pearl is the most elusive person I have ever known. A genius of charm.

Pearl was also, as I haven't explained, raised on a faith-healing religion, not the gloriously dramatic Temple of Aimee Semple McPherson, but the stubborn doctrines of Mary Baker Eddy. *Christian Science.* After Raymond took off, Mabel Margaret found respite in a reading room. Eventually she founded her own, in her living room, for herself, her two daughters, Pearl and Lydia, and an elderly bachelor named Ronald. This little group of four were the only Christian Scientists in town. During their evening studies, they mumbled and moaned and passed the book from lap to lap. Then, on weekends, Pearl and Lydia went door to door with pamphlets, two lovely girls with soft cheeks and shining hair. Never in need of medical care, the girls were implicit testimonies to the power of faith and prayer. But no one converted.

Faith, as a form of insistence, is an oddly stable construct, given that it brings in relation two contrary mental formations—pouring emotion (some form of religious exaltation) and an intellectual framework designed to provide stasis, as a necessary stabilizer. Its electrifying core can transition from religion to politics with little more than a change in vocabulary.

In a hypothetical marriage between a faith-healer and a hardcore leftie, the latter would seem a little like a dumb lug out of the movies. Part thug, but also oddly innocent, in the way that stupidity can seem comically blundering. You know how straight men can be innocent of themselves, their fantastical drives cloaked by pseudo-technical terminology? It's so boring. The intellectual left has that problem. Anyway. In my scenario, Blanche DuBois rules simply because her drive towards emotional extremes wounds and confuses everything around her. Poor Stanley. He's paralyzed by her spectacle, as well as his own befuddled desire to *do right*.

The covert fantasies which motivate the need to believe—these are the muscular terms in a language of transformation. That's the burn. It's the first spot in this essay where class explicitly slips in (look quickly or you'll miss it). Fuck everything else. My mother's side of my family teeters right on the edge of self-dramatization and self-destruction, and since everybody winds up dead, you know how the story ends.

> Or perhaps it's impossible to mark the ending of family stories. Too much clutter. I was intrigued to find in a recent biography of Aimee that one of her 'kidnappers,' a charming but unsuccessful prospector and gambler from Nevada, sounded much like Raymond. Receipts for food and dry cleaning (which were evidence in her perjury trial until they vanished under mysterious circumstances) showed Aimee and this man holed up in a hotel for several weeks. Hijinks of the spiritually gifted. It's unverifiable but it feels like that warm trough in the bed next to Aimee was filled by Raymond—is that true enough?

Still, I have to insist on my argument. Can we stop piling blur on top of blur? As a goal, people. Of course, I've never told a story straight in my life (and in this essay, I haven't tried). This is not hypocrisy, because consistency is not my point. I'm a seamstress of blur, performing nips and tucks on the empty center. But I need to know where it is. Is that just personal taste, like clean underwear?

3. First Comes Love

Pearl met my father at a Communist Party meeting in the early fifties. I like to imagine the ardor of their first glance across a smoky room, crowded with people engaged in passionate political conversation. Youth being a plush velvet suit, deep and soft, yet lacerated with the rigorousness of all those sexual impulses. But this wasn't Paris, with its aestheticized frenzies. It was the South Side of Chicago, a place that hangs you upside down and whacks the sentimentality right out. They moved in a community whose (exhausting) urgency came from the streets, the factories, the union halls.

My parents met at a C.P. meeting. That's all I know. I never heard what they said to or thought of each other. No personal touches. Somehow that didn't qualify as 'material.' (Is this a Marxist definition of *material*?) But I heard another story, over and over. It was a late night story, when the household temperament went from coolly intellectual to soft and sudsy. This one was a little drama with Pearl's shrink. Before Pearl met my father, she had been sticking her toe into the murky waters of psychoanalysis. Introspection was not her style, but her boohoo intellectual friends were doing it, and since it was the fifties, the shrink was Freudian, and since she was broke, Pearl had an analyst-in-training who charged twenty five cents an hour. This man was fond of telling Pearl that her life was a fantasy. This was his response to everything she told him about her childhood, her first failed marriage, her political beliefs, her friends. When she came in with tales of my father (talldarkandhandsome, smart, communist AND social register), he calmly told her this was also a hallucination.

It was to be Dr. Cornfield's last such pronouncement. With sweeping gestures Pearl described the wedding announcement that ran in the Chicago dailies. It took up a whole page. Why her wedding announcement took up ten times more space than anyone else's was never specified, but the implications were clear enough—it had to do with the shock communism of a son of the ruling classes and his inappropriate divorcee wife-to-be, Pearl. In any case, Pearl didn't go to her last session with her shrink. She snuck into his office and left the clipping on his desk.

Perfect moment of revenge, possibly invented. Any invention being possible, especially when we are sexually soiled, wild, fruitful, & poor. Being the wrong favor, yet being chosen, Pearl went adventuring. It poured out easily, warm companions found in the doorways of the city. I can picture my father's mother, Ethel, watching my parents through the window of her elegant Gold Coast apartment, her green eyes half-closed as she lifts an ebony and ivory cigarette holder to her lips. A barely audible sigh as she releases a thin snake of smoke.

This I know is true: having chosen one another they believed they were free.

With a feeling like yearning but more vague, I used to check the wedding announcements in the Chicago papers. Everyday I'd sneak a glance at that page, looking for any announcement, just one, that was over-size. Not that I was fact-checking my mother—I only wanted context. I wanted to be located in relation to some other over-size wedding announcement. But they invariably looked the same: a small paragraph of copy under a mug shot of a bride.

Once a mug shot of Pearl did appear in the paper.
It was because she was a pipe smoker. We all gathered round as she pointed to the excited caption:
"No more Lucky Strikes: Pearl is a woman who
swears by her small yet sturdy Norwegian pipe."

Thomas married Pearl at City Hall. They exchanged gold bands in front of a judge named Bogan. It was early on a Friday, in order to avoid the worst of Chicago's July heat. Still, the breeze off the lake was like a warm scarf. Pearl wore a blue suit of light crepe wool, but no hat or gloves.

There are no photos of this event. Due to my ignorance, I've made up every detail—*stonewall* being a shimmer that repulses. This was more my father's response to questions than my mother's. It sounds rather stiff, but it's really a form of motion, like a fine breeze in the sails of a little boat. You don't question the breeze; you just keep moving.

It's not what is told, but what is withheld, that creates suspense, so storytelling is partly the art of not telling. My household was greasy with that kind of suspense—or is that something all children experience? It may account for the flatness of childish expressions, their diffidence, a wariness around adults. I, at least, remember that emotion parsing everything I said. It took effort to detach facial expression from the act of speaking, but as much as possible I blanked my own face. With that kind of carefully contrived innocence (which I felt guilty about, but which was, in fact, ignorance), I remember remarking to Pearl that I didn't know anything about my father's father, since he had died before I was born. I was perhaps eleven, and we were having dinner. The adults were a wee bit sloshy. Pearl seized my idea, exclaiming to Thomas that he must must must instantly entertain us with tales of Thomas, Senior. Thomas replied, "There is nothing to say."

Pearl tried beguiling it out of him but Thomas was stubborn. After awhile Pearl's voice quivered, bluster melting into hysteria—"How can there be nothing to say about your own father?" Over and over again, Thomas would only respond, "There is nothing to say."

No way into that matrix. The argument dwindled off. In fact, nothing was ever said about Thomas Senior—his name never crossed my father's lips.

Thomas told me only one family story that I can remember, and I go fuzzy when I think of it, so I'm not sure how much of my memory is correct. He lifted his head up from the newspaper one night and told me how, when he was fifteen, he'd gotten a call from his aunt. As it happened, before she made the call she had drowned her son in the bathtub. Michael was a little boy with red hair and tender skin. A baby, perhaps? Was it two children that she murdered? I vaguely think that it was, but I'm not sure. In my memory the murders just begin with Michael and then take in, like a cloud of pestilence, whatever other children there were and the husband Jack, and then the murderess herself. I don't know her name. What went through my father's head when he hung up the phone? What was said in that conversation and what was implied? At the time, I was so shocked I couldn't think of any questions. Eventually I went to one of his sisters, and she told me her version of what had happened, which was distinctly different, but which had the feeling of truth. Like a godmother in a fairytale, this aunt is gentle and wholesome. Refreshing. Nonetheless, I've forgotten what she said.

This is a story I could get to the bottom of by going to the Chicago Public library and researching through the archives of the *Tribune*. Murderesses, especially double or triple with a possible suicide thrown in, tend to make the news. But would you want to play *Clue* with your own family history? Perhaps you would. For me, the prospect is inexplicably irritating.

> A friend questioned me on this—what is at stake, he wanted to know. Would the truth undermine the sense of myself I've constructed from these family histories? I'd be violating my own cloud of uncertainty, that's for sure. My self of no sense. Perhaps I like the cloud, and even believe in it. It's a habit—*I have always lived in the castle.* It's expansive, oddly permissive, as a form of identity. The irritating part is the work required to manage it.

Families trail off like the ghosts to whom we are all connected. They don't have a bottom. And it's not only ancestors, but other ungraspable relations which shadow me—from my father's silence to mother's dreamy milk. That's a sweet one.

It's not that Thomas never talked. What he said and didn't say never failed to surprise me. What he uttered came from a territory of silence. It entered with complete confidence but felt alien.

Once, eavesdropping, I heard Thomas and Pearl talking about a recent neighborhood rape, of a new girl in our neighborhood. Age-wise, I was somewhere in my slow descent through high school, and this girl was not much older. A stranger had broken into the her room, raped her, then he let her leave to do something oddly childish, I think she needed to feed her guinea pig. He let her out on the promise that she would come back and she did, and he raped her again. After a few weeks of mulling this over, she pressed charges. In my neighborhood, being streetwise mattered intensely so I could barely think of this girl as a person. Pearl responded to the story with complete impatience—perhaps she found the girl's inability to handle her circumstances threatening. Thomas' opinion was the surprise. He was sympathetic to this mysteriously stupid girl. He thought that perhaps she had come *from the country*. Sexually innocent, as well as innocent of our local racial politics, of the lacerating hostility that was part of our daily life, she suddenly found herself cluelessly adrift inside that (inside us), and was lost.

Thomas had more than a few such moments of sympathy, but they were as unpredictable as his little fits of irritability. I grew up in his city, in the city his parents had been born in, but there was little context. It was missing, and that was the loaded message. In our deep and disorderly photograph drawer, we had one picture of my father before he became my father. It shows a boy of about nine, wearing shorts and holding a pail. He is standing against a wall and grimacing awkwardly for the camera, as he squints into the sun. No one else is in the photo. It's just Thomas, but his fixed frightened eyes are on someone standing behind the camera, so that I feel that person—her hysteria. I think I know who it is.

4. The House of Ethel

Ethel. For me the word conveys a fine-tuned state of paranoia and high dudgeon. She was unbeautiful, despite her elegant figure. Her nose was a little beak, and her chin was awkwardly receded. But she had style. Observing Ethel ordering a cab over the phone was an electrifying experience. "I am

. . ." She spit and hissed every syllable of her long married name into the phone as if. . . as if—what? Vengeance, power, money, style were all at stake. And yet there was an impossible sheen to her speech, a melody. It was brutal, really, just the way she said her name. Had there been a time when random cab company dispatchers knew Ethel by name? Who am I to say, but probably. In any case, Joan Crawford's accent and style, in fact the vocal style of that generation of actresses, was a whole-cloth imitation of women like Ethel, for whom it was bred in the bone.

Ethel was always ready to meet the cruelty of the contest. I'm glad I didn't know her better. What I did know came from afternoons, maybe once a year, when Thomas and Pearl would load me into the car and drive with mysterious urgency to her north side apartment on Astor Street. The prospect of being five minutes late to Ethel's made Thomas tight and crabby. We had to arrive on the dot. I felt breathless.

Her building had a doorman. Her apartment was like its own climate—tones of soft, saturated beige, imported from the fifties like that was a foreign country. Snowy white wall-to-wall. Stacks of *Vogues*, in Italian, French, and German. The afternoons always followed the same pattern. Our coats were dispatched to an enormous closet. Then we were led to the living room, where we sat around an inlaid mahogany table on round upholstered chairs with no arms but odd little skirts, while Ethel reclined upon her divan, tiny feet crossed. She was inordinately proud of her small feet—size 4 1/2 before marriage, and five afterwards. From a mirrored cabinet, drinks for everyone (mine with the maraschino, ginger ale, and grenadine) and then, a round of cheddar cheese puffs, served on a silver tray by a maid who endured.

Delores. Ethel took a martini, and smoked one Kent after another, in a long ebony and ivory cigarette holder.

These afternoons were conducted like interviews, in which each person sitting on an armless chair would have to describe, in a manner amusing to Ethel, what they were up to. The goal was to raise a dry, appreciative laugh from Ethel; at stake was social humiliation of a degree so peculiar and yet severe, it was utterly mysterious. Each eroding second, every witty remark was part of the burnished display of her total control of social intercourse. Yet her eyes sparkled with pure fear. Ethel was a breath of terror inside the artifact of personality. One afternoon she asked me about my tennis, and I told her that I didn't know how to play tennis, then she said, but tennis is the best way to get bows, and by the way did I have any bows, and in distress I murmured WHAT? and she said BOWS and I cried out HUH and she said BOWS again, and this went on, with increasing agitation, until finally Thomas broke in and said *Mother, that is not a word people use anymore*, and *Camille, it means admirers*.

I didn't get it. I never did. Around Ethel I turned into a sloppy version of nice, which was obviously fake, and in any case, Ethel didn't appreciate sloppy. I assumed the guise of stupidity, which was protective, even if inaccurate. Dumbness can be sweeter. Stumbling down her halls, lined with photographs of grandchildren in tennis whites posing on their private courts or in country clubs, I never noticed there was no photo of me, or Pearl, or even Thomas.

The stupidity was feigned, but my cluelessness was deep and pure. I sailed through childhood sustained, on the one hand, by a combination of maternal fable and paternal missing links, and on the other by a strange belief that everything told to me by an adult was an un-truth. I believed in a sort of principle of opposites. The statements of adults were a kind of signpost, indicating that the reality I should act on was the opposite of whatever it was I had just been told. This boiled down to *I'll do whatever the fuck I want.* It took six years for the public school system to beat this out of my behavior (using the usual tools of suspension, flunking, etcetera), although of course it lingers in my beliefs today.

Let's get to the basics. When we speak of rules we are referencing contested territory. That includes not only injunctions on student behavior enforced by obscenely poor public school systems, but all the unwritten codes, the ones relating to unspeakable divisions and unbridgeable gaps. When they're violated, it's like invisible writing that appears when you hold the paper over a flame. There they are, the codes which describe intelligible experience. Since no one ever talked about them, I thought maybe they didn't exist. Hah. Break them and an a transformation happens. As the rules become intelligible, finally specified and visible, the person who violated them becomes unintelligible, slides off the map towards strange.

One example is the rule about what happens when the asphalt play lot of your elementary school erupts into a gang melee, ten-year-old girls imagining themselves to be representatives of Chicago's illegitimate armies, swinging at one another in a seething mass. The rule was that all the girls fighting were Black, and all the girls watching were white. But it looked like fun, so Camille broke that rule, jumping into the pool of flailing arms & fists. Then everyone acted embarrassed, so she got out. There was another rule about double-dutch, a great jump rope game that came up from the south with the Black migration to Chicago. The rule was that only Black girls played this game, but Camille discovered that if she slunk around in the background long enough, her participation became tolerable. It was as easy as two-four, six-eight, ten-twelve, fourteen-sixteen, twenty-two-thirty-two. . . Once Camille was established, the other white girls wanted to play too, but (being pussies every single one) they only wanted to play with Camille.

We were different. The family, I mean. Being of the left, we were somehow outside the necessity of following all these stupid rules. We were made out of broken ones. Yet breaking rules brought a kind of shame, because in truth there was no outside. I, at least, never got there. What I found was a kind of defeat in my own sadness, when the first girl I loved moved away from me, deeper into the ghetto, unavailable.

Getting a clue meant being indoctrinated into social pain. What I learned was how to walk down a South Side street. The task of pleasing my grandmother, or even the basic chore of washing regularly, remained inscrutable—in fact invisible. I was a dirty, scraggly, skinny child, which I now recall with a dash of regret, because it leads inevitably to the reflection—that perhaps, if only—I had been different, there would have been a place for me (in Ethel's will).

5. Stefan and Charlotte

Chicago's ruling class was larded with unrecognizable relatives, but who knew. (At least, no one was talking.) Stefan was the one who enlightened me. In our neighborhood of mostly

Blacks and Jewish Communists, we were neither. He was the son of a Polish leader in the United Steelworkers Union. Stefan had none of his father's gruff confidence. Already, he was the male half of one of those odd couples, composed of a gay man and a straight woman, although Stefan was in his early teens, and Charlotte was forty-four. Stefan had that indefinable homosexual quality of *languor*. By twelve, he possessed an exhausted worldliness.

In fact, languor was the characteristic Charlotte and Stefan shared. They relaxed well together. Charlotte maintained hers by living in darkened rooms, eating only chocolates, and drinking only coffee. She was very slim and pale, with a wedge of shiny black hair that hung to her shoulders. Both Charlotte and Stefan were soft, with the kind of white skin which seemed a bit vaporous, as though if you bumped it you might enter them. Charlotte was the girlfriend of Stefan's father, who had become a very lapsed Catholic after his wife left him. He was a beloved big bear of a political figure. People were forever knocking on Stefan's door, needing his father to help them with something or other.

Stefan managed to escape Chicago for his last year of high school, choosing an 'alternative' boarding school in San Francisco where each student cared for their own chicken. I visited him there, staying in the tiny room which he claimed he never left. He confided, *I don't do anything here except listen to Billie Holiday fourteen hours a day.* Draped over his bed, purring irony and detachment, he whispered huskily, *San Francisco is Sodom and Gomorrah unleashed.*

I recall Charlotte and Stefan in a living room, probably her living room. Why was Camille in Charlotte's living room? My memory is foggy on that point, but it seems to have been a place I spent significant time. Charlotte was stretched out on her sofa, with her slender ankles crossed just like Ethel, but Charlotte was tranquil to the point of murmuring torpor. As always, there was an open box of chocolates by Charlotte's side (she ate them slowly), and a cup of black coffee. The room was dim but very warm. Stefan drifted slowly from the turntable, to the window, to the chair, to a book. And as he sidled this way and that, he told me the story of my father's family.

He started out with his usual tone of ironic boredom, but as he went on Stefan perked up. Since I quickly fell into incredulity & speechlessness, the momentum of the conversation depended entirely on Stefan, and he did not flag.

They weren't big, it turned out, they were gigantic. How many monuments in the city? *Most Large Monuments.* One in particular commemorated a labor riot in which more than a handful of workers were shot in the back by company goons. And of course, hall after hall in the museums bore names which I suddenly realized were the same as one of my father's names. I couldn't keep track of the businesses founded, even whole industries. And since Chicago has a second city complex, a tendency to build the biggest whatever in the world has resulted in some edifices so fantastically enormous you, reader, probably have heard of them. Perhaps you have even been inside them.

I know Stefan was getting off on his story, because he didn't just throw me one dry bone, but a whole pile. I suspect that leads to the expectation that I'll dump the truth here, in one of those enactments of life's mysterious parallels. But I don't want to. I won't tell which family monument you are most likely to have been enclosed by. It's that irritation again. I just can't make myself do it.

6. Princess Me

How did Camille take these revelations? By mumbling, *Wow, that is so weird*, over and over. I think that's what she said. It was a shock. Her greasy dreadlocks quivered. She was just coming out of her schoolyard fighter years, and all other forms of human interaction pretty much floored her. She thought her hair had to form big oily clumps—years would pass before she learned to wash regularly. But here was Stefan, offering Camille the possibility that she was a princess in disguise.

She began to look around her city with a new appreciation for the solidity of its monuments. They seemed to carry a *for-your-eyes-only* message, pointing secretively to a castle in the sky, the one which was completely inaccessible, but which had her name on it. Being an unknown princess in a city of hog-butchers was a melt-in-your-mouth sort of secret—delicious, private, and oddly sanitary. Nothing actually showed.

The fantasy had no connective tissue. It was as impersonal as Disney. But that didn't cancel it, just like communism didn't. It only thrust those theatrics of class onto a series of tiny, almost invisible stages. One year, a scary but glamorous relative surprised everyone by sending Camille a Christmas present. When she opened it, Pearl snatched the gift and held it to her bosom, inhaling, exhaling. . . *Oh, but this is an elegant brand*, she exclaimed. It wasn't. It was just another cheap new cologne that had been getting some recent hype. In fact (Pearl was too thrilled to notice), the bottle was half-empty.

Rescue me. Isn't that what adoration of ruling class style is really about? And they are so not interested—otherwise they wouldn't be ruling class.

What I'm attentive to is the desires that get stirred up. That's the rustle in the grass, that little snake. All those shiny spreads in magazines, jewels and silks, they're the froth of a basic craving—not for stuff. Forget stuff. The craving is for recognition, pathetic hope of every masochist. And, *elegance is refusal,* the only smart thing Diana Vreeland ever said.

I speak with authority because I've been mixed up all my life. . . those incompatible elements. Nonetheless, the mix remained surreal to me until the day I was prowling for luxury goods with Thomas through Ethel's apartment. She had died, finally. The excruciating but hilarious reading of the will had just taken place. A cousin had found the old photo albums, and we paged through them together. I, at least, was shocked. The photo I remember best showed my father in a tuxedo and his sisters in white satin full-length gowns, snapped as they were emerging from a limousine. Depression-era America never looked so stylish, curvaceous, limber. The white satin on those girls was as thick and luscious as Niagara Falls. You could get lost in it. Their smiles were warm. At sixteen, my father, leaning against the big curvy Packard, was terrifically elegant in spite of himself, and sneering. I felt a pang—envy? disappointment?

And what does the ruling class want from everybody else? What's the emotional hook? The same relatives who would call Thomas up to relay Ethel's suggestion that he leave Pearl at home, would then leave Pearl befuddled by their confidences. Pearl would come up to me with a dazzled look after a dinner encounter, and tell me some horrible secret. She's probably forgotten them, but I remember every single one. Don't you think it's best to keep some ammo in reserve? They seemed to think Pearl, the most elusive person I have ever known, was safe, familiar, even, in some way, 'earthy.'

Putting your secrets into someone who is lower class is an odd form of hoarding. It's a bit like stuffing a person as though she were a piggy bank, except that this kind of piggy bank might waddle away. I'd like to think that's one of the things this essay is doing: waddling away with those secrets. But a friend pointed out to me that secrets aren't really told unless they're told to another ruling class person. After all, the servants know everything and no one cares.

7. Poem Interlude

Girlish cloud condensed along wire
With two ghost feet
And a brain of
Feathers. All nerve and
Wanting the real the
Impossible.

My whiskered genitalia. My future as a slut.
With these I went crawling through the whole
crabby army.

8. A Lady of Fashion

I'm not built like the women in my father's family. They are thin enough to seem wind-whipped. Tough but delicate, like whippets. I do have his eyes, a family characteristic so marked it's a little creepy. Not just the color (we share precisely the same shade of yellowish green) but the thin arched brow which thickens and sinks slowly with age. We had lunch one day and regarded one another over bowls of minestrone. He had my eye, but bigger, I thought. I couldn't differentiate myself in the river of his ironic gaze.

If thine eye offend thee pluck it out. Then, buster, hand it over. Theft and gift indistinguishable. In that tangle is the reason Ethel called up one day and told Thomas and Pearl she wanted me for a weekend. She was going to teach me how to select, and shop for, "an outfit." I had been in college for about a month, and while I hadn't come out as a dyke yet, I was beginning to gear up for that. Nonetheless, I got a princess rush off the idea (wouldn't you?). Plus there was the festive prospect of free clothes.

My first mistake was to arrive a little late. Two-and-one-half-hours late, in fact. I cannot remember why this happened, or how I justified not calling her. It got our weekend together off to a rocky start. From the moment she walked up to me in the train station, I learned about breathing deeply and exhaling calming phrases. . . *Oh Grandmother, I am so sorry. <Excuse inserted here.> I should have called, it was terrible to leave you waiting*. . . I was to repeat these apologies for hours, with such minor variations I felt dizzy.

That evening, we began going through the motions of an education in selecting fashionable attire. Sitting next to Ethel on one of her spotless white couches, I was a rapt student as she did some compare and contrast with the French, Italian, and British editions of *Vogue*. The following day, we did a grand tour of the department stores, and I ended up deep inside some luscious wools, feeling lost, in fact. I recall the sleeves of the plush mohair wrap had to be artfully rolled up, or they hung down around my knees. The skirt was tight around the waist, but so generous down below I felt like a lady emerging from a lake. Tottering with Ethel through the racks, I ran into only one person I knew, and it was my best friend. We stared at one another in shock. Later that evening, I got to wear my new clothes out to dinner with a retired ballerina.

But the apologies never stopped. It was the weekend of *apologies without end.* I began to identify with Little Red Riding Hood, in her failure to placate her wolfish grandmother. After returning from dinner with the ballerina, Ethel fretfully catalogued all the insults I was guilty of over the years. A long list, I'm afraid.

With each new item, I tried again to soothe the wounded Ethel, but nothing I did could stop this grief and paranoia from escalating. I don't recall everything on the list. I do remember Ethel frantically gesturing at a place on her white living room carpet, telling me that at the age of five, Camille (thinking no one was looking) had dropped her cheddar cheese puff precisely there, and ground it in with her heel.

But Ethel had spotted it, and had lived with the stain (which I couldn't see) ever since. The climactic accusation occurred in the dining room. Ethel turned with a ferocious suddenness and described an incident years before at the Thanksgiving table. Ethel customarily served roast beef. All was well, until the wild Camille began spearing pieces of roast beef and carrying them to her mouth with her knife. This brought sighs of horror, as everyone turned to stare, transfixed by the image and possibility of blood gushing from Camille's mouth all over the holiday table.

Uh-oh. I was out of my depth. My melody of apologies trilled on and on. I left her apartment the next day as one flees a prison. I had worked hard for my clothes, it turned out, and I never wore them again.

9. I, Claudia

I want to wrap this up, I really do. It's like what parents say before they spank their children—*Trust me, this is harder on me than it is on you* (although you were right to suspect the parents of having more fun).

What was the matter with Ethel, anyway? Her own mother, of course, Claudia. She hated Ethel. I have a portrait of Claudia, a delicate turn-of-the-century pastel of ungodly size. When I was very small, Pearl told me that I looked like that lady in the picture, with the peacock feather and pearls and elaborate hair. The cooler perspective of adulthood brought the realization that there is no resemblance at all, but the attachment had been formed. Now Claudia is with me. I snatched her from her spot in the dining room during that posthumous tour of Ethel's apartment, then had her shipped. She arrived in a crate so big, opening it was like breaking into a coffin (which was a lovely moment, if a little spooky). I leaned her against the wall in my shabby Victorian apartment, which had rotten window sills but a marble fireplace and a chandelier dropping flecks of gold paint. Perfect.

Claudia was a big slut, despite her long marriage. Between the wars, she particularly liked prime ministers of deteriorating European republics. In the portrait, her expression is grim, reserved, a little disdainful, but photos show her with a devilish smile. Cruel but sexy. She did the most romantic damage when she was in her fifties and quite stout, wading through society in her embroidered velvets and ridiculous hats. As for what she did to Ethel, only one story came down to me. She made Ethel receive her gentlemen callers in the ballroom in the winter, which was unheated. That puts the temperature at about twelve degrees fahrenheit.

When I was a kid, I'd heard rumors of Claudia writing something. A sort of diary, mixing her escapades with various literary and political musings. I wanted to get my hands on this diary (wouldn't you?), and after some surreptitious searches, I eventually found it, all ten pages. What remains of it in my memory is her jocular attitude, which struck me as arrogant and overly familiar, and her observations on class in the United States, as compared to class in Europe. These boiled down to—it matters over there, isn't that yucky, but it doesn't matter here. Aren't we lucky?

10. Striptease

After I moved, I put her away. There was just no room on the wall for her big self. Claudia is now in my closet, growing mildew on her eyelashes. She died long ago, and I never even met her. An easy subject. Why didn't I stick to her? Why, in other words, this orgy of trashing the living?

Hmmh. . .but I've hardly begun! I. . .rather, Camille, could go on like this indefinitely. For this house of incongruity has many rooms, and each has a place for my shadowy presence, but also has no place. The result being that I'm unnerved by my own disappearing acts and startling reappearances. What is American class? What elements compose a class-based identity, and what happens when those elements are mixed?

I detail the experience without making it intelligible. The class codes become visible, but that's hardly comforting. There's nothing homey about a set of rules. They were there before I inadvertently broke them, and they're still there.

One observation emerges from this which seems worth pointing out. Silence is one way of negotiating the unacceptable. Transgressive romantic fantasy is another. They're tools for managing the survival of self—the first maintaining it, the second an act of invention. But you can't separate the tools from their context, in personal necessity, social power, and class.

I'm reminded of a story Lydia told, about Pearl—yet bear in mind, Lydia was not the soul of reliability herself, especially when the subject related to slippery Pearl. She was too tempted by comeuppance.

Lydia was visiting Pearl. Older sister Pearl was escorting younger sister Lydia about town. Younger sister was somewhat intimidated by the witty communist mathematicians who comprised older sister's 'set,' but, being plucky, along she went, here and there, including, late in the evening, a foray to a strip joint. (This was in the late forties.) Something happened in that bar which Lydia never forgot. They had microphones wired in unpredictable places. After Lydia discreetly disappeared in the direction of the ladies room, Pearl told the bartender to turn the toilet mike on, and the club was doused, so to speak, with the sound of Lydia pissing.

It seems to me that the writer's role has similarities to the role of that microphone. Given the alternatives of silence or fantasy, ruthlessness becomes the middle way, inescapable, if not always truthful. What do you think? Where would you draw the line... What part of your life belongs to you, and what part belongs to me, should I happen to find out about it? Would it be different if that weren't Lydia pissing, but just a tape—a simulacrum of Lydia pissing?

I used to believe the key to getting to the heart of the matter was a willingness to be ruthless—an impulse that doesn't move me quite as much anymore. Where has it gotten me? I am the only one in my generation who knows there had been a murder in the family. Over the years, my father and aunt discussed it around me. They thought it was likely my great-uncle Jack, a hapless man who only had a job because of my grandfather, had also been a victim. Because of timing, and the fact she used poison, this could never be substantiated. She was nailed for the murder of her son. He hadn't been a baby at all. She poisoned Michael when he was eighteen because she didn't want him going away to college.

Lately I've been thinking that I am a wave, and all the stories in the world are the water. I'm among stories, just like all the other waves. Which part of the water belongs to which wave doesn't actually matter. It doesn't apply. Personally, this means I can't fall apart without changing into something else, other stories, different ones. This finds a solution in dissolution. Somehow it relaxes me.

LYNETTE #1

I am waiting in line for a movie at the Castro when I see them in front of the ticket booth. They are leaning towards one another; there is an atmosphere of indecision. The tall one, the one I love, looks just like she does in the ads. She's even wearing the same outfit. Thick wavy hair, soft toothsome leather jacket, spotted leopard pants. Big heels. Her date motions with a hand and runs off using short steps. This signals a short absence. The woman in leopard print stretch pants walks over to me. Her name is Lynette; we've been introduced. She has a wide mouth and wide eyes; large brown irises. She hands me a folded piece of paper. 'A party,' she says. 'I hope you can make it.' 'This weekend?' She nods, I nod. I put the paper in the pocket of my jeans jacket. She walks back to wait for her date. She puts all her attention into that. I take this as a sign that she's at work.

I bring a friend to the party. I am feeling insecure and my friend has a low, husky laugh. She isn't moved by much. Small and hard like a hazelnut with lovely facial bones. Many people are attracted by her aura of experience.

I recognize some of the women at the party as strippers I've seen at the Baybrick's show. Wrapped up in red or black lace, they are noisy and demonstrative. It's a screen I can't penetrate. I am vaguely uneasy with the amount and variety of drugs being consumed. My friend and I wander through the crowd with cigarettes and glasses of gin.

Sometimes I see Lynette. She's wearing big dark clothes, kind of sloppy looking. I assume this means she's not working. Clothes are conductors in the electrical sense. I want to slip my hand under her shirt.

I am happy when she looks at me. Some sort of recognition, then waiting.

Sitting on the carpet eating a carrot stick. Lynette walks over, quickly nudges me hard under the throat. I lean back on my elbows, her hand slides over my shoulder, presses me down. I feel very hot, I think this is what I want except I also want to finish my carrot stick. She is sucking my neck, which has become soft and elastic.

In my mind I say, 'I am the beloved of the whore with a heart of gold.'

'But I don't love you,' she says.

'You're some other whore,' I say.

I'm only doing this because my beloved is unavailable.

She comes back from the conference with Lucy, a woman I am jealous of. They are agreeing that the conference was peculiar: paying eight dollars to hear one male psychiatrist present his handling of a case while two others attack him in minute detail. I am curious whether the psychiatrists, by attacking one another, can come to be on the side of the client, who is female. Then, if one changes his position, does his relationship to the client also change, or is this fixed...

I'm not in the habit of revealing my thoughts. Privacy is a service I perform; it's arbitrary what I reveal and what I don't. I say, 'Silence is drainage.'

> One of the most interesting ways of making narratives within narratives complex in gay porn is the use of films within films. Many gay films are about making gay porn films; and many others involve someone showing gay porn films to himself or someone else (with the film-within-the-film becoming for awhile the film we are watching).
>
> (Richard Dyer)

Interrupted. My erratic motion toward the 'sexual fringe' means the characters fall off before we get to see them fuck. Anne flicks her wrist when she says, 'I can't understand why my friends don't invite me to see them fisting.'

> Anti-porn, where the narrative is taken out.
> My tongue is a fish wife, flowing and stuck.
> Messages sliding over glove-like intrusion.

I decide my beloved ought to be more jealous of me than she is. First, I get my waist cincher, which has an amusing way of making me sit up straight, and other underthings in a matching color (black). Then I dress up in a long forties dress with black paisleys and bits of turquoise, a sort of black jacket with a jet-beaded collar, a pink rag around my head and a blue scarf around my neck. Next are the rhinestones. Rhinestones have to occur in sets in order to be really effective so I wear the bracelet, earrings, and necklace. (Last time I was in my favorite old clothing store, my friend Renaldo who works in there started hissing at me about, 'Did I see that rhinestone bra?' I could have died for it.) I put on white lace gloves and go out to buy a card for my beloved:

something with roses and gold. Since that sort of thing isn't in style anymore, the only thing I can get is Chinese, but it looks romantic and there's no greeting to cross out. I take my beloved out to dinner and give her the card. The little story inside is about my previous lover:

> Randy Raye was a sweet thing I was happy to love. Dark hair and brows in even strokes across her face. Her lips lifted back from her teeth when she laughed, uncurling a quick and sometimes nasty wit. Girl with a cigarette and leather jacket, so fifties and all mine. Slim firm legs I wanted to bite and did. When she worked at the pinball parlor, her co-worker—a blond boy named Bill—started on hormones and grew breasts. One day he asked her to call him Luann. When I saw him he seemed unsettled, more vagueness across his face.
>
> Later she worked at the parlor. Not as a prostitute of course. She couldn't take that on, though some of the butch girls did. After we broke up I thought of her sitting at the table at the top of the stair, saying, "And these are our models tonight," as she introduced the women. I couldn't go up there since we were on the outs. Twice that summer I circled the block in my waitress uniform and padded shoes after a long day at work. Wanting to see her so bad was like a groove laid into me that I had to learn to live with.

My beloved is a prostitute and thinks I should try it out. 'Would you clean toilets for seventy bucks an hour?' I'm not interested, but I listen to her stories which are flat, like the drama has gone somewhere else. So and so comes in when he can't stand it anymore because his wife won't give him sex. He hates himself for this and won't touch her, but masturbates while she undresses and lies around. They talk about sex roles and she says he's kind of a feminist. Every month or so he comes to the house and I take a walk for forty-five minutes. I walk around the wide flat streets of our residential neighborhood and look at the trees. The suburban silence is irritating.

I go to the promo event with my friend Shelley. I find myself edging up to Lynette with a plastic glass of champagne. She is talking to a tall thin gay man who is dressed like an Eisenhower engineer, except the crew cut is too long and sticks up, bristly with dippity-do. Circling them inconspicuously, I hear Lynette say, "I can make love to a woman like her very best lover." Instantly I imagine her in my grainy cotton sheets and flush, decide to head back towards Anne. I pass Lynette's partner, Cheryl. Blond, wearing a red satin merry widow and fishnets, she's dealing with the radio reporter, a rather anxious looking feminist. She speaks soothingly into the microphone: ". . .a luxury item, in the same vein as getting a massage. You pay for my undivided attention. There's no responsibility or performance anxiety for the client to deal with, because it's all for her. The woman's pleasure is our only concern."

> When a stripper's show is going well, the air is thick, charged with sexuality, and she is in total control. This pleasant feeling of immunity is close to contempt. As in the fantasy of the passive man,

> the stripper takes pleasure in being a tormentor. While I think all of us strippers felt some disdain for men, the only women I ever heard admit to feeling that pleasure were gay women.
>
> (Seph Weene)

As a sensualist living under threat, I have incorporated threat. My complicity is violent. Head unwinding newsreels of gore where I am never the victim, sometimes the sadist. My switchblade my first boyfriend gave me is always in my pocket (I made that up) and so on. For practice, my beloved and I often fight with rubber knives. We are deliberate. For example we were both wearing leather jackets, crew cuts, and eating spaghetti in a roomy restaurant called the Grand Piano when she told me this:

> You know the Panhandle. Big streets rim a basketball court, a bathroom used by local communists who for years have refused to pay their water bills, and eucalyptus, cypress, also bushy thickets. Were you aware those thickets are inhabited by hermits who never come out but who can be seen with paper bags over their heads muttering in the interior. She leans forward and talks out of the side of her mouth. Well, several years ago one of the hermits ventured from this sanctuary, and his head fell off. He was found sitting on a park bench with the (McDonald's) paper bag still on his head, and it wasn't for several months that his head was found, by some kids, playing in a clump of uninhabited bushes.

I respond by telling this story:

> This is a story about the SUPERIORITY of fear. If I only had a brain. After you've eliminated everything else, what you're left with is the truth. I'm no dummy. "No one saw him upset but he was very upset." The postcard he sent me had 'Black Mischief' written in pretty script on the bottom. Two black kittens had their eyes scratched out and blood was dripping out of the sockets. The next card showed Jesus knocking on a door; he had scrawled "Time & Time Again" on the back. Finally he quit trying to stomp on my feet and started to chase me. It fascinated me the way his mouth was moving up and down but no noise came out. I crossed the street. He didn't know what hit him. He landed on all fours splayed across two lanes. The next car swerved but flattened his head. It crunched like a vase and the blood splashed out thin and watery. There was a long red tire track. I thought of the scarecrow stuffing straw into himself. Someone on the other side of the street looked like he was trying to run but couldn't move his feet. His fingers wiggled. There must have been noise but I don't remember any. It felt like my body was touching itself in relief, all over hot flashes, and I sat down on the sidewalk behind a parked car and waited for the police.

My beloved and I go to Mitchell Bros. to see Fran's act. Fanny is her stage name which I ought to use here. Fanny Fatale. A bush of yellow hair in the shadowy warm room;

the men all have flashlights. We do too, but I feel obliged not to use mine. Her beautiful legs give me a swelling feeling of contentment. The pleasure of looking where all the men are shining their flashlights. She strips as she works the room, giving us more and more honey-colored skin. The men are inaugurating a young man in some sort of sexual ritual. One says he'll be a snot with his girlfriend now that he thinks he knows something. Fanny approaches him with arms straight out; his smile is painfully stiff; the other men giggle and hoot. I've heard about how obedient they are. She lifts her leg into his face, plays with herself, takes money. When she comes to us she lays in my girlfriend's lap, grabs her breast then rolls onto me. I'm a fool like the men. She whispers do you like this place, I say yeah I like the temperature.

Touch is relatively untouched, why is that. Perhaps what we see is more heavily constituted by ideology. Describing my beloved, I am consistently opposed by some (sexual?) incongruity. Writing her 'looks,' her body is an underivable effect. Until the image leans down into touch (shadow meets body) this is porn. Otherwise it is like trying to match what is visible through the keyhole with my desire.

Mobility implies sharp judgement, ideological pressure.

Writing touch, I am hardly opposed at all. It enters the text, fills it up, slices it like conversations. An aggressive democracy of fucking. Is this idealism?

> An individual can resist only to a certain degree and at some point necessarily succumbs. But it is

> the way in which they succumb, the angle of submission, that is often interesting. . .
>
> (Charles Bernstein)

I lean back on my elbow, take a long drag on a cigarette. My beloved—slack, casual—leans thru the doorway. Telling a story which recedes in the middle, her brown irises drift away like slow breath, irony disperses to points. She wears a coon cap and baggy charcoal pants. Her hands have a way of sliding up; self-deprecation takes a sexual edge. Eyebrows arched away from me, what slips out between her even teeth: a faint hiss.

> Shelley, dressing, hides herself in the kitchen.
> The spectacle presents itself as something enormously positive, indisputable and inaccessible. It says nothing more than "that which appears is good, that which is good appears." The attitude which it demands. . .is passive acceptance, which in fact it already obtained by its manner of appearing without reply. . .
>
> (Guy Debord)

When she comes out, Shelley is wearing a tight shiny red dress. She gets up on the rippling bed. We all watch round, high, round breasts appear as she pulls it off. Watching a body acquire itself—linked, smoothed—nude is an idea of unity smeared across the joints. The torso sliding out, a warm paste. Grinding hips and shoulders. Everyone leans forward, wondering how much we'll get to see. A garter whizzes past my head. I lean back in my lawn chair, gratified, laughing. She gets it all off, lip synching to a song about men, furs, opera: "The pleasures of being a woman." Then my beloved tells her she's running out of time. Rolling her hips, she pulls on fuzzy sweatpants, soft as her moustache. Next a t-shirt. As the song ends Shelley swings towards us grabbing a baseball mitt and cap.

In Shelley's story, the monster metamorphosed into an ordinary little girl. She's trying to make the distinction sticky. *That narrow smile means he thinks I'm too cute to be single.*

> Consider the word "gay." Like so many terms in the homosexual lexicon—trick, number—it owes its origin to hooker slang. In the 19th Century, the word was reserved for "fallen women" who could be found in redoubts of lust like "gai Paris."
>
> (Richard Goldstein)

After the parlor was busted, Randy Raye moved to San Francisco and began film school. The mother of my beloved locked herself in the bathroom and called us, sobbing into the phone. Later, the trial. When we got to San Francisco, we moved into Margo St. James's place and slept in her bed as Margo was touring the country giving lectures on prostitution. She had a white Manx cat with one blue eye, one green eye and a sleeping bag covered with ripstop nylon which we unzipped and used as a (drafty) blanket. Her apartment building was poured solid concrete, immune to fire. She had more porn magazines than I had ever seen piled under various tables, a professional collection which she picked through while wearing her reading glasses. The magazines interested me for a while, then I ignored them. Better was her poster collection, which had the promotional posters of every Hooker's Ball ever staged. One poster on red paper showed a woman reclining, tickling her genitals with a feather. A big woman, her thighs already sliding out of the picture, and high in the corner that wavy smile, like a flag's stripe.

SEX TALK (WITH ABIGAIL CHILD)

1. Sex Talk

From my table in the cafe I watched her walk up the pavement, with a curious stiff-legged stroll. She was wearing a man's suit from the '40s, baggy pants, blue smoke curling from the tip of a thin cigarette. Her round cheek was so soft it reminded me of one of those pictures of Colette in drag.

> Among lesbians the story is a form of sex talk—a joint whereby the community and the couple are of the same body. Proximity is difficult but brings us tongue to tongue. "Fetish as disclosure."
>
> My relation to fetish:
> bigger here are importantly hugely infantile
> I could feel my body proffering a leather
> nipple. waiting to plus anemone
> Lean identified rubies loosen

Lévi-Strauss argues tattoos are the sign of a defended tribe. A tribe facing extinction or being threatened. Fetish works in that direction. One might say in a defended world, identification becomes the uniform feature.

I ordered espresso with a piece of lemon peel. When she ordered the same thing, I slapped her face lightly, as a joke. She tilted her head, rubbed her chin thoughtfully as her eyes closed and a smile came onto her lips. "That was interesting," she said, "but you only slapped one side."

Narrative seeps from the broken privacy of the couple. It is a disturbance of intimacy, a betrayal, which accounts for its dramatic effect. . .

Yes! The dramatic effect lies in the transgression. A matter of identity equaling control, and then pleasure in the diffusion/breaking of the pattern. A pleasure of violation. Broken expectations.

So, I slapped the other side of her face, with my whole hand instead of my fingers. "You did it differently that time," she observed, and I watched her soft cheeks flush. "I want to keep you off balance," I said.

Intimacy fastens like barrettes—

Intimacy fastens, to be inserted somewhere inside the head.

The other is recognized by means of fantasy, so that intimacy itself is a fiction, dreamy as sky writing, a slogan in white cloud. . .

or perhaps an architecture? An absence underlined. You speak of skywriting. . . Narration in the twentieth century had been permanently formed by cinema and the photograph. Now. . . how to dislodge their control?

2. Real Charm

Sit on my face
See how wet I am

unmistakable juice and smell and hair
innocently sweetheart clit scream breath blue
thighs hot swollen fully
Look has abundance
Lying played pulled cooed and fatted
  focused
suddenly dry

kiss me
fuck you
returning real charm

IF I WERE ATTIRED TO RECEIVE THIS WITH
ANY ACCURACY—
MY GARMENTS WOULD FALL STRIDENTLY
INTO ME.

Eroticism in the West proceeds through a strategy of striptease as moral tale.

Fantasy bends it out of shape
twists in my face. not a nice ass
but a great heart-shaped butt
the bottom
what's written out

HONEY MINE

an unassimilable

Conventional narration must contain her.
His little death does not detain me. Determinism
holds us all down. . .

The smiling faces of ads are a form of control through resemblance. A community of female sexual perverts resembles nobody, and nobody wants to resemble us.

What I love in MAYHEM is a notion of backwards. The fact that I could retreat and reorder without feeling sacrificed. The filmic codes are clipped—which has the curious effect of separating the image from its portent of 'accuracy.' Recognition torn. . .

"Go on and suck. Suck the life outta me. I wanna feel my life in somebody else's mouth."

Following this line of thought, power verbs shape
faces on
your own prism
cunt the civilization of the ass
unseals
becomes like you when you come and wear
the kind of smile I want to take home.

SURFACING ON THE BED AMID RIOTS
I LOVE TO BE FILLED WITH TIME/
IMPROVISATION
OF YOUR MOUTH BETWEEN MY THIGHS.

3. Story Line

Her hand on my shoulder, that first gesture of invitation, was so characteristic of her. Circular as a huge conscience, something to follow indefinitely. Her fingered goodbyes marked my body, a sort of sexual technique. Even this story, its thin crust, marks her evasions.

INCAPABLE OF BEING USED UP

The progress of tensions through narrative 'line' has parallels in the maps we make of our lovers' bodies and the moments of exposure and vulnerability on the way to orgasm.

IT'S BEYOND SURPLUS

FULL OF HOT and chronic satisfaction
soaked cause I'm stopped between love and a third tongue
girlfriend   sexy buttons popping twisted
I'm visually them physically the unreasonableness of the
situation
                                        this world

It is tension more than line that interests me. I see a field—promises—an array of conjugation—the wish you want. Line, if you must, is a focus perpetrating depth. The line as line exists on the surface, is habit perhaps?

The **idea** that I'm telling a story is what I'm attached to, not the linearity or anything else. I'm attached to this idea because it establishes contact—which can be appropriated, misused, disrupted, eroticized. Like this one:

Terry was a big-boned whore, a lesbian, and an incest-survivor. When she became a fundamentalist Christian, she married a carpenter. Everyone wondered how much did he really know? One day in a rage, he was heard yelling, "Well at least you were never a prostitute!"

Erotic error kissing my impeccable cunt

Order in time (or the 'linearity' of narrative) doesn't necessitate a patriarchal ordering of consciousness. I prefer an implication/integration of loss: what happened in the beginning (or middle or end) won't return.

Forget repair, even if minimal. If loss is a part of life we are missing nothing.

Then what is pleasured in the telling of a story?

The wind in fact an instrument of excess, prone to gorgeous. Or, sex as disclosure—a manifest and metaphorical stripping.

4. Audience

And what about the relation of recognition to desire? As in this quote:

"To desire the Desire of another is to desire that the value that I am be the value desired by the other: I want her to recognize my value as her value. I want her to recognize me as an autonomous value. In other words, all human, anthropogenic Desire—the Desire that generates Self-consciousness, the human reality—is finally, a function of the desire for recognition."

What of the desire for another—not to be loved, but to love? Do I want to recognize me in the lover? Do I want love to recognize me? Do I seek to be lost in love? To be its familiar?

I think that stories have all the sneaky pleasure and mutilations of intimacy hidden within what we call narrative structure. Narrative moments are always coupled and involve multiple manipulations of deceit and recognition.

"When I'm having sex, it's like I'm having a story. I hear things like 'She spread her legs as her lover's tongue softly ran across her vagina.' The third person! we exclaimed."

Perhaps what's operating here is distance—the shadowed sex IS taboo, when its appearance is only in books.

Or could this be, 'I story myself so others will witness my sex as desire.' The third person is present only to satisfy my need to be observed. . .

If the observer is my need to satisfy my desire, this is voyeurism as identification. If the observer is my mind, I have fragmented myself and this is separation as identification. And if I borrow your rules of attraction, I reintegrate opposite sex identification, try on your power.

AGREED: what is functioning is the NOUN of narration, mirroring the sense of self.

I distrust devices of plot and linear time and character relation. I want both process VERB and person NOUN to be tilted. I ask for more 'takes' on the body, so that reality is approached in excess of enumeration.

softer bigger whiter breastier
remake the elaborate identity of her
or of her him
elaborate your identity

So it was easy to let her carve it, warble wobble. Only by turning on her with all my teeth bared could I recover ground already lost. Of course I did not. Of course yearning made it impossible. Pleasures of the rupture, rack, and screw.

5. Close Enough

Perhaps what is happening between us is an opening of a kind of erotic conversation. Here, at the margin. Because a community of sexual perverts resembles nobody, and nobody desires to resemble us.

As a lesbian the differences are multiplied, the possibilities mutate, taking on all kinds of genuinely new procedures. This is not borrowed habit, but a "kind of loving" become, in the presence of wit and intelligence (the head screwed *on and on*), genuine alternatives

---

The room is either dark or light or is two rooms. There are implements beyond my consciousness.

Breast high partitions cover the linoleum floor, creating a maze through which workers stroll and softly talk. At either end of the vast warehouse are sealed rooms whose roaring ventilation systems cool the computers. You are allowed in these rooms, because you wear a special identification badge. Between the computer rooms stretch two rows of windows that face twin lines of young olive trees whose leaves are covered with fine greyish hair. Beyond these trees the workers go to sleep and have sex.

Shadows tip the lover onto circumstance.

I want to be touched, or touched continuously.

The sun makes close enough open. Let me drink my bathrobe, skirt a retinue of clings, a sanitized restraint gives way to luster's substrate

Bent over the edge of the body, there's no telling who we are. Lattice handiwork, the roseate palm smacking our tin flesh.

HONEY MINE

We're getting rosier and rosier.
These large sensations come and go. We want to be a
star, we want to be adorable. Instead the larger
sensations, so open there is a sense of leveling.
What is inside slips out and vanishes.

In any kind of joking, a system that's given as isolate
liquifies, falls suddenly into another

There's a tangle of questions all over the floor, stepped on

TANYA

TANYA

*"My argument of silence—what else could it be—
negated the presence of others."*
—Mike Amnasan

New feminist slasher narratives, I thought while watching the "Revising Romance" program of Cecelia Condit videos at New Langton Arts. It felt like opening the post office package and finding an actual fluffy white cloud dripping with blood. In these videos the narrators sound like sweet white girl waitresses telling us about disasters in the kitchen. We are compelled—after all this is the story of our food. But the narratives become unhinged at the place where we expect the waitress and the enraged chef to be separate people.

"No one saw him upset but he was very upset."

In the first video (*Beneath The Skin*), a woman tells us her boyfriend's ex-girlfriend was discovered in one of the closets in their apartment. Dead, in a smelly locked box. We get nothing solid (fear, shock or rage) to encapsulate this, but rather a narrator whose voice reminds me more and more of mall music. It's a kind of decorative scroll, contained, elaborate—a vocal style reminiscent of Patsy Cline. Images of this scene are spliced with bald mummies, muddy blood-like stuff, and finally the narrator herself in a swing, her smiling face tinted with pastels that slide across her figure.

"But people just don't go around killing other people."

Now her red lips are speaking through a plastic mask and she is in bed.

"We are very different. She was epileptic and I'm diabetic."

"He was just incredibly magnetic, and he has a huge body."

Trying to move towards a point, while skirting the issue. Turgid and cloud-like resolution. The narrator is no author—but so what? The purpose of narrative authority is to contain the audience. Take that away and what happens? Logical relations are points of contact as events spin out of control.

There's one plot point after another, each more perfect than the last. For example: she murders her husband and then says he abandoned her. He was a space that wasn't being occupied so, she absorbed him. He murdered her. Then she found the body. And so on.

In the next video, the male character wears a mask, a distorted face with a gaping mouth. *Possibly In Michigan* opens with two women in a shopping mall being followed by a man. The women are well-groomed, white, their skin has a shiny video moistness. These are attractive images disconnected from any soothing qualities—the representation is both totally flat and excessive. They strike stewardess poses and speak in sing-song rhymes while they shop for perfume, oblivious to their follower with the huge mouth. Their indifference to danger erases our relation to them, so that hysteria—not suspense—slides out into the audience. The video stays at the verge of violence of a particular feminine type: being consumed, eaten alive. It seems to be making a paranoid argument: dismemberment lurks at the mall. Is this what makes the video "feminist"? A lurch towards the surreal stalls consumption at the point of contact. No one can do anything. Then the grid shifts inside the black screen frame as the elements decompose. Eventually, one of the women is captured. The man in the mask tells her she has two choices: he will eat her, or he will cut off her limbs one by one and eat them. But her friend arrives in the nick of time and she shoots him dead. They cut him up and eat him.

A theory of appetite begins where contamination rubs consumer into

object, contradicting itself.
Desire and nausea are dog-like myths, guardians to a boundary
which shrinks to nothing.
The quarantine of menstruating women begins private life.
A consumer's only defense is appetite, engorging objects to
prevent loss of control.
Oscillation between consuming and expelling the maternal image
characterizes his sexual response.
As Sherlock Holmes says, after you've eliminated everything, what
you're left with is the truth.
The role of discipline is unclear.

Why?

My tactic, vis-à-vis narrative, is really just to bring abandonment into the relationship.

Darling X marks the beginning of my story, before theorems arrive. At that time, cheap food was very important.

HONEY MINE

My beloved was on welfare, which required that she apply for several jobs a day. In fact, this was the equivalent of a job. Making sure she remained jobless required certain tactics, for example her bomber jacket and rolling stride. Only several years later did I find out she had been turning tricks on the side. I was living off a check from a magazine and fantasizing a career in journalism. The room we shared had no heat but a Crockpot which all day every day transformed whatever we put into it. Potatoes, leeks, and ham hock for example created thrilling society, and embellished our room—in fact the long hall of little rooms, padlocked like bicycle sheds — with a fragrant signature.

Only later did we find out that Tanya had worked in the restaurant when she was a member of the commune. Margo had told us it was cheap, and it was practically under her apartment. One evening, we walked in to check it out and found live jazz and mounds of food steaming on low black tables, with a few quiet people scattered among the pillows. They served a full, cafeteria style dinner for $1.50—beans, rice, soup, yogurt and tea, carrot juice and sweet potato pie extra. Some sort of political group ran it. A tall Asian man and a stout Jewish woman ladled out food with grim expressions, making them unrecognizable no matter how many times I went there. I peered at them, as if into a haze of arguments.

The city had taken on a ruined and post-war atmosphere, there was an undercurrent of agitation and distress. In my area, there occurred a proliferation of black berets: one for anyone. Tanya, uncovering her head, slipped forward thru the dark streets, past the rosy medallions, past the storefronts with Germanic emblems. Bars on the basement window did not conceal the peeling paint of the window frame. At the end of the street, the auditorium sat like a granite fist. Tanya sat by herself. The auditorium was nearly empty, implying decisions, a chain of command. A few journalists lounged like sackcloth. I was waiting under the red exit light when my beloved mounted the podium. She spoke in the style of a Marxist revolutionary, in which every muscle is connected to every other in short sharp strokes. (A few years later this becomes a robotic style of dancing.)

My beloved told me the commune had guns in the basement. "They had the tools to do it," she said.

Returning to the memory of the scene, there were several disturbing odors. Climbing the stairs to Tanya's room in the Tower hotel, I found her sitting outside her room with the padlock hanging on the open door. Her shaved head is a round spot in our conversation, there are also nervous gusts from her mouth. It's hard to get the whole story from her. She sort of peels off at the edges of her sentences, while holding the red bandanna in her hand and rubbing it back and forth across her scalp. A fast series of smiles indicates that her information may be unreliable. Or, she is ashamed of what she knows. She says she sure she's not a druggie because whenever she wants drugs she's usually satisfied with a cigarette. She says her father is a Berkeley psychiatrist. This is the context: someone got murdered, or possibly three people. I can't remember if I saw her only before or also after this occurrence.

The truth of a story becomes evident in its anatomy, in the bones of narrative structure. Like the drag queen who says to the straight audience, "I'll take it all off and dance in my bones for you." Gestures of mercy proceed from either side in staccato bursts.

Tanya's thick waist and then branches, as X precedes Y, leaving each white foot paler than before. Rumors of her death preceded her death. The smear left on the pavement exhibited interference patterns, but the sound is hard to recognize. My hand-held wrist, so cool and sucked dry.

It was Tanya, because of her placement in the middle, who had the child's position. Crouching down, she held her hand over her mouth as the man and woman paddled the aluminum canoe. This went on for too long.

Someone else in the Tower Hotel was killed by a Canadian Mountie, the victim was a small guy who was manager at the time. He was an indifferent man with curly hair, I don't remember his face. The case involved either drugs or diamonds, with a South African locale. If it was diamonds, there was also a blond involved. The story was so bottomless it detached and turned into fiction the instant I heard it; that made it tolerable.

The murdered manager was replaced by a friend of Margo's, part of a very large circle, all of whose members were peripheral. This friend was a big scarred Bohemian, his face seemed to have tiny chips knocked out of it. After his girlfriend dumped him, he carried on for months in stunned and silent grief. Then she came to visit. She looked like a diesel dyke with lead eyes, gliding up on her motorcycle, then clomping up the stairs in her heavy leather chaps.

A Conversation

Three women are sitting in a cafe at a small round table, spotlighted by a low overhanging lamp. The table is in the corner by the window. The cafe name, a scroll in red fluorescent light, hangs in the window.

"A long time passed before I was able to regard these feelings with relief, a sign of liveliness in adverse weather, as it were. All the brows I had ever admired were now like bird tracks on the beach, or loose change. In the beginning, of course, there were uneasy transitions between conversation and sexual activity. But eventually she built a nest of aromatic twigs at the foot of my bed and every evening accompanied me on a stroll, perched on my wrist. What a creature. Leaning towards her delicately feathered neck, gently entwined in the smells of musk and cedar which emanated from her, I grew oblivious to the outside world."

Tanya drew a long sigh. "How slowly one recovers the sense of smell, which is how I recognized her." Rosa smoked a Marlboro, tapped it on the edge of her saucer with a wry smile. "I would never court oblivion for a girl. We've all lost the love of our lives at least three times by now." The overhead fluorescent light lined each wrinkle on Onya's face with shadow. She was tired, but when sincerity overcame her she became soft and rather smaller. "What sort of lover evades description?" she asked. "Or is he really pink and long-limbed, as I sometimes think."

"Having been in similar situations, I know I possess remarkable nerve," said Rosa. "I would venture a hardy and unequal transition to enthusiasm." Tanya had lowered her head and was staring in the direction of her espresso. "That time, after a certain point, I shut my eyes. Not because I didn't want to see what I was doing, but I wanted to hear, smell, and touch what I was doing." For myself, at first, I simply followed the custom. Feelings of pleasure, however insubstantial and transitory, caused me to feel disorganized and therefore at a disadvantage.

Tanya said I was too eager to take personally the attentions of any person with money.

The End of the Commune

Tanya did try to leave the commune. She wanted to embark on a course of study. Her tool was employment as a bicycle messenger in the canyons of a large economy. She felt attached to a line of communication. One shake and she knew illusion, the bright and colorful underside of her father's psychiatric certainties. Her smile was her advance into silence, wiping clean the sentences she shredded. The vowels peeled back, unable to fit her. Riding with traffic, from business to business, thru uniforms of prosperity, she understood her journey as implicated in, and identified with, techniques of coercion. The guilt she felt weakened her.

A Drive in the Country

Mud as red as your head, with scalped cliffs. A kind of donkey toughness (stuck to you) but there are also leafy sections.

The roads lead to an indentation along the outer rim. The cabin in the woods emits a kind of musical groan, but there is something insect-like about the grammar. That resemblance fades when I remember where I am. My speech fibers. Trying to wrap a tree. The leaf world whitely barking. And cottonwood by water yessing like her little boy as he mouths a thistle's purple bud.

The dirt road led thru a grove of eucalyptus along the top of the Marin Headlands. Their crisp brown leaves clicked at the approach of the sea green Mercedes. Sitting back on the quilted leather, while Hal drives along the shadowed road. I just listen as Hal says he likes women and boys until their skin gets rough. When he draws his lips back in a smile his teeth are shining—he runs his tongue over them. His eyes slide towards mine, offering an apology. There are rosy tips on his cheekbones, in contrast to a sharp humorous gaze. He slaps his palm on the steering wheel as the car stops. My beloved is standing with her back towards us, her long thin legs seeming to drop from her leather jacket. She has spread a white tablecloth on the ground, high above the gleaming bay dotted with white sails. There is bread, fruit, wine—some plastic containers of chicken salad.

My beloved was working for Hal, the moon geologist, painting his house, while he was at the NASA office, drawing topographic maps of the moon. He said drawing the maps felt like having webbed feet on the moon. He was another friend of Margo's; it was a curious friendship which seemed to recede entirely and then reappear under new circumstances. By the garden in the dry valley, for example, with its messy plumage of black-eyed Susans, blue sage and larkspur. Hal had laid out a large map on the red sandstone patio, under the shade of a twisted cedar with shredded slivery bark. Margo with a martini was stepping gingerly thru the garden, peering at the flowers. Hal rapidly circled and hunched over the map. He said it was a triumph of state-of-the-art computer imaging technology.

My beloved was a strong woman with small breasts and a sensual roll in her walk. Skin so soft it would yield to any touch, then foam back and enclose it. Struggling to emit sound, one after the other. She is not leaving me alone; she nibbles at my lips. Waiting for the white belly to fold back into sky, as fog sheepishly grazes the low hills. I avoid what I want to do tonight and instead lie down with a magazine.

We had two rooms in the Tower Hotel. Her room was on the street. When we slept in her room the garbage men woke us up at 6:00, shouting in Italian. The scent of yellow broom slipped in from the hill down the street. The hill's steep slopes were gravelly and seemed parched, but it was the only green spot for miles. A proliferation of waxy leaves on unrecognizable plants and bougainvillea so brilliant it left a blank spot on my retina. In the street, I passed the shut-in faces of people who lived next to the park, their small houses tucked in livid tropical gardens. Fingering items in various stores, occasionally I stole them: a blue macramé star which I tied to the string hanging from the lightbulb in my room. On the street below us and slightly to the right was a fortune cookie factory. A strong and sickening sweetness came from the place, a smell of quarantine. The sign said, "We have adult X-rated cookies."

Her room overlooked the street, mine overlooked a pebbled roof that stopped at the sidewall of a larger building. Dingy lightwells make the border of the world. Curling up under her covers, crying and relaxing, later draping myself in newspapers in the cafe around the corner, I explained to everyone that I was preparing for my career in journalism. Everyone was indifferent, a sign of erosion I thought.

Each morning, Lonny swore and screamed, at the police, at "faggots," his preacher's voice thundering. Was he a rude man at flashpoint, or just wringing out emotion as a side effect of his position? He lived down the hall with two women in one room, a tribe. They had been together seven years and were all under twenty-one. "Girls in a commune in a love bed," that line stuck in my head. I imagine a bare mattress the fog drifts over. Fog, mattress, windowsill, all the same color. Little and Beanpole were the names he'd given them. His screams, always directed outside, created a buffer of silence around the women. They worked as cooks in a team, thus limiting the amount they'd have to talk to anyone else.

Little was bright and hard enough for a better story. A small woman, she swaggered right into my face when she spoke—as if she were looking at me, but her eyes had always found some spot just to the side. But when Beanpole passed me in the hall, hatred grazed the floor like the uneven hem of a long skirt. A false modesty, lowered eyes. She had the thinness of a long depression, and a body that receded like a hairline. Her way of seeking shelter silenced her, was out of her control.

I wondered what shape the three of them took over that foggy bed.

The words break up under pressure into small distinct clods: hardly something I can listen to. Fear, I am someone who is supposed to have that characteristic. Weaving it back in, a breath down the horizon of an incalculable mistake. I see Beanpole leaning against the wall by the pay phone, where the wall is covered with scrawled messages. I finally spoke. I said, *Girl, you never look at anyone, how come?*

"Our eyes met—her gaze told me nothing but that I had passed across it, as close and as remote as a figure in a dream."

FRIENDS

1. Social Life

It was because of Gray that I got to know Alice. Gray Loving. That was his actual name. He loved me in his own weird way. If I had been capable of normal responses myself, I might have found it creepy. But I was new in the school, and going through a bad period: stunned, speechless. I didn't eat. I got thinner. My only social characteristic was an amazing invisibility. The more wrecked I became, the more the air seemed to eat me alive. Gray had a wasted quality that was a kind of a throb. His hair was stringy, greasy, and long, like mine, but his skin was bad, and he was always clammy—due to illicit substances, probably. He had that toxic sweat. He followed me through the halls, and when I stopped and turned around, he stopped too. He gazed at me longingly like we were *twins of the spirit.* His eyes filled up and dripped—like grief sloshing. Tears magnified his pupils and irises, so they seemed to swell in my direction. I never saw him talk to anyone.

Gray didn't make me uncomfortable, because I didn't have that feeling. I lacked the internal scale that distinguishes comfort from discomfort. In my social paralysis, I was composed of tiny habits, such as what I would eat (cottage cheese with sprinkled wheat germ, stiff-skinned sour plums). In between, in the cracks in my daily routines, were those utterly random moments I lived for. One morning, I didn't go to school because I discovered three little black wiggling tubes had hatched in a puddle on my window ledge. I named them: Riddle, Giggle, and Smack. They were mosquito larvae. I pushed them around with a tiny stick, trying to create a scenario that would demonstrate whether or not they were intelligent. When this became frustrating, I tried to read them like tea leaves. The fortune I read in the worms seemed to be that if I went to school late enough I'd avoid running into Gray Loving at lunch.

Just after the noon siren, I slipped through the school's large front doors and saw Gray drifting at the end of the hall, lost, probably looking for me. Our eyeballs connected and he made a major lurch in my direction. I turned down another hall, pretending that I hadn't registered him, and found a stairwell I'd never noticed before. I swerved in that direction, my feet clattering downstairs into a warren of halls, the walls of which seemed to be sweating, or perhaps it was just the gleam of brown enamel paint, and there were rumbles from the pipes and certain closets. Hot air gusting from ventilation ducts. Locked doors leaked smells of cleaning fluids. I thought about the pride I felt in breaking rules that no one cared whether or not I followed. I was in the basement; so what? I relied on such peculiar things.

I wandered until the zeal of exploration wore off. Just then (finally) an open door, and there was Alice, looking at me through the swamp water of her aviator sunglasses. She was sitting in the middle of a broken-down couch in the center of the room. She had the skin of a baby, and her long straight hair was ash blonde, so heavy it hardly moved. I must have seen her in motion all the time, because that's what bodies do, but I don't remember it. When she was at rest Alice became vivid, a teenage Buddha, impenetrable and serene. She patted the seat next to her. I went in and sat down. A half-dozen other students were scattered around the room, quietly eating.

—It's hard for me, Alice was saying. My dad says it's because I was kidnapped. But I don't know. Was I really kidnapped?

She smiled gently at me.

Flummoxed, I leaned forward to check the reactions of the kids sitting on the other side of Alice. But they were blinking like dazed monkeys. A guy and a girl. Their arms and legs were twined around one another easily. I pretended not to notice. I opened my lunch bag and pulled out a sour plum.

—You don't know the story, Alice said. Everyone but you knows the story.

She looked at me with a tender note of remonstrance.

—It was after the divorce. I hadn't seen my mother in two months. But when she pulled up in the Buick outside of school and told me to get into the car, I did. Twenty-four hours later, we were in Texas. It was like a dust bomb, driving down a little dirt road for miles and miles, a dry irrigation ditch, dead cottonwoods. At the end of the road was a little house. The door opened, but the windows were covered with boards. What does that tell you?

—You were squatting, one of the kids commented wisely.

—At night, I slept in a closet. My mother said, *Aliens don't know about closets, so this way they can't abduct you.* During the day, she opened the front door a crack and scanned the horizon, watching for the feds.

A small mountain of cans was piled on the old kitchen floor. For meals we sat next to the mountain, selected our cans and ate out of them with plastic spoons. There were no lights, no toilet, no phone. After a week someone did come. I watched the cruiser throw up dust for miles. My mom gave it one hard look and then began wiping the counters with a rag. I wonder if she gave up right then. Texas Marshals. They strolled up the walk in their gleaming black boots and knocked on the door. Howdy, ma'am. Please open the door, ma'am. Their voices were calm and low. I couldn't see their eyes behind their sunglasses.

Alice pushed her glasses up her nose, tilted her head back and looked at me.

—I surrendered, she said.

—To the real world, a girl added wistfully. Cheryl.

Cheryl looked at me, blinking tearfully over her hard contacts. Her black ringlets seemed to tremble around her pale face. With her big nose, I thought she was an interesting mixture of delicate and rough. When she laughed she leaned forward and cackled into her palm. The boy next to her was Erik. He was huge, awkwardly squeezed into the student chair, with waves of tousled, surfable blond hair. In the lull that followed Alice's story, we regarded one another with a tinge of unease.

Erik. Cheryl. Alice. The entwined boy-girl pair. This was the beginning of social life and it caught me unawares. It was sort of like getting new furniture. I would forget I knew anyone until I stumbled into one of them.

It began the next day, when I turned, alarmed, as a load of books crashed next to me at the start of second period Social Studies. It was Erik, giving me a look of curious significance.

I had someone to sit next to. As Erik settled in, I stared with shock at Mr. Gibbs, our teacher, as he thumbed through his notes for the day. I noticed, not for the first time, that there was a repellent quality to Mr. Gibbs. It wasn't a personal characteristic but something more off-hand and natural, like the way a penguin repels water. Mr. Gibbs was also pear-shaped like a penguin, and he had a penguin-like layer of fat, and rheumy eyes. I noticed these aspects of our teacher with an intensity bordering on grief. Mr. Gibbs waddled to his place in front of the class and began talking about the cotton gin. What kind of thing would have a name like that? My mind foamed up. Erik and I did not speak.

Deeply skeptical of any social encounter, with chilled waves rolling in and out of my heart, I dashed off at the bell to my next class, clutching my books. Nonetheless, passing the stairwell to the basement at lunch, I lingered for a moment, thinking of Alice. Her smile, Cheshire-like. It didn't attract me exactly, but compelled me with a sympathy purer because the smile was so bland. I carried my lunch (as always, stiff-skinned sour plums and cottage cheese) into the basement. They were all there. Alice nodded at me for the second time, and I took what had begun to feel like my seat on the orange vinyl leatherette couch, next to her.

Alice inclined her head in the general direction of the boy-girl pair on her other side.

—We call them The Pretzels.

The pair looked at me with speechless melancholy.

Happiness blazed in my chest, and I grinned.

Days passed, social life continued. I rarely had to use my words. I spent lunches well inside the circumference of Alice's honey smell and the soft gush of her voice. Second period every school day, Erik's books crashed onto the desk next to mine. He was taciturn but his body was symphonic. His sprawling frame overflowed our little chairs, and his blunt cut mane of blond hair, that hair, was beautiful.

Giggles make wiggles in your face, Erik printed with a pencil on the margin of a handout, and pushed it towards me. When I laughed, he added, in even smaller letters, *YAY*!

Erik was yards of relaxed boy, with only the stiffness of his neck to convey suffering. In the hallways between classes, he barreled by without looking at me. Or so I thought. One day a dim apprehension led me to glance back after he'd passed, and I found his neck twisted, his gaze locked on mine.

I discreetly checked if Erik was flashing me one of these glances every time he passed. He was.

Get me out of here. His eyes buzzed mine like radar beams.

Out of what? Our world, the interstices of school and home and the floodplain of friendship. Was that it? Or was it the body? So big and mysterious, really its own planet.

He thinks we share a chunk of the same bloody heart. This thought popped up of its own accord. I didn't know what to do with it. *He could be my alien, if I wanted one.*

Soon after this, Cheryl pulled me to the side in the hall. She leaned against a locker and shook her ringlets of black hair down her back. I looked with interest at the bright green contacts that slid around on her muddy green irises.

—Guess what I heard, she said. About Erik. You know his dad is a chemist, she said. He's kind of a frog, and he works with a lot of other frogs, down at the sewage plant. Well, his mom was a fashion model. She's just a gorgeous babe.

There was a pause as Cheryl and I struggled to imagine Erik's mother.

—Poor Erik, I said. So that's his problem. There's an ugly person inside, struggling to get out.

There was a long snide girlish moment, followed by withering laughter. I'm not sure what got resolved, but afterwards I just stopped wondering about Erik.

One month slithered into the next, and then the next. My social life acquired a little solidity. There wasn't much to it, but it did continue. One day I overslept. Late to school, I walked through streets deserted due to the cold. Erik came up to me as I climbed the front steps, a biting December wind at my back.

—Hey, said Erik.

—You're late, I observed. Let's be late for Mr. Gibbs' class together.

The wind was blowing his hair all around and the tips of his ears were pink. He looked like a model in front of a wind machine. But it was the emotion that leaked out of him that, as always, caught my attention. Some wad of feeling that was sullen and stunning. I felt a sudden pang in my heart.

—Uhh, he said. D'ya have a moment?

—Sure. But can we go inside? *Brrr*. . .Erik frowned as he gazed fixedly at the ground. I sighed, rocking from one foot to another. I understood that we could not go inside.

—I'm bisexual, he mumbled.

I looked up at the winter sky, through a few filmy clouds, into a pale expanse of blue. This sky touches down everywhere, I thought. Amber waves of grain and purple mountains, etc. Now that's promiscuous.

Then I looked at Erik and frowned. What <u>was</u> a bisexual? What was <u>sexual</u>?

—How do you know you're bisexual?

—Well, I'm having an affair with a teacher.

—Wow.

We sat down on the freezing cold steps.

—Is that complicated? I asked.

Erik didn't answer, which confused me. If he stopped answering altogether, my curiosity would never be satisfied and would turn into suffering. I decided to jump right to the point.

—Who is it?

—Mr. Gibbs, he said quietly.

—But Erik—

—What?

—That's impossible.

—Why?

—He's. . . He's a penguin.

Erik gave me a cool, appraising look.

—You should dump him, I said. He must be thirty years old.

Erik shrugged and got up and I followed him into class. Mr. Gibbs eyed us but said nothing.

For the next few days I felt like I was caught in a whiteout, snow swirling all around. The actual weather was dreary, a late fall paralysis of clear and windless cold. The snow was my thoughts. I couldn't fit the new information about Erik into the known world. When I looked at Mr. Gibbs, he became a wall of skin, a barrier with pores and body hair behind which lay an *Unknown Lande.* I wanted and expected him to disappear. Yet there he was, day after day, meaty and mundane, waddling and droning above us during second period.

Erik seemed a little glum.

Anything in life, is life. Anything at all. Gradually I absorbed this uncanny fact.

As I was drifting down the hall shortly before Christmas break, Erik stepped in front of me. He cleared his throat and his whole body seemed to rustle as if a wind was passing through it.

—Where are you going next year? he asked. Like, college.

—Dunno, I answered, shifting uneasily.

—You should go somewhere. Maybe here.

He handed me a state university application.

—That's where I'm going. The app deadline is Friday.

He sauntered off down the hall. I didn't say anything. I was too surprised. I recognized my future as soon as the paper was in my hand.

2. Obvious Thing

It was the obvious thing. The school was cheap and good and very big. Forty thousand students attended. My whole social life migrated there: Cheryl, Alice, Erik. But I never would have if Erik hadn't put the paper into my hand.

My new home was located between a factory district and a small dreary metropolis (Toledo, if you need to know), with strips of pasture on either side. On a hot day, I could smell cows. The cornices of the school's low red brick buildings were decorated with yellowed stucco knobs that looked like art deco frosting. I liked to stare up at the knobs and let the rivers of students (mostly in engineering and agriculture) turn into a smear.

It was perfect for me. It was an uprising for me. It was a blur.

Cheryl appeared in my doorway several times a day. She'd slouch there, staring at my floor for long moments, unable to talk. Horrified. I watched her moments of pain but they didn't last long. Then her loud self came back, and she moved like a party, shaking her long hair.

We gossiped. Rumors, unconfirmed, that Erik had found a girlfriend. Our reflections on Alice, who'd moved into the room opposite mine and then was hardly ever seen.

I kept my most important decision a secret: I'd decided that it was time for me to try to process heterosexually. *Squish. Boy on top. Squish.* There was the boy whose mouth tasted like oysters and one who thought I was a German exchange student named Ingrid (I faked an accent). Tangles. Just so you know: I really did those boys. My mind foamed up when I thought about it.

My logic felt pure, based as it was in action. Our shared circumstances (of dorm, school, bodies) led me to believe that everyone else felt pretty much the same. This made my talks with Cheryl endlessly provocative, as there was virtually no one whose actions I found comprehensible. Why had Gray Loving followed me around for months, crying actual tears? Why, come to think of it, did Alice always smile at me beatifically? A smile that was unwavering, like a principle.

I told Cheryl about Gray Loving and she said firmly,

—Gray crushed out on you doesn't mean that you have anything in common with Gray.

Then she gestured with her head towards the wall in back of her.

—That painted foot in the hall? Alice was out there in the middle of the night, painting that foot.

I peered over Cheryl's shoulder into the hallway, and there it was. A giant well-made foot. The yellow paint blended with the dingy wall, making it both inconspicuous and spectacular.

—No one knew she could paint. Now people are saying she's a genius. 'She never goes to class and she's doing reasonably well': voila, genius. Well, I think she's on acid.

As the days passed, the foot grew into one leg, then two, then a figure, a reclining male nude. He looked like a landscape of rolling yellowish green hills, spreading outward from the genitalia, which were a fruit arrangement: a banana and two plums. The nude floated dreamily at shoulder height down most of the length of the hall, his eyes half-closed. Then, on the opposite wall, another figure began to appear, a woman, in the same queasy yellowish tones. Her pussy was a little snatch of dark red cherries. The figures had small faces, shaped like cantaloupes, and that bland.

—I love the colors. They're so ill.

—Sammy thinks Alice must have hepatitis.

Snicker, snicker. Cheryl continued,

—I knocked on her door and there was no answer. It was unlocked, so. . .I went in! Alice just smiled her Buddha smile. The window was covered with a tie-dye sheet, making the light purple and orange and blue in shafts.

I couldn't believe that it was so simple for Cheryl. I hadn't seen Alice in weeks.

—What did you talk about?

—Acid, like I told you.

—And she said?

—Saturday. She'll do it with us.

It didn't seem like a bad idea. Saturday came and Cheryl and I stood in front of Alice with our mouths open and she put little tablets on our tongues. I waited for mine to dissolve, waited to get off, then I couldn't move. *No wonder Alice hardly talks anymore. Where she lives now. . . speech is boulderish stuff.*

Insurmountable. I lay pinned against the bedspread by the weight of possible words. Trying to think in boulders, flitting between shafts of blue and orange and purple light. Finally my eyelids fell with a thud and I went somewhere. Into the interior, which was pure white, and I was lost in a fog. My blood ran around my body like rumors in a forest.

Perhaps I slept. Perhaps the hours rolled over me with such intensity that my memories were demolished. In any case, it was morning before I opened my eyes. I found myself sprawled on the floor. How had I gotten there? On the ceiling there was a long scrawl; I stared at it for quite a while trying to decipher it before I realized it was a crack, actually. Then I saw Alice sitting in her rocker, sipping tea. She smiled, though it was nothing so definite as a smile, more like an effusion. It filled the air around her. Mildly, she said,

—Your cunt tasted like orange pekoe.

A thrill collided with my chest. It rose like a bright bubble and burst and I felt like crying. I looked around for Cheryl. She was gone!

—I don't remember anything, I admitted.

Alice nodded wisely, then said,

—Cheryl already left.

What had Cheryl seen? Was it possible I'd had sex with a girl and didn't remember it? I lay there as uncertainty filled me and turned over and over until it finally became a slavish form of love. Such extreme feeling demanded sacrifice. I went to my room, which had a small sink in the corner with a mirror over it. I leaned over the sink and cut the letter **A** into my tongue. *A is for Alice, the acid queen of my dreams.* I watched in the mirror as the firm lines turned watery and dribbled red over my lips. It tasted like salt water. Then I rinsed off the razor and lay it in the sun, on a window ledge.

I went back and knelt by Alice. I showed her my tongue, blood on my teeth like a vampire. Her smile was calm and kind. She ran her fingers through my hair and I glistened with pride.

I began slipping into her room whenever I could. I'd scan the hall to make sure no one saw me before I opened her door and darted inside. The door was never locked, which I took personally, a sign of welcome.

Alice would nod at me from her rocker and smile. I sat down on the floor as her nods tapered off into the rhythm of whatever music happened to be playing. One day I started massaging her shoulders, and I just kept going, pushing her shirt's large white buttons one after another through their holes. The dark purple shirt slipped down and spread out around her waist. Her tits looked beautiful above it. Her areoles were large; when I gathered up her breasts her nipples hardened. Then she put her shirt back on, like that was the end of a thought.

I kept expecting something more to happen. It had to, because she'd led me to believe it already had, or something.

A visit with Alice possessed so much calming emptiness that I left her room with nostalgia for emotion. Was this good? Well, I told myself, at least it made sense. Where other people had history and personality, Alice had nothing, at least nothing that showed. She had become simple, like an abstraction, with intelligence humming somewhere under the drugs.

3. Stalker

I needed a holiday. When Cheryl appeared in my doorway, slumped and gossiping, I told her this, and she said,

—What, are you having difficulties adjusting?

—Not really. Are you?

We had an uneasy silent moment. Words push up when they're ready, you know? Think of all the hours you spend not speaking, living without words, in the lather of your incomprehension. . . Cheryl is probably fucking Sammy, I thought to myself. I envied Cheryl the blazing certainty of being straight. Even though heterosexuality seemed like a sort of suburb, she was one with that planned community. Whereas my little stab at queerness amounted to. . .a possibly imaginary escapade. I shuddered in the doubt of not knowing what had happened. Uncertainty such as mine was the lowest form of sexual life.

How Sammy had appeared was something of a mystery, but he was the boyfriend, with his pressed slacks and soft New Jersey accent.

I liked Sammy. At nineteen, he was utterly adult, and weary, and so dry that his jokes made the inside of my mouth pucker. People like that sometimes pop out of the grinding machinery of ancient religions. *Fuck homelands*, he used to say, the way that other people say forgeddaboutit. Cheryl was Jewish. Sammy's parents were Christian Palestinians and he regarded religion as part torture, part embarrassment.

If Sammy wasn't around and his name was mentioned, Cheryl's face wrenched into an odd grimace. At one of those moments she said,

—Should I tell my mother I have a boyfriend, and he's from Palestine? She loves Palestine, hah hah. Cheryl seemed to sag, with a look more nausea than love, as she did whenever our conversation went anywhere near the topic of Sammy or sex.

And there she was in my doorway, sagging. The stricken look had come back. Whatever she was thinking about, she was making slow and difficult progress. Finally she shook her ponytail and said,

—Come home with me for the weekend.

We left on Friday in a borrowed car, and got to her parents' house by dinner. They lived in a brick bungalow in a development of bungalows, the post-war type with lots of tiny bedrooms. The streets were wide and curved and empty. Cheryl's parents' house was nearly overshadowed by its front yard bushes.

—Pot roast. Oh, fabulous, Cheryl said sarcastically the moment she walked in the door.

—You're home. Home. Where you belong!

Cheryl's mother smashed Cheryl against her apron. Cheryl's brother raised his big hands and clasped her. I noticed that he was. . .slow. Had she told me that?

—CHERyl, CHERyl. . .His voice cracked and soared eerily.

Cheryl's father quietly glided into his reserved spot next to her mom. He shook my hand.

I enjoyed everything: the tiny dining room, the grainy pot roast, the little red potatoes, the green beans, the floury yellow cake with strawberries just for Cheryl. All I had to do was eat and watch and listen to Cheryl and her mother carry on about all the usual school topics, interrupted now & then by Cheryl's brother Henry's ragged inquiries. Cheryl's father said nothing at all.

Henry looked great, so it was a big surprise every time he opened his mouth. His hair was thick and black and his skin was smooth. He had a large square Republican jaw. I judged him to be a little older than Cheryl. In fact, he wasn't that mentally disabled. He didn't have a job, but he did volunteer for political campaigns. He had a collection of buttons in his room, all advocating fiscal responsibility.

—Henry is a Republican, Cheryl said, her face twisted up with regret.

It was hours later. Dinner was over and everyone had withdrawn into their tiny rooms. We were in Cheryl's, which was soft yellow and creamy pink and plushy. Her pillows had fur.

—Well, Henry is not completely. . .

—Sammy's not Republican. I wouldn't fuck a Republican.

That word. I skipped a beat.

—I wouldn't either.

The silence smiled on our agreement, or so I thought. But Cheryl had entered one of her moods. Her features glazed over, distracted by drama within. I waited, and when she came back, it was with a new quality: stubbornness. She told me she wasn't using birth control.

—I just don't want to.

—Do you want to get pregnant?

—Of course not.

Whatever. I didn't say, Hmm, I had the impression that not using birth control could get you pregnant. Why push it? The truth was I had never used it myself.

She gave me a blanket and a furry pillow and I curled up on her soft rug and listened to her breathing deeply and regularly in her sleep. I was a pea, and this was my pod. Cheryl was my sister pea.

In the morning, I sat with the males of the family, watching a golf tournament on TV while Cheryl and her mother fussed over waffles. At some point Cheryl's mother walked into the living room with the day's mail. She stared at a postcard, puzzled.

—There's a postcard for Camille.

My heart, or something. Nubs of dread sprouted on the broad fields of my tongue. I took the card, which was post-office issue, no picture. On the back was the message *Time and Time Again*, in shaky spooky-on-purpose script, then the initials *W.S.*

—What is that? asked Cheryl.

—I've been getting weirdo cards, I said, sort of helplessly. They're all signed W.S. but the handwriting is never the same.

I didn't tell them this was one of the tame ones.

Everyone shut up and looked at me. I felt crushed. The idea I'd been clinging to, that these cards were related to some wacko but not unfriendly art project, I finally acknowledged to be unlikely. Especially after the W.S. card I'd gotten earlier in the week. I described it to them: a postcard of two black kittens, their eyes gouged with a red ballpoint into gaping blood-stained holes.

—How did she get a postcard here? Cheryl's mother asked. Someone must be watching her.

—You're being stalked, Cheryl declared.

—Somebody hates me, I said, frowning uncertainly. I kind of want to kill him.

—Don't kill him, Cheryl's brother bellowed. That's wrong!

Over breakfast, the family discussed what I should do: ignore it, or not, seemed to be the choices. What can I say? It counted, but it didn't add up.

In truth, heretofore attraction seemed bizarre, anyway, and these cards were just illustrations of that fact, like heavy breathing in a movie. They'd come in the mail, I'd toss them in a drawer and go out.

But now fear arrived. It scrambled my memory of everyone I'd spoken to since I'd arrived at school. On the drive back, I wondered whose rubbery smile, or blank stare, or carefully averted eyes concealed an insane obsession—with me, of all people. I had an enemy. I felt like gagging. Malice as miasma had drifted into my life. I discussed various possibilities with Cheryl but we couldn't pin anything down. It irritated me terribly that this was by intention.

Little by little, fear was transformed into something more bearable, a weird and electrical edginess. I did all I could to hold it in as we walked back into the dorm, making a beeline for my room. We passed Erik. Cheryl grabbed him by the arm and told him to come with us. Erik, looking pained, permitted himself to be dragged along.

I showed them the kitten card. It had a title across the bottom in delicate script: *Black Mischief.* Red teardrops fell from the kittens' red eye sockets and dripped from their little white teeth. There was a poem written on the back:

Thoughts of you
cling like dog shit
to my shoes.
—W.S.

I emptied the drawer where I'd been stashing the cards, and handed them over. I hadn't realized how they'd been piling up. One card showed Jesus in thick 3-D, murky irradiated browns and greens. He was knocking on a cottage door, his eyes soulful as a puppy, with yellow rays spilling around his head. "O earth, earth, earth, Hear the word of the Lord," was printed across the bottom.

—This is so weird, Erik said solemnly.

—Camille you need to get a diagnosis, Cheryl ventured. For these cards. You need to figure out what you're dealing with.

Diagnosis! The word itself shone with a bright medical light.

—How do we get that?

—Erik, you're in a psych class. . .

—Dr. Marshall? I don't know. She's peculiar.

Erik was reluctant to go to Dr. Marshall because. . . she brought food to class that she hungrily watched her students eat, as she talked about her diet, which was very demanding but which had enabled her to lose over 200 pounds.

—She's a matchstick with lots of loose skin. That's okay, but she talks about it in every class. It makes me uncomfortable.

—Well, this isn't a food issue.

We all looked at the postcards spread out on the bed. Erik sighed.

—Alright.

The following Wednesday I put the postcards in a brown manila envelope and we all walked to Dr. Marshall's office, which was a few blocks off campus. Erik knocked and we were called into her office. It was tastefully furnished with a walnut desk set and dark green armchairs, atmosphere dabbed with air freshener. The doctor strode from behind her desk, clasped our hands firmly. Her beige suit of heavy crepe hung loosely on her shrunken frame.

—Sit down, she said, with an expansive wave towards the chairs.

Her gestures were still those of a much larger person.

—So what can I help you with?

She carefully studied me. A thin brown cigarette trailed smoke.

I repeated what Erik had told her on the phone. She listened without comment, flicking through the postcards one by one. Then she spread them out on her desk in a fan, examined the postmarks, and sorted them in the order in which they'd arrived.

Finally, deliberately, she spoke.

—These postcards are from a male. I don't think he'll try to hurt you. However, you might find a dead cat in your closet.

She put the postcards back in the manila envelope and patted it.

I sagged. My breath released in a gush.

—Thank you, Dr. Marshall, I babbled.

Dr. Marshall gave me a crisp, sympathetic smile, and ushered us out. The whole appointment took less than ten minutes.

—What the fuck was she talking about, Cheryl said under her breath after the office door clicked shut.

—I told you she's weird, Erik said.

—Guys, stop.

They looked at me.

—This is what we wanted, right? She told me what to expect, and I can handle it. It's sad of course. . . but I'll get janitorial services to clean out the closet.

4. Nadine

It was a peculiar couple of days. Cheryl, looking grim, left town, this time with Sammy. Erik was holed up with his long-rumored girlfriend. He finally told me her name: Jill. I was left alone to wait, with no deadline, for a postcard or dead cat. The waiting dragged on all Friday night and through Saturday morning until I opened my door and found Nadine, her blunt-cut blond hair swinging against her neck. I had met her at field hockey try-outs. I was taking a whack at the ball when she showed up dragging a hockey stick. Neither of us made it to the second round, and we had bonded over that. Now she grinned in my doorway, a lean girl in jeans with skin the color of honey. She came in, we sat around in my room and nothing much happened except her lips pressed into the flesh under my ear. I got so excited I felt sick. I didn't know what I could do with her, but I thought it might be a long list.

—Be sweet, lady, she said, after I mumbled goodbye.

Sunday afternoon I heard another knock. I opened the door and it was Nadine. She ran her slim hand around my crotch, right in the doorway. Her kisses were almost bites. It was hot and appalling, standing there with Nadine-who-looked-like-a-Breck-girl, my thrills and confusion pulsing outward from her thin, hard lips. Nobody saw, but I was ready in case they did. I felt weirdly legitimate, legs spread to her fingers. Was that the power of her good looks?

We messed around awhile and then went for a walk. One of the frat houses we passed was having a beer bash and Nadine insisted on going in. She entered their wet t-shirt contest, tottering down a plank held up by two chairs, the pink flush of her nipples visible through white cotton. Of course she won—Nadine was perfect—and the frat boys toasted her, beer sloshing over the rims of their plastic cups. After we left, I told her I thought the party was horrible, and Nadine just cackled.

—It could've been worse. I could've lost the contest.

At my door, she gave me a quick hug and sidled off down the hall. It wasn't what I expected, but she'd turned the corner before I had time to react. Then I didn't see her for a week. All that week, whenever I thought of Nadine, the pleasures of girls opened in front of me like a pit. I resolved to just do things with her, like whatever she wanted, if she ever turned up again.

Knock, knock.

—Hey you.

—Hey.

She pulled out her wallet and showed me her hottest latest thing: a fake I.D. that said she was twenty-one. It was greenish and laminated and had a photograph and a thumb print under the title, 'Official Identification Card.'

—It looks cheesy.

—It works. And I know where to get more, at only ten bucks apiece. I'll take you. Then we can go to the gay bar tonight.

It sounded like a reasonable plan. We borrowed a car and drove into Toledo, past blocks and blocks of houses with bars on the windows and mismatched shingles. The fake I.D. guy was in his sixties and moved like an old turtle. His garage was full of decaying appliances that at one point had perhaps been candidates for repair. He did his fake I.D. business on a table in the back of the garage. He typed my info onto the card, then inked and squashed my thumb into the box labeled 'Thumbprint.' He slapped the laminate on it and handed me my card.

—Wow.

The parameters of adulthood expanded to include me. *Touched by the honor.* I stuck the card in my rear pocket and walked out of the garage with a bit of a swagger.

Nadine was right about the bar; we flashed our cards and got in with no problem. I wanted to sit and crowd watch, nursing my whiskey sour, but she had other ideas. So I sat in my booth and watched her: Nadine flitting from dyke to dyke, running her fingers through her blond hair and jerking her head back as she flashed her grin. I watched her stop at someone tall and butch, with blue eyes so dark they were strange, and a smile that was right there—direct and warm. Nadine thrust one breast out and stood with her hips cocked, concealing her slightly crooked spine. Her posture pressed her perfect nipples into the white cotton t-shirt. A dazzled shudder ran through me.

Did I like being with her? Could I stand it? It did get me into some sort of beauty bubble; I had to qualify just to get an invitation. That was something. I watched Nadine slide into a booth, and lean over the laps of some laughing dykes. What was she nuzzling?

With an effort I looked down. There were orange & blue lights reflecting rainbows in my glass. Then I watched the different groups rub across one another. Fags clustered at the bar, in a bubble world of sports jackets and jeans. Occasionally one would break away and prance, the others laughing. The women were raucous and more shabby, sprawled in the pit and the wings off the dance floor. Nadine had told me in this club the dykes were impossible to tell apart from the whores. They looked as though they were all wearing the same mask, and that interested me more than anything. It was the mystery I wanted, I could feel myself headed towards it though I didn't move.

It's hard to explain. There was the feeling of my body moving faster than my thoughts—simple forward momentum. Then a drop-off. When you stop you go splat, or something. That's how you learn what you're doing.

At last call, she came back to me. I got her home in a cab and we made out in the back. It felt like practice, her thin lips swimming against my neck. I could sense Nadine's willingness and disinterest at the same time. When the cab stopped I pushed the door open and leaned into the darkness; there was a garage looming out of a grove of white trees with papery bark. Nadine was already trotting around the cab, headed for a side door, up a narrow flight of stairs—her room was over the garage.

I paid, then followed Nadine up into a small studio with not much in it but a mattress, white boards on cinder blocks, and neatly shelved books. Most were by 19th Century American writers. I picked up a book that was on the floor by the bed—a collection of essays by Emerson.

—So this is your private life.

She cocked her hip, lifted the beer, ran her fingers through her hair—the whole bar vocabulary. But she was talking about quiet evenings and philosophy. Jazz, with a background of crickets. I couldn't even follow what she was saying, it seemed so out of character. She rolled her eyes in exasperation and began pulling at my shirt. When she'd uncovered my belly button she ground her knuckle into it, sending nerve pulses into my gut that grated inside. Nauseating and sexual. Then we were wrestling.

I caught a glimpse of a black window with bare branches pressed against it and her face floated by with a look of weird romance. Somehow my shirt came off. It landed with one shirt sleeve stretched out while the rest made a white cotton pile on the floor. As I jerked my foot around the sleeve she got me off balance, bent over. In a headlock, I let myself fall. I thought we'd roll around among clothes, two girls, smooth and jabbering.

Then she pressed a blade against my throat, and I went blank. Breathing hard, bent over towards the floor, our bodies gently rocked together. No feeling, just silence and curiosity, a deeper level of attention.

She sprang away, shaking her hand out, laughing a little hysterically. I looked for the knife but all I saw was her right thumbnail, long and curved like a horn. It was yellowish, coated with clear nail polish. She held it up like she was exposing a secret.

—You're playing with my head, I told her.

Nadine sat on the couch and hunched over, staring at her hand. It lay there like a little claw.

—The last time I did that, this guy was dragging me out of his car and into a cornfield. We were somewhere outside of Toledo. The fuckwad let me go after I stuck my thumbnail into his gut. It was dark, he couldn't see what I had or didn't have.

—That sucks, I said, sort of stupidly.

I stuck my thumbnail against my throat. It felt convincing. I was filled with admiration.

—You're so streetwise, Nadine.

She just looked at me. Smells of belly sweat and fear. Real fear clears my mind, I try to remember that. I sat down next to her, and awkwardly, buddy-style, put my arm across her shoulders.

—Where did you sleep after that?

—I didn't sleep. I sat until dawn under some bushes at the edge of the field, listening to the trucks.

Appearances were dazzling and indecipherable. I believed they hid real experience. So of course I still wanted to have sex, whatever that was. *Choose me, out of all this blur.* But don't you need to remember pleasure in order to have had it? I remember Nadine curled up next to me, running her fingers across my stomach, breasts, neck. I think I remember that. The rest tumbles from my brain in a swirl of before-and-after. Clothes on the floor. The bare branches of a birch tree pressed against the window. I raised my head and heard a scratching sound; it was the branches. I wanted Nadine to be blond all the way through, I really wanted that. Or maybe I just needed reality to finally arrive, and what could be more real than sex? At least it would make her my girlfriend.

Her lips were thin and difficult to get hold of. She wrapped her legs around my waist and rocked and twisted rapidly. Orgasm launched her away from me (like everything else she did). That was what I expected. But in fact afterwards I kept hearing a sweet far-off drone: it was Nadine telling me stories as she lightly ran her fingers across my shoulders, stomach, thighs. What was she saying? I felt almost drowned, like I was swimming against everything into a black sheet with stars.

5. Postcard

The card was waiting for me the next morning when I stumbled into the dorm and fished around groggily in my mailbox. I flipped through the announcements (class schedule changes, cafeteria menu) and found the card at the bottom. I knew it was from him; something about the odd finality of the picture. It showed a little boat in the middle of a lake in autumn at sunset, with the silhouette of a man and girl facing one another. The lake surface shimmered orange and yellow in circles around the boat. The scene conveyed a sinister peace, but something seemed about to happen, because neither could get off the boat without moving. I felt a shiver of hatred. It passed through me, like background radiation. I turned over the card and this is what was written on the back:

> Who is the true bridegroom?
> If he hollers let him go, bitch.
> —W.S.

I made my way to my room and went to bed. Or, rather, I fell into bed, and kept falling. If I'd had thoughts, I'm sure they would have been dramatic ones, wild voices calling across the rocky embankments. But I just lay under my blanket and let the marbles fall out of my head. I pulled my knees to my chest and cried harshly.

There was a knock on the door. I looked up and it was Cheryl, with Sammy just behind her. Their faces wore an expression I didn't recognize. I rejected it. I raised my head and screamed like a banshee,

—Get Out Get Out GET OUT **GET OUT!!**

The door clicked shut. I guess I slept. I opened my eyes and stared at nothing for awhile. Felt tender, sickening lassitude. Eventually I noticed the postcard lying face down on the floor. The postmark was unfamiliar. I picked it up and realized: it had been mailed from Brazil.

The stamp seemed to glimmer in the dreariness of my room. It was a rainforest parrot, tropical pink and green and yellow, styled as a paper cut-out. The lovely word *Brazilia* was stamped in tiny letters on the wings of this bird. Could it be. . . that my stalker had left the country?

I had to take this strange fact out into the world, which meant talking to Cheryl about it. I threw on some fresh clothes and set out to find her: I tried her room, then the Snack Closet, the Fresh Fried Cafe, all the vending machines. I trolled the halls and found Erik, feeding quarters into a Coke dispenser.

—You didn't know? Maybe she couldn't find you. Cheryl got an abortion yesterday. She's probably at home or off somewhere with Sammy.

His soda clattered down to the opening.

I watched Erik pop open the Coke and gulp, gulp. I didn't say anything, though my thoughts tumbled. Greasy, radiant shame.

Erik drained his Coke, tossed the can, and left, while I still stood there stupidly. Eventually I slunk back to my room and put the postcard in the drawer with all the others. I looked at it one more time and a thought occurred (which didn't feel like mine): *Now my collection is complete.*

6. Dream life

Cheryl wouldn't hold it against me, I knew it. She just wasn't that kind. But I felt dazed. Was that unexpressed regret? I never did ask Cheryl about the abortion.

I never did, I never did...

It didn't feel like a failure. Something just emptied out. My new condition, once it arrived, was oddly comfortable. Paralysis can be languid, even relaxing. Cheryl and I nodded when we crossed paths, which turned out to be surprisingly seldom. She moved in with Sammy that spring, somewhere off-campus. Then I never saw her.

I was the faithful one. I possessed a stubborn faith in my tumble after the elusive Nadine, and I would not stop. I wanted to fill my adulthood with adult-type experiences. What I got was screwy tortures and never enough sex. To be fair, Nadine threw her arms around me now and then and tried to give me—love, I guess.

In a lot of ways, I never bothered to relate to her. Whenever I made a joke, she looked at me sideways and a discouraging dead space opened up in our conversation. Nadine was too skittish and headlong to get the humor of any situation she wasn't the center of. As my real friendships had fallen away, I mostly ended up having fantasy conversations with other people. Especially Cheryl.

Like when the picture of Alice and her fiancée arrived

one day in the mail. They were posed so that Alice appeared to be shorter. What a stretch! *Cheryl,* I wanted to say, *Remember the Texas Rangers who rescued Alice from her schizo mother? She's marrying one, only toy-size. Alice is marrying Ed. Remember Ed? The one you used to call the tiniest Texan imaginable, the pocket-size Texan.*

In the photo, Ed wore a cowboy hat and Alice was positioned as the loyal little woman at his side, absolutely clear-eyed and beaming, as if to say, this is not an acid trip.

I dropped that photo in the drawer with all the weirdo postcards.

I missed Cheryl so much it was annoying.

Dream life with Nadine. We were at the bar almost every night. One day I woke up and she was already dressed, smoking. Maybe she had never gone to bed. She looked tired and careless, slumped in the chair, in her jeans and cowboy boots, taking one drag after another as she stared levelly at me.

—I can't deal with you anymore.

I felt agreeable. I think I went back to sleep. I still saw her everywhere, possibly more often than before. We shared the same shadow.

Nadine was just a girl in a pile of girls, swarming. She grinned like a drunk. Yet something true about her still seems so beautiful to me, perhaps it was the light behind her skin that spilled out at her elbows, her lips, under the arches of her feet. Or was it her deformity, the spine which knitted her back into a slight twist so that her tits protruded, high and separate? It's a strange way to touch the world. Years later, I read something about the appeal of blonds—they bruise easily. I put that thought next to Nadine, as though I were putting a piece of her hair in a locket. But it's nothing like the way I really feel.

SEX LIFE

SEX LIFE

It was an August day, hot and clear. I stuck out my thumb as cars zipped by. After they passed, I started walking down the tarmac road, through a county of red dirt and warped tiny pines. I was going to work. Eventually a dusty hatchback skidded to a halt at the shoulder. When I opened the door there was a shiny revolver on the passenger seat. The driver said, *I'm an off-duty policeman*, flashed a big goofy grin and stuck the gun into the glove compartment. That's the way it started. I remember there was a light at the end but no tunnel.

Bright blue sky reflected in gun metal.

My sex life begins later, in a tiny loft above Sam's Health Foods Store. The whites of Sam's eyes were yellow as scrambled eggs, and his wiry hairs seemed about to spring off his head. Sam employed me and Max, his brother. Although Max was only twenty-two, he had a musty old man smell and hair grew out of his ears. Sam let me sleep in the store's loft when I worked till closing. After I wiped the counters and dropped the day's wad of cash in the bank slot across the street, I'd climb the ladder up to Max's pile of porn.

Why are there so many body parts? I wondered as I fingered Max's magazines. The only body in that hot crawl space was mine. I gently touched the women's cunts, scalded pink cracks. On these nights, my mind rose out of my body and floated around the rafters, dry as dust. It's that sexual specificity, like rocks in the brain. Do you know what I mean? I was eighteen and it was stunning. Fantasies lurched through my mind like drugs. Any feeling was appropriate because my head was empty. I started carrying a knife when I hitched rides to work. I'd sit in the back of the car and imagine playing their throats like violins. *After I'm done with you, confession will be a relief.* Lots of guys had ponytails then, which made it easier.

Twinkle little star, give me your revolver—that's what I said to the off-duty policeman as I opened the glove compartment. I giggled when he threw me out.

There was a dyke story in one of Max's porn magazines. It was my favorite, but not because I liked it exactly. Reading it by the light of my flashlight was like examining a photograph of dead relatives. On the first page there was a drawing of the author, Lisa V., grinning crazily as she rowed a small boat on a stormy ocean. The dizzy feeling of the picture had something to do with eating pussy, which was explained carefully, step by step, to the male audience. The story reminded me of Anita, only because it didn't resemble anything we'd done together.

Anita was a small person and her moans sounded like soft hoots. She cracked out shaky orgasms that left me clutching her fingers. Hers was my first pussy and I enjoyed playing with it. I tried flicking her clit with my finger as I listened to her breathing. But sex with Anita was mild, like a survey. We did this-and-that—whatever she'd spent her marriage fantasizing about. Once I tongued her asshole, because she wanted me to. Then I felt nauseated. "Why'd you make me do that?" I said. She giggled and grabbed my tit. "You'll do whatever I want you to do," she said.

Anita had a husband, Mark, and me (before I left the state), but they kept me a secret. I was eighteen, and Anita was my first.

What's with the body anyway, I said to Anita, and she said it has to do with space, occupation. *Give it a try,* she said, backing me into a corner. *Put your legs and arms up—expect a circus.* Is it possible to walk away if you don't like it anymore? Anita's legs were lights underwater. I stood as still as a butler; I didn't know where I was. The husband, Mark, replaced me, but not before I'd tasted her cunt.

Mark and Anita picked me up in the cafe where I worked. It was pretty easy, I guess. They sat at a table in my section for several hours, swapping stories of payoffs, political vendettas, feuds between the police and fire departments, and I drifted by, listening. I noticed Mark first, actually. He had a cynical way of nibbling at a cigarette. Anita stabbed little pieces of cheese with a toothpick and drank white wine. When she looked up from her glass, she was usually staring at me. It turned out they were newspaper reporters. And they knew a good bar, etcetera.

It was a nearly empty jazz club. Anita danced by herself, spinning around the small dance floor with her arms swaying, while Mark and I leaned against the back wall, watching her.

Mark was neat and compact with dark hair. Anita had small perky tits. Even sitting back on the couch, after we got to their apartment, her nipples pointed up through the soft knit top she was wearing with jeans. Her torso was square atop long slim legs, and she had a big pillow of wavy auburn hair. But her face was distractingly broad, a fat person's face. Mark took a hundred dollar bill out of his wallet, rolled it into a thin tube, and passed it around on a mirror with lines of cocaine.

Coolness at the back of my throat while I tried to fall asleep. Murmuring from Mark and Anita's bedroom, then quiet. Dim streetlight bled through the curtain over the couch, where I was curled under a pinkish yellow blanket. Every time something happens, I adjust to a different kind of silence. Perhaps they had tense words as I was sliding gently out of consciousness, but I heard nothing. I woke with a start to hear Anita's slow sobs, a low throbbing like a cello. Her cries were bleak beyond disclosure, though their door was open a crack. It flooded me with excitement, a sexual disturbance. As it went on and on, she began to sound like the rhythm of my breathing, and I fell asleep.

Nothing much happened for the next few weeks. The three of us hung around together and I spent more nights on their couch, while the point (which even I knew was sex) didn't seem to be getting any closer. Not that I cared very much; I wanted experiences. Was I going to turn into a lesbian? Anyhow, I wondered where the sex was—Mark and Anita didn't seem to be having any, at least while I was lying out there. Then, suddenly, they did. I heard every moan, because the door was open a crack, as I sat by the coffee table wiping the mirror clean with my finger and rubbing the leftover cocaine on my gums. Buzz.

Weeks later, Anita asked me what I thought. I didn't know what she was talking about. *Just tell me your impression.* She was pushy like that. So, I told her I was amazed how much noise Mark had made, those moaning noises—it sounded so femme. She laughed at my inexperience. *In the movies men don't make noises like that when they're screwing,* I said.

The next time I spent a night on their couch, Anita began sobbing again. Then she stopped, and Mark came out in his bathrobe. He lit a cigarette and sat down in the chair across from the couch.

"I'm going away for two months," he said, "I understand you are going to fuck my wife." He jabbed his cigarette out in the ashtray and sighed. "Anita's had the hots for you from the start."

Their door was open. I imagined her listening, curled in their bed, eyes open and face wet.

The next time I came around their place Mark was gone. Nothing changed except Anita seduced me and we started doing it all the time. What I mean is that the connection between us didn't intensify. When she wanted sex, a glare would lurch out of her, a kind of cold pornographic light. It embarrassed me. Once afterward, she looked at me with an amused expression and asked, *Are you a dyke yet?* I mumbled something and she said, *Well you choose your apples.*

I was her idea, the fix for a wife with lesbian dreams. She never told me the details, but I could feel them pushing out at night, in the way that there's a ghost town inside every city. It made her ferocious but not personal. She really thought I'd be grateful later. *Adolescence is a form of brain death,* she told me. *Thanks,* I said, and she laughed. Now she's silent because she's in the past, like someone dead.

Once she wanted me to tell her my sexual fantasies. *Confession is good information*, she said, stroking my clit with her finger. I shuddered, then recoiled. What could I say? My mouth was unconscious. I should have whispered, *It feels like your nostalgia.*

Anita was supposed to make me a dyke; that's what I was waiting for. It sounds so stupid, she put out in almost every manner I could want. But I felt I was sticking around because I didn't get it yet—was this lesbianism? I had wanted a different surprise; I kept waiting for her to give me one. I wish I could say I got fed up and left. But Anita actually told me it was time, once Mark got back. I don't remember exactly what she said, but it was something along the lines of *Don't you have better things to do, now that you're all grown up?*

Anita hated writing journalism. She really thought of herself as a poet. Once, after reading her own article in the newspaper, she said, *You can't pummel vivid into a normal sentence. It's hopeless as marriage.* So, I wrote her a note before I left. "Thanks for everything," it said, and then I tacked on a quote she'd found in some magazine. It was Gary Gilmore, interviewed by Norman Mailer. "You want to learn how to be an artist? Then learn how to eat pussy. That's the only art you'll ever need to learn."

It's scenic around here. People come to bathe in the desert springs. Red rock cliffs splinter like icebergs. Outside the store, a forest of pinyon pines grows as high as my knees, and the dust is a fine red sand. Sam's customers are mostly tourists, they sit at the tables outside with their bags of carrot chips and herbal iced tea. The breeze smells like sage. I rinse the sponge and wipe the counter, then take a bite of organic cream cheese coconut cookie. It's tender as clouds.

I'm still working my way through Max's porn. I wonder if he knows. Nasty Max—he makes cracks about my hitch-hiking. *Then drive me to work,* I say. I call him Trash Can behind his back, because of the junk he eats. Max says if I don't watch my ass, the local psycho killer will pick me up. *Who might that be,* I ask, and he snickers.

Sex life, sex death—I don't have an opinion. I've got a waist and a knife instead. Anita said the difference between a violent act and a sexual one was that if you chopped all the fantasy out of the violence there'd be something left over: *damage*. But sex without fantasy—is nothing. When I read Max's porn, I like to think of that particular nothing and what falls into it. That reminds me of my life.

FETISH

1. The Female Boyfriend

When I was twenty-two, I was fucked over by a bisexual. Alternate Wednesdays and weekends, when her husband was on business trips. I liked it. Her name was Kate. As Kate stroked my lips, she said,

> *An ideal surfaces. Interrogation is what's left after you spread your legs.*

Kate was a successful journalist, and she wanted me to be a journalist too. She said I could break into the business with either sex or politics, but sex was easier because it required less analysis. She arranged for me to interview a prostitute named Becky. Kate said,

> *Whores accumulate privacy. What you do with it is your business.*

Becky was a dyke. While I interviewed her, she was washing her pickup truck. I didn't know what I wanted. Was there such a thing as a female boyfriend? So I asked Becky, "In the lesbian world, what is the difference between butch and femme?" Becky said,

> *Femme means making pink the color of your interior, and then drinking a lot of fluid.*

When Kate was out of town, I snuck out to a gay bar. It was all men until midnight, when a female boyfriend walked in, wearing a satin tux the color of blood. She approached me, and all my hairs grew wet while purses opened their tiny mouths next to my skin. She said, Touch me there. I said,

Which is the fold, the dot, the persuasion?

She answered, Accent the positive. So I did. But there must be something inside.

2.

An ideal sniffs my rust.   An idea surfs crust.

My mistress cuts & tucks one silicone 38D into my chest and then another, while I'm bound to our massive brass bed. Her kinky breath is soft as suede.

When I cry she tells me,
    The best titties are raised on the farm.

When I scream she says,
    Pain shreds & relaxes. You'll stumble over the real thing.
    Think of scrub brushes and the perfect ending.

When I sob in agony she comforts me,
    Later we'll take a tour of the castle.

My mistress is cruel. She's bright as breath.
    She whispers to me as she cuts,
    I'm a fan of the flesh—tits, stuffing, sweetmeats.
    I suck the juice from the roast, I'm a pig with a straw.

3. Becky

Kate asks me about my interview with the whore Becky. I told her about the female boyfriend in the beautiful red tuxedo. Kate said,

I'm not prejudiced but I just like men better.

I relaxed. Relaxation is a cruel mistress. How many kinds of lace do I have in my pocket? One, two kinds. The princess in the castle showed me her precious garment: black panties knit from pubic hair. He plunged his face into my hairs, the princess reported. Great, said my mistress, We'll make a sex video from crushed lips & your razor.

When I'm scared, I remember what the female boyfriend told me. She said that sadomasochism makes theater from the alienated boy—I mean body. I know that. I mean, We've always lived in the castle, but true love is more subjective.

I think about the "lower stories" when I glimpse their fluids. Vulva is bright noxious atmosphere, gleaming below. Don't you wish you had a more stretchy wish, and a little privacy for your skin? It's easier than thinking, & a few stripes cover the living room. One day, you'll believe your couch is your leg. Think about which is the female. Remember, it's that or nothing—I mean a whipping.

Don't eat anything in this room. There are too many visuals.

EXPERIMENTALISM

1. Methods

Writing I find exciting often gets called experimental. In America, this is another word for marginal. It's patronizing. Other countries distribute legitimacy in literary culture differently. For example, while living in the U.K., Kathy Acker wrote for the *Times Literary Supplement*. Can you imagine Acker writing for the *New York Times Book Review*!? Just the experience of reviewing her work in the *NYT Book Review* caused several reviewers to spontaneously combust. On the other side of the Atlantic, debates on literary aesthetics are part of public—not just academic—life. Not so here, which means the conventions of representation that underlie mainstream fiction in this country can't be effectually critiqued. (I don't consider academic debates to be part of public life.)

So what conventions of representation am I talking about? Consider identity. Mainstream fiction tends to assume separate and coherent individuals, each with a single body and character which is built, rather than destroyed, by conflict.

I believe it is possible to have one identity in your thumb and another in your neck. I think identities can travel between persons who have an unusual mutual sympathy. Let's not even mention multiple personality.

But what I want to talk about today is the manipulation and construction of social distance. Mainstream fiction assumes a position not too close, not too far away. A situation is implied, an entire social horizon, which is speckled with white individuals who maintain distance from one another and from social "problems." Containment. Segregation. A narrative structure which covertly mirrors the growth of white suburbs since WWII, where there is no discomfort around racism because only white people are present. Breaking this long chain of social convention at any link can easily result in personal and literary deformity, which is another term for experimentation.

My sister said I shouldn't have sex until my nipples turned
brown, which I figured she thought would never happen.
She was older, and kept her drugs and screwing

in the basement the same way she kept her jewelry there. Her
lovers were thin white men whose trouble was drug-related.
When Paul left Cook County Jail he carried an odor of rape

he had large nerve spots in his eyes. Fear moving like a breeze
in a prison yard, I could feel that in my stomach when he was
around; otherwise I didn't care. I thought about Monica.

Her sharp teeth and brown cheeks. The way her greed
slid across my hips could be scary but her palms were
narrow as slots, that made it okay to have sex with her.

Monica was Black in a segregated city; so the closer we got

the more transparent I became, my longing vicious

as wavering lights of association. Relation—the spot where

we're the same, or at least rolling downhill on a boulevard

lined with palm trees and novelty shops.

So when Sam said, *Any real man would rape a 14-year-old*

if he saw her naked,

it shut me up.

(My X Story)

The well-modulated distance of mainstream fiction not only distances social conflict, it also doesn't represent lesbian relationships very well. Mainstream literary forms reflect conventions of identity that are dominated by the masculine and the heterosexual. I am not arguing for femininity in literature here. I don't find those essentialist positions very interesting. But I think relations between women have the potential to strain conventions of representation. HOW exactly? Consider the characteristics associated with women: weak boundaries between self and other, heightened capacity for intimacy, identification of self with other, and a more fluid sense of self. In mainstream contexts, these capacities are exploited until you reach, at the limit, erotic positions which have been emptied of subjectivity, e.g. BIMBO/CUNT. I think it's quite difficult, perhaps impossible, to represent a dyke as empty in that way. The corollary in the lesbian world to the empty sexual object is an erotic position I think of as invaded subjectivity.

I was her idea, the fix for a wife with lesbian dreams. She never told me the details, but I could feel them pushing out at night, in the way that there's a ghost town inside every city. It made her

> ferocious but not personal. She really thought I'd be grateful later. *Adolescence is a form of brain death,* she told me. *Thanks,* I said, and she laughed. Now she's silent because she's in the past, like someone dead.
>
> (Sex Life)

I take it as a given that the well-modulated distance of mainstream fiction is a system that contains and represses social conflict, and that one purpose of experimental work is to break open this system. But experimental work can require a context of aesthetic ideas which many people who might otherwise be interested in it don't have. In this context, intimacy, autobiography, and direct address don't function just as content but are strategies for pursuing a reluctant audience. So are genre narrative forms, such as sex writing or horror.

There are many roads into the succulent interior. How can the mechanisms of genre fiction get us (the cabal of experimental writers) there?

Consider porn narratives. Usually people do not appreciate being taken apart. They rely upon having an ego, enjoy feeling integrated and in control, and experimental work that questions this can arouse distaste. What is so interesting about pornography is that losing it is the point. People want to be taken apart so that ego control (resistance to pleasure) is subverted. Where there was distaste, there is now desire mixed with dread. *Pleasures of the rupture, rack and screw.* The audience becomes an unwitting collaborator in its own disintegration, in the interest of pleasure, or just feeling, period.

Genre fiction is not about representing experience but producing and organizing feeling--sexual excitement, horror, mystery, fear. The aim is to invade the reader's subjectivity. To control, and then to release. The desire of the reader to be aroused or to otherwise escape is the keyhole through which all the mechanisms of the narrative operate (note, this turns the writer into a kind of spy!).

Because genre writing deals in something as low as feeling, these forms are relatively easy to use in other contexts and for other purposes. They are already degraded, so their resistance is weak. Experimental writers using genre forms are like drag artists. *Let us acknowledge the camp aspect to our more extreme performances.*

> My mistress cuts & tucks one silicone 38D into my
> chest and then another, while I'm bound to our
> massive brass bed. Her kinky breath is soft as suede.
>
> When I cry she tells me,
> *The best titties are raised on the farm.*
>
> When I scream she says,
> *Pain shreds & relaxes. You'll stumble over the*
> *real thing.*
> *Think of scrub brushes and the perfect ending.*
>
> When I sob in agony she comforts me,
> *Later we'll take a tour of the castle.*
>
> My mistress is cruel. She's bright as breath.
> She whispers to me as she cuts,

I'm a fan of the flesh—tits, stuffing, sweetmeats.
I suck the juice from the roast, I'm a pig with a straw.

(Fetish)

How to pass suffering, eroticism. . .from one person to another? Where does coherence fly apart? The answer to these questions does not lie in one or another particular strategy, but in the sensual devotion of the writer, taken to formal extremes. We explore our narrative tools, discovering *exactly* how they manipulate or release the contorted social body—because it's the one we live in, the one which feeds off us, the one which has swallowed the visible horizon.

2. Monsters

One of the forms of narrative I write is software. It's lucrative. About four years ago, I used stock options to buy a house right around the corner plus one block from one of the worst housing projects in San Francisco. A couple thousand people live there. It gives my neighborhood the highest child hunger rate in the city. Our first night in the house someone got murdered, just before midnight. It was a block away but the shot sounded like it was in our back yard. One shot, a pause, then another. Purposeful. Somehow I knew it was intended to kill, and not just a couple of kids shooting at the moon. Plus the neighbor told us he'd had his car stolen three times.

Impenetrable poverty plus dumb fuck rules, class and race segregation: I'd moved into the only San Francisco neighborhood that duplicated on a smaller scale what I grew up with. It annoyed me.

Locality, forever. *Skewed*. Something huge gets mutilated as it slides through a stuffy tube. We're on the beach very far to the west, watching what pops out. It contains all of American culture. I came here so tightly wound. Born on 43rd Street, South Side Chicago & haven't been back since I left the hospital.

From my dining room window, at the rear of the house, the project looks strangely vacant. There just never seem to be many people around. The buildings proceed down the hill towards the old industrial port like giant shabby steps, but there is never anyone on the racks of balconies. I've rarely driven through it. Structurally, it's sort of a dead-end place, the way it's laid out, like a suburban subdivision: streets point into it, then twist up like spaghetti. The few drive-through streets are dotted with dealers scoping out the passing cars. I'm just talking about the roads.

When I first moved in, I often found myself dreamily staring out the dining room window. I wanted to check out one of those balconies. The view would be amazing, they practically hang over the bay. Developers have been salivating over that piece of land for years. Nowadays they are nibbling at the edges of the project, building expensive live-work lofts for software designers on adjoining vacant industrial land. It's weird. Different economic classes get spliced together via crimes. The mode of interaction being criminal. So, one day, I mentioned to a friend of mine that I didn't get it, how did dealers get kids to work for them, playing courier, or delivery boy. What would a dealer have on a kid? Why get involved with some jacked-up, scary asshole? I felt like an idiot as soon as the words left my mouth. Patiently, step by step, my friend explained how it was done, until I could have done it myself, as obviously he had. All I had to do was ask. Knowledge. The getting & taking and the tearing up. Did I want to go there?

Of course I did. One day I walked in, took a place on the balcony next to all of my friends & drank their salty water. I listened to the radio. I watched as a crack lady ran down the street behind a white dog. Then the dog was scratching at the door. When I woke up, that sound was the shade, bumping against the window frame. And I was thinking, as I am always doing and my thinking told me this: *This is what I want. It's inside my system of attractions. I'm penetrated by the present and it's always the same: chronic anger. Awful but refreshing.*

From up here, it is all visible. From down below, also. Radiant contradiction. Eyeballs: the severely vivid mechanism. Finally what is seen is not a target but just circumference, expanding. Highlights scatter across the field.

I walked into the projects a couple of weeks ago. It's right around the corner, why not just walk? It was a friend's birthday. She told me where she lived, but it wasn't easy to find. The apartments didn't have numbers on them, you had to just know. I asked a bunch of people. Kids were running everywhere. How come I hadn't seen them from my back window? I look whiter than usual, I thought, looking at my hand. Up here and not even shopping, that made me odd. People looked at me skeptically. I felt skeptical about myself, but slick, as in greased. I wanted to fall off my little ledge.

Bored with what had gotten dished up as myself. The backwash of swallowing it. That nausea.

The balcony was great. I hung with my friends and listened to the radio. They played that song I like, the one about money. Later, we went out to eat birthday steaks.

California is shallow. That's true. Though it thrills me that I can walk across the city without getting beat up for crossing some invisible dividing line of racial turf. Of course, I could get beat up for something else. *I'm so easy to please.* It's the instability at the heart, which is to say the heartlessness of just washing away faster.

I'm supposed to write about narrativity but these problems of locality are where I get started. For me, writing grinds itself into what's familiar yet unbearable. Add mobility to that and, voila, narrative. Disjunction is the formal consequence of this ripping and tearing, and it's packed with information, almost to the point of being insensible.

The streets I walk measure me. They measure you too, through mechanisms both criminal and friendly. Including that knowledge is a kind of spectacular innocence—the moment of saturation feels dazzling, but there is probably no point. Still I love it, formally and erotically and intimately. It's all about nested structures. I entrust my twisted little pieces to the warm nest of the sick social body, and I feel our bond. It nourishes me.

To theorize my point of view, to pursue critical formalism as a ritual and as a grasp for power, let me put it this way. Narrative provides context so that the rupturing of identity is recognizable. I think we are impossible beings. We ruthlessly evade scrutiny, yet recognition is the beginning of transformative emotion. It's a feeding process. You don't know if you're creating a monster.

As a narrative writer I improvise recognition. It's like a location from which mutant beings emerge. This feels true, in life they never stop emerging. Look—they even swarm through this text. I allow it because I'm terrified and seduced. To encounter them via narrative is to formalize a moment of surrender.

BABY (OR WHOSE BODY IS MISSING?)

BABY can't stop himself from being born. Cut from a knotted uterus then jerked free, he's so sick he can't breathe. BABY's grey as a rat & limp as a noodle. Rivulets of blood run through his toes & puddle on the blue sheet covering his entire mom. The doctor and nurses are wearing blue sheets, with white latex fingers poking out. Metal implements hang from the white walls. The doctor lifts BABY up before the witnesses and says,

> *People are looking for solutions however reluctantly, because drugs are unfashionable.*

BABY looks down on his large flowing blue mom. He cannot see anything of her body but a red slit and blood sliding across the blue folds.

Someone takes hold of BABY, lays him on a metal shelf, and puts a plastic bubble over his mouth. BABY begins to breathe oxygen smoke as he looks up at the blue masks of his doctors. BABY's eyes are hazy. But it's not a result of wanting money or drugs. Before BABY learns how to think, he has a thin grammar.

Meanwhile, conversation passes like plates among the white asses of the doctors. No one is listening to BABY, who says,

> *I feel I'm just the logical result of certain families breeding with each other. History has something to do with it, but not as much as you think.*

BABY will never remember his first breath.

He won't remember his body arriving, either.

All objects ARE frustration (is a theory about art). The body is plumbing and consciousness, so you feel your toast before you taste it. Pain folds a person's cranium.

I'll explain circumstances to all you minors.

i) The picture is big,
ii) The picture rains on us,
iii) I'm coated with picture.

Understanding requires free time, and no one's time is free.

(Restless stratification.)

Here is a picture of BABY:

His skin is soft as butter.
His eyelashes peek like little lambs then curl up.
He is quiet as a pocket.

Mom is dripping, little puddles of white form in her nipples and the whole house smells of milk. Mom's understanding is perfect. She knows that the nipple is the only object that ISN'T frustration, so she puts her nipple in BABY's mouth.

Mom says, I'm so glad the BODY arrived (kiss kiss).

BABY is sucking. Then BABY lifts his head & says, "I'm the only one whose body isn't missing."

I was a bar dyke before all this gender-theory crap came along. I kissed and fucked like every other girl in my invisible world, and I stuck dollar bills in the G-strings of all the strippers in town. That world is still invisible, because I left my body there.

> *If you believe that, find the burial at the end of this sentence. Do you know whose body is waiting for you there?*

No one can see anything before I get dressed. After I get dressed, I am a sex toy. This happened even before I became a lesbian, or a mother, or a girl. It is a very personal, very feminine thing: minimalism.

It's simple. There's less private and MORE PUBLIC in everyone's life. How can you see yourself, when you can't even see your information? Is it local, or does it start in Los Angeles and expand outward like an orgy?

If you think you look like yourself, look for the hole you make in air. That's what I wanted, when I began these sentences. Now I'm afraid of poisoning.

I see BABY's grammar brain spreading from his big blue eyes across his face. I'm waiting for tips of intelligence. Recognition begins somewhere, maybe in language, before any mass starvation. Maybe recognition is moistened by visuals.

When I talk to BABY, I'm talking to the future, with the perfect understanding only a MOTHER can have. I know, for example, that to restore theatricality to language (that modernism tried to destroy), BABY'll write a script for a horror movie starring the little wonder slut of Hollywood, Drew Barrymore.

Which objects are the most scary? Think very delicately, then put those words into Drew Barrymore's mouth. BABY's tiny pink lips are the beginning of language, but when he reaches for her nipple, Drew Barrymore screams. There's a gulf between milk squirting into BABY's mouth and a moving picture. Why are objects frustrating? Here's something to try in the privacy of your own home: compare the neck and lips of a Hollywood slut to the neck and lips of a mule.

BABY doesn't know the difference between mother and monster. He doesn't know that purses hide money. He can't tell why.

PERILS

Before my expulsion, for immature and morally reprehensible misbehaviors as well as academic failure, Dr. Wittig had never bothered to look at me. I wasn't surprised. Very few people looked at me. It was remarkable how many people seemed to find ordinary social intercourse with me actually unpleasant. I rarely failed to observe that when I spoke to a fellow student at the Institute, his eyes would dart at my mouth and then jump hurriedly away. Apparently my mouth had become some sort of stain. So I quit speaking and crept like a wraith from one classroom to the next.

My only sustaining interest during these last months at the Institute was to observe Dr. Wittig. My opportunities for these observations were limited to her lectures and her daily marches through the halls, and I was careful to station myself in the hallways at those times when she usually appeared. She was a small woman, and in order to see her I had to stand on my toes and peer into the coterie of lanky senior male physicists who always surrounded her. They advanced in a phalanx which exuded a trail of deep and furious conversation. My back against the wall, my eyes riveted, the impression was inescapable—I was staring into the bloody heart of Science.

This I did with a strange quiver of satisfaction. I felt she owed me something. I was one of a handful of female students, and she was the only female physicist. I never spoke to her, for in one respect I was like every other student: I found her terrifying. This was not due to her physical appearance, which was unexceptional. She was round as a mushroom and an untidy fringe of brown hair covered her bowl-shaped head. Her clothes were sensible. True, her cheeks had sagged down over her lips, creating a permanent scowl. But the kicker was her voice, which crisply sliced into any student's idea and extracted just what was stupid. Then she would turn and look the questioner in the eye, as though she had just given him back his kidney on the tip of a knife. After this ritual humiliation, a soft collective groan rose from the mass of students which could be heard even in the hallway. I left her classes sweaty and drained, but relaxed.

Before I finally got the boot, before the session with the Dean in which the failures of my character and intelligence were coolly identified as though they were constellations in the night sky, I had become obsessed with the idea of having an audience with Dr. Wittig. It made studying impossible; my thoughts kept wandering from my books to that office door. I pictured myself opening that door and walking through a labyrinth of stuffed bookcases and journals piled high to a surprisingly orderly desk. I'd nod courteously and she would look up with a keen expression of interest. Laying my large Optics textbook before her, I'd show her the footnotes I'd found, and we would go over them together, side by side. At this point in the fantasy I usually managed to stop myself. I knew the scenario was inappropriate and even embarrassing, because she taught Quantum Mechanics, not Optics, but the visions recurred, especially in dreams.

The footnotes in question stimulated me highly. I turned to them over and over again, and each time they rewarded me with a peculiar sense of refreshment. They appeared in a textbook which bore this dedication:

To The Student, with the hope that this work will stimulate an interest in Optics and provide an acceptable guide to its understanding.

There were three footnotes in my textbook. The first one began,

The student who is interested in further experimentation will find that she can refine the value of Planck's constant through the following procedure. . .

After I found the first footnote, I paged through the whole textbook and found the other two. Each one identified the student as SHE: "She who is interested in further experimentation. . ." I was stunned, and sunk in one of those moments of hyper-real recognition. This girl, adrift in the footnotes, her wandering thoughts captivated by formal descriptions of the behavior of sparkling light, was known to me. *Reader, I was that ghost.* This was the hypothesis I wanted to present to Dr. Wittig, and which, in dreams, I did present to her.

Expulsion quieted these fantasies. Of course, I'd seen it coming, and I'd collected a few part-time jobs to prepare myself for my separation from the Institute. Once separated, I found I had to force myself to leave my room. My only desire was to sit all day in the glassed-in porch I rented as a bedroom and watch the sun pass over the squash plants. Our back yard, like most yards in town, was a field of squash plants. An Institute experiment gone awry had contaminated the town's soil, with the result that only two varieties of plants thrived—squash, and a curiously misshapen pine whose trunks tended to twist like corkscrews. The trees gave the town a name, used only by students: Armpit. In any case, as it was early June, the squash plants beneath my window were eagerly growing, their firm yellow tendrils spreading over more of the yard every day. By August, they would have formed a dark green wave several feet deep, and the town would have grown enough squash to last for centuries. This prospect was the final amazement which the Institute offered me. Only with difficulty did I manage to tear myself away from it in order to perform the duties of my new jobs.

I had to give up on ever speaking to Dr. Wittig, or attracting any notice from her whatsoever. But the end of my dream left me melancholy and listless. It was weeks before I could even muster the spirit to return to the Institute to pick up the last of my things. I finally went one evening, just before the buildings were locked. It was after all the students had left for the summer. As I was rushing from the building, my notebooks and papers in a shopping bag, our paths crossed.

"Camille," Dr. Wittig said, "What are you going to do now?"

I blushed hastily when I felt her hand on my arm. "I'm not sure."

"Have you got a job yet?"

"No," I lied.

"I need someone to help me file and sort my experimental data. I'll pay you. Thursday afternoons, from one to four." She spoke briskly as she wrote her address on a slip of paper and dropped it into my bag.

The effect of this meeting on my spiritual state was nearly indescribable. Suffice to say, desolation was shattered and my fantasy life began to bubble and churn anew. This time, I decided, I would conduct myself differently. I would pledge myself to Dr. Wittig's task in the spirit of obedience, and attempt to follow the rules, whatever they might be.

When I stepped through her door the following Thursday, I entered one of those states of clarity that belong to another life and spirit, one which has been dedicated to a higher pursuit. My peculiar overheated personality simply drained away before her stern and superior gaze. She looked me over, and then her smile, with teeth, was gleeful. I followed her into the cool darkness of her house. The drapes were closed and, in the dim light, the furnishings seemed swollen and furry. Everything was upholstered in something soft. A Bach violin concerto, played with passionate rigor, seemed to emanate from the very walls. Dr. Wittig tossed her head lightly from side to side. "David and Igor Oistrakh," she said worshipfully. "The Russian violinists are the best."

She ushered me into the study and bid me to sit in a small clearing among the papers on the floor. It was a sight I thought I'd left behind forever—wave functions beyond number, in heaps, all mockingly inscrutable. Suddenly I was filled with dread and exhaustion too deep to allow for even a polite expression of interest, and I sank to my knees in the appointed spot.

She looked at the mess of papers with amusement. "Somewhere in this pile, Camille, you will find an exhaustive description of all possible interactions of strange quarks with tops and bottoms. I find it rather interesting, when I'm not utterly bored by it. But what about you? Are you stupid, or do you just not like physics?"

"I don't know," I said.

She smiled dryly. "I doubt you're stupid, but I'll tell you what to do." She then described her various catalog systems and gave a list of their inconsistencies. It was a long list, and as she recited it, she seemed to be observing me. In the pause that followed, I realized she'd given me a difficult task, not a filing job. But I tumbled into the problem humbly, each breath beginning a new train of thought.

In part, this was because the problem was difficult, but Dr. Wittig also distracted me, as she persisted in strolling restlessly about the room. She poked journals with a finger, picked up objects and set them down carelessly. Finally, she settled at her desk.

"My father was a butcher," she said, at length. "That's not what you expected, is it?"

I turned to reply but she was really talking to herself. "Butcher and Bitter, I called them. My parental influences. Physics got me out, and for that, for a long while, I loved it passionately. It took me to Vienna, where I studied before the war. One step ahead of the Nazis, I followed my professor from Vienna to Princeton. Through it all, physics had for me a steely glamour. It was a winner. War couldn't change that. Nothing could." She looked at me. "What is it like," she asked, "to not be any good at it?"

"Oh," I said miserably. How could I explain? When I received official notice from the dean, failure poured like honey from my throat. As the letter fluttered to the floor, my head fell onto the table and I closed my eyes to let the prospect of expulsion take on the shivering gleam of the newly real. I expected to feel broken, and I did. What I didn't anticipate was the sickening warmth gliding through every fiber of my body. Failure can be a kind of massage. Everything stops, and then all that forward momentum is replaced by a series of tiny choices. . . I decided to try honesty with Dr. Wittig. "I think I'm a lesbian," I said. "So I'm going to work on that. I need more experiences."

She didn't seem to have heard me. "Girls," she said, "never last at physics. Somehow girls are ruined for physics, even the ones who have a Talent."

"What about you?"

She sighed. "Yes. What about me? I can only say, some vices are so private their very existence is questionable. . ."

She then opened a desk drawer and took out a rectangular silver case, from which she extracted a cigar. "Do you mind?" she said. Surprised, I rocked back on my heels and then found myself locked into her steady gaze. Her irises had green rims with a yellow core, and they watered. I was reminded me of ponds, the shallow kind, a little scummy.

"Go ahead," I said. I resumed my work.

When she spoke again, it was in a deeper voice, somewhat husky, as if she were finally going to set something straight. "Let me tell you a story about a girl who actually did become a physicist. It was a mistake, of course. She should never have come here. Everyone was terribly distracted, and I not the least. She was my student. It was the late forties, and the Institute was filled with young Marxists studying mathematics. All the political arguing gave the Institute an atmosphere of openness which was, in the end, illusory. Socially, it is physics which is the dismal science. But Marjorie seemed to think she could belong here. She floated in like a pink lollipop."

Dr. Wittig scowled at me. "You are odd, but she was a terrific spectacle, Marjorie. That lovely name belonged to a girl who walked into the Institute at the tender age of fifteen, wearing capris and a sweater set. She attended the open house with her father and shook everyone's hand, peering up into each stern face with a polite smile. Her hair was astonishing. It was so shiny it looked wet, but it was thick and soft, a sort of auburn cloud. It exactly suited her personality, which was soft and drifting. . .

She was quite brilliant, that was the most surprising thing. Marjorie was quick as an eel at any depth. She didn't seem to understand how peculiar this was for us. She had the expectation that we would simply be pleased, and she wasn't sensitive to the ambivalence she aroused. It was with considerable relief that we granted her a Ph.D. in physics when she was nineteen. Everyone thought she'd go away. Instead she got married, and that seemed, well, equivalent. She married one of our most promising mathematicians and quickly had a son, named Jonathan. She became a housewife. It all seemed normal. Those of us who didn't do that, the women who were serious scientists, were really just freaks. I don't mind saying so. It's had its rewards.

"Anyhow, poor Marjorie was left alone with her young son. Her husband committed suicide, a few years after he got a job teaching at the Institute.

Dr. Wittig paused for a long time. "At that point, we should have given Marjorie a job. I'm sure she needed it. I wasn't the one who argued against it. But then she got married again, to another mathematician, and we were saved from having to make such a decision.

"She accompanied her new husband to Pakistan, which was where he was from. That was when I started to get her letters. I still have them. They're in a box in this very desk. I intended to give them to Jonathan, once he was grown, but now he refuses to speak to me. There's a lot in those letters about his first steps and words and the little games he used to play with his mother.

"Ahh, this story," she said sadly. "Once back in Pakistan, her husband came under the influence of his family, and when Marjorie seemed to have trouble getting pregnant, he took a second wife. She was simply expected to live with the new arrangement. I didn't hear from her for months, and then a terrible letter arrived, filled with despair. She told me the whole situation. The new wife wouldn't look at her, and far worse, neither would her husband. 'I've disappeared,' she wrote. 'I'm a stranger in my own life. It's all I can do to speak even to Jonathan. He has no one else here, believe me. . .'

"I didn't answer her letter for a good while. I'm unfamiliar with this sort of problem, and I wasn't sure what to do or say. Finally, I sent her money. No strings attached. I simply expressed the hope that she would leave Pakistan. She wrote me back immediately. 'Your help means more than I can say. Jonathan and I are leaving for Paris in a week and this terrible episode will be over.' I will never understand what happened in Paris. I visited them two years later, over the weekend after a high energy physics conference to which I had been invited.

"Jonathan was very well-mannered. Children seem to be like that in Europe, they're so polite I find it somewhat eerie. In this respect Jonathan had become European. He wore a sailor suit and had tea with me in the kitchen. 'Dr. Wittig,' he told me, 'My interests lie mainly in painting and music.' He was about seven at that point. Their apartment, in a poor section of Paris, was sparsely furnished. Marjorie kept Jonathan's clothes in a cardboard box. I inquired delicately into her employment situation, and her replies were vague. Perhaps she was the kind of person who simply needed to be given something to do. As I said before, her character was oddly cloud-like, soft all the way through. A lovely person. I gave her more money.

"Over the next ten years, the frequency of her letters diminished. I wasn't sorry. They were troubling to me, those letters. She seemed to write whenever she'd met a new man and was bursting with enthusiasm over what the relationship promised for the future. But these relationships never lasted. Each letter described a new one, and as I said, they arrived less and less often. It became apparent that she was living off of a series of men. I'm ashamed to say that when I was invited to Paris for another conference, I did not look her up. I didn't want a closer look. Three years had passed without word from Marjorie when I received notice that she was dead. It was a barbiturate overdose, whether accidental or intentional I do not know. She was forty-one. Jonathan had just turned twenty.

"I went to Paris as soon as I could. I believe I got there about three months after Marjorie's death. I was concerned for Jonathan, of course. He had no one. When I arrived, he was hopping mad, full of energy. He looked like a wild man, with that head of red curly hair. He must have gotten that from his father. Jonathan seemed to have absorbed Marjorie's death without any effect. He'd become a Marxist, he told me. I accompanied him to various meetings and cafes, and I observed that he was treated with respect, despite his relative youth. He had such intensity. He was very articulate. Marxism lasted a few years, then he became a poet, and forswore politics. I wrote to him before I visited Paris again, and told him I would love to read his poetry. But he was in a rage when I arrived. He had just burned it all. He told me he was leaving behind every shred of his past, and I was never to attempt to contact him again."

Dr. Wittig opened a drawer in her desk and took out a shoebox. "Here are Marjorie's letters," she said wistfully, "You can read them if you like."

I looked at the box in horror. "I can't believe that story is true."

"Every word is true." She glared at me as if to say, *Do you think you're worth lying to*?

I said nothing. In fact, I bent my head humbly and received her contempt with the strange sensation of letting myself be chewed, of being nothing more than crumbs falling out of the side of her mouth. After a few moments, it became apparent that her spasm of bitterness had exhausted itself, and she rubbed her eyes wearily. "Well," she sighed, "Have you made any progress with my data?"

I confessed to having made no progress at all.

"I've been distracting you." Her tone was neutral, as though she were simply articulating a foreseeable and inevitable fact. So, I was surprised when she went on give me something like an apology. "Camille, perhaps a little extra attention would have helped you at the Institute. Perhaps I should add my failure to give you that attention to my list of regrets. But, nowadays, I'm bored by students and I never take special notice of any of them, including the boys. As I get older, the peculiar passions stirred up between teacher and student interest me less than tending to my squash plants.

"Now you've failed. . . Try not to take it to heart. Physics prides itself on the lions at the gate. But the lions don't matter. The field itself has become, for me, curiously discouraging. Fundamental physics is in danger of becoming, and perhaps has already become, merely a form of religion, albeit one motivated by mathematical aesthetics. What we study is either so small or so large, it's intrinsically beyond the reach of measurement. We can speculate, but in our rambling and often awkward theories we are no more than priests, mumbling our secret language. . ."

She ground the stub of her cigar into an ashtray. It seemed to struggle for life, releasing a few more puffs of acrid smoke. "It's not what I wanted," she said sadly, "To be a priest. . ." She collected herself and looked once again at me. "Perhaps next week you will make more progress with the data."

"I'll just have to work harder," I mumbled.

Dr. Wittig said nothing. I got to my feet and bowed. I'd never bowed to anyone before. It felt awkward, but once I'd bent over, I found it even more awkward to straighten up. She watched me gravely as I backed out of the room. When she finally nodded goodbye, I leapt through the doorframe as though a spring had been released.

Her front door closed gently after me. Cool sheets of river mist hung across the street. It felt like incredible effort just to get walking, so I sat for a moment on her stoop. I needed to stop and think. Especially I needed to think about Marjorie, her mysterious sex, being that. Juggling everything else. It choked me up. She must have had a beautiful mind. Then she went to Paris and dissolved in a glass of water.

I've had moments, occasions really, separated from all other moments, when the ground tilts. It surges up, then seems to pause as if to make conversation. Perhaps it's physiological—just another one of my brain vessels breaking and then waving frantically at all the other brain vessels, who are still quiet and neatly tucked in, sound asleep. I had a moment like that, sitting on the stoop. A ripple moved across Dr. Wittig's sidewalk, then something like long fingers or hairs curled under my breasts. A cool sigh down my neck. There was a little jerk as two nearly weightless legs settled around my waist. I sat up straight.

"What is it?" I spoke loudly.

"Don't look," murmured the icy violet. "But it's me, Marjorie."

Can lips be vacant? Made of nothing but breath. I was listening to the air running up and down Marjorie's throat as her chin rested lightly on my shoulder.

"I think we're twins." A sweet voice slipped like a breeze into my thoughts.

Ohhhhh, twin-ship. The word tugged at my eardrum, as though attached by invisible thread. It calmed me. "All right," I said, softly. Somehow, I was ready for this. I relaxed my spine and told her amiably the first thing that spun off the top of my head, "You can be my twin until I take off my hat."

"You're not wearing a hat," she pointed out.

"Yes," I said. The point was inarguable. "Come with me, then. But just until I get to my next job."

I got to my feet. I clasped my hands together at my belly so that her stick legs, rather like the legs of a skinny nine-year-old girl, protruded from the crook of each elbow. At first, I lost my balance, although she was nearly weightless. So, I stopped and started over again, more slowly, placing one foot ahead of the other, then carefully shifting my weight. Gradually, I picked up speed and we made steady progress past the bungalows that peeked up behind mounds of squash plants. She kept one hand around my throat.

"Where are we going?" she asked. Her voice had the trusting lilt of a child.

"To work," I said, sternly. "Happy Hour. I'm going to dump you at the door."

"You tend bar," she said thoughtfully. "Is it an interesting life, Camille?"

"Life is just whatever happens. And if it's not something I want, does anyone care?"

"Camille needs a bright spot," Marjorie mused. "Paint your toenails. That's what I always did." She stuck her little foot forward so that I would be sure to see the tips of her wiggling toes. They glimmered an opalescent pink.

"Nice polish," I said. I observed that her legs consisted of cold white fuzz. White stockings have a different effect, because they veil the meat that you know is there. Marjorie was entirely without meat. Suddenly I had to ask her. "What is it like, being what you are?"

"Shabby. Just another way of being sick and making trouble. Why do you think I came here? I was tired of hanging around my son in Paris. I sat in the middle of his every dream like a spider, talking to myself and wet with the effort. Poor boy. Each day, he had to sweat out adrenaline from the nightmares of the night before. It was time for me to leave him in peace. So, I came here to bother Dr. Wittig, and now I've found you. I'm not heavy, am I?"

I paused to consider this, then I had to confess I was enjoying our walk. Carrying a weight, even one that was mostly imagination, gave my steps a little stagger. It was a town of science, and so clean. So spartan. What could be better than to watch my shadow stagger through it, with a ball of peach fuzz resting on its neck?

In this manner, we followed the street as it curved down towards the center of town and the river, which ran through it. We passed the insurance office, gold lettering on a black window, a barber shop. As usual during the summer, no one was on the street. It disappointed me. I wanted everyone to see whatever it was—the face I hadn't seen myself, so I staggered and wove with a little more frenzy. It must have disturbed Marjorie, because she sounded breathless when she said, "I need a story. An ordinary story. About anything, but you have to be in it, and it has to be true."

I don't know why I picked the story I did. Why does a dog wag its tail? I reproached myself later for not choosing a story that highlighted some interesting feature of my history or personality. Perhaps I chose this one, about a girl with a deformed face, because I wanted to see the face that rested on my shoulder, small and pink and filmy. A lozenge with pretty features. That's what I'd imagined, but I hadn't dared to look.

I began: When I was fourteen, I had a job working in Bernie's ice cream shop. The manager, Louie, hired me. Louie despised Bernie. It was the murky hatred of Polack for Jew, plus Bernie was Louie's boss. I heard about it and felt it, but I never saw it directly until I came into work one day and there was the new girl that Louie had hired, her arms already deep in the vats, crusty with dried ice cream. Between her nose and lip, there was a cracked vertical snarl. It drew you to look into it, like a car crash on the street. It was lined with fresh blood that seemed to have worn its own path into her mouth. Lisa, for that was her name, had no upper lip.

Later that morning, Bernie walked in. He had to push his way through the crowd of ladies with strollers who'd collected near the entrance. When he saw what they were murmuring about, he fired Lisa on the spot.

Lisa ran sobbing into the basement. Louie, who'd set the situation up, ignored the whole business. He stood at the sink and rinsed out all of the rags. Bernie turned to me. He slapped his arm around my shoulder and squeezed with such warmth he almost lifted me off the ground. "Go make her feel better, Camille. *Be a woman to her*." My gut fluttered; I was so thrilled. No one had ever called me a woman before, and the mystery of that, being a sex. I wore it down to the basement like my princess crown.

Lisa was in the corner curled up on a big case of chocolate syrup. The lower half of her face was all shadow; it was her forehead that I saw, wide and clear, and her eyes, bright with resentment. I sat next to her on a carton of peanuts. "You're a pretty girl," I said, "except for that one part."

"No, I'm not," she said.

"You'll get another job."

"No, I won't," she said.

"Why don't your parents get that fixed. Stitch it up or something. Then you can come back and work here." Lisa pulled her knees to her chin and sat there, fiercely silent.

"Bernie had to do this," I told Lisa. "But actually, he likes you. Everyone likes you. . ."

Marjorie's laugh turned like a worm in my ear. "Everyone likes you," she echoed. "That's what Dr. Wittig used to say to me. She never understood how I could get myself into such a fix, time after time. 'You're a nice girl,' she would say, and hand me money to prove it. God, it was never enough money. I'd see how much there was, and I'd swallow a shout. But then the money stopped. When things got really bad, she didn't want to see me anymore."

"Marjorie," I said, "I'm dying for a look at you."

"Please don't," she said. "It's my voice that you should remember. That's the main thing left after death; didn't you know?"

I trudged on, frustrated. I had been hoping a peek at her face would tell me whether her looks were a mark that had drawn her life to her. Some people are target practice for their era; it's important, I thought, to understand the wider causes and effects of personal disaster. "Were you pretty?" I said.

"I don't know. I never knew what to make of myself. At least I died before I lost my looks."

"Something you had in common with Marilyn Monroe. . ."

"As a matter of fact, yes."

"Well," I said hopefully, "I'm a dyke. At least I think I am. So, none of this will matter for me."

"Surely not," Marjorie said, "It doesn't even matter to me anymore."

I settled into a firm rolling stride. As we cruised along, I found myself rifling through my filing cabinet of dilemmas. There must be one which needed supernatural assistance. "Can I ask you a question?"

She said of course, and I kept looking, and eventually I found something. Wouldn't you? It was lodged deep in the recesses, a thorn. Pulling it out, that would feel good. One drop of my brain blood could fall from the point onto the pavement and break into a million bits. Why hold onto these things?

I began to murmur the story, the one I hadn't told.

Six weeks ago, I got the call. Come to Dean Ratcliffe's office, I was told. This was it; he was going to throw me out in person, as well as via certified mail. Well, why not. At the appointed time, I walked right in and sat down on the fat leather chair that faced his desk. It was a substantial desk, mahogany with brass. Rain streaked the window. He had his back to me, and his hands were in the pockets of his slim well-cut suit. His head gently nodded to the beat—try to imagine the strains of a Mozart flute concerto as prelude to disaster. Then he turned to me. His eyes were pepper, gray and black. "Camille Weed, is that you?" he said.

I nodded casually.

"You have been causing some consternation around here. How do you feel about that?"

Without waiting for a reply, he launched into my various misdeeds. "You are an incredible girl, in all the wrong ways. Being at an institute of higher learning, especially on a scholarship, means first of all you must follow A Code of Behavior. We all do that around here, Camille Weed. It is a requirement.

"You and your pal—Mr. Don Silver, isn't it?—the one who flunked out last year, why did you two think you could just rampage through the dorms smashing bottles in the middle of the night? Making a ruckus. Creating a hazard for our tender-footed students who stumble to the bathroom in the wee hours. Two people went to the infirmary with glass splinters that night, Camille Weed, only because they were trying to answer nature's call. Why did you think you could do that?"

His brow was flat—ready aim fire—and he pushed each word out like some sort of turd. What could I say? The drugs were good. Once we'd started it was impossible to stop. The bottles burst silently into ice blooms and hung like that in space for what seemed like hours. So, of course, we ripped them one after another at the walls, looking for that same moment. It was so perfect. Why couldn't Dean Ratcliffe understand this? He was one of the physicists at the Institute who had done the original work on the atom bomb. He knew the value of a good explosion.

I said all this to Marjorie, or maybe it was just my thoughts rushing in a flood. She murmured something faintly, only breath perhaps. I became anxious. "Are you okay?"

"Don't worry about me." But her voice didn't break a whisper. "As for your question: this is what I think. Stop worrying points like a dog. You have a point Camille, but from where I sit, points don't matter."

With that, I felt a slither down my back. Dazed, I looked around. How had I made it this far? All the way to the parking lot of the mini mall... There, in the right-hand corner, was Tommy's Tried and True Tavern in black script under two neon martini glasses. They blinked erratically. And, in front of the bar, was parked a single car—Ricardo's big blue Buick, with whitewalls and a gleaming red and chrome interior. That old fag was my one regular and, usually only, customer. He was waiting for me.

I pushed open the big wooden door and walked through pools of honey slush, kicking the dust. It was late afternoon, and the light filtered through panels of amber glass that were stuck high in the walls and around the door. Tommy's was a cheesy diva kind of bar, vaguely homosexual. Happy Hour was always drenched in that pissy yellow light. Sticky pop numbers flowed from the speakers, covering everything: the cracked vinyl booths, the chairs with stubby legs pulled up to empty tables. On that day, I looked around. I listened: my life was talking to me. I found myself thinking about Don Silver, my partner in crime and Patti Smith concerts. Big shaggy Don who played his saxophone like a greedy dog chews a new bone. He was my best friend, and I was his only friend, but he would have to go. That was something Dean Ratcliffe and I could agree on. If I was going to switch from being a wannabe physicist to some sort of full-fledged dyke, I needed to learn things—stuff I could pick up if I was just around the right people: how to carry on a conversation, remembering to wash regularly. I needed a girl gang.

Ricardo was sitting at the bar in his usual place, languidly sipping gin, straight up. He was the kind who drank extremely slowly, all day. "Happy Happy Hour," he said solemnly, after I slipped into my post. "How's my girl?"

"I've had a long day, Ricardo. This is my second shift." I crouched and began searching the miniature refrigerator on the floor for an empty among the cans of pressurized whipped cream. At the beginning of my shift, it was my ritual to do a nitrous oxide hit and then take a moment to contemplate my Future.

"Ahh, Camille," sighed Ricardo, "I don't even work anymore. I paid that debt to society by selling insurance for twenty-eight years. Now with every passing day I roll deeper into that retirement rut." He leaned over the counter and peered down. "What were you working hard at today, Camille?"

"Filing," I barked. "For Dr. Wittig. She's a physicist." The gas made my voice shrill.

"Dr. Wittig! I haven't heard that name in years. She was one of the first people I met at the Institute. I picked her out right away—those flushed cheeks and that rapier instinct for the heart of the matter." He added slyly, "Unnaturally vigorous in a woman."

"I thought you sold insurance."

"I was a biochemist, girl."

I stood up and steadied myself against the bar. Ricardo had the amphibian eyes of a steady drunk, and often reminded me of a frog, but listening to him was part of the job.

"She and I got hired here at the same time. Biochemistry was a new field at the time and considered absolutely a bastard. Mix bio and chemistry and send up a rogue sprout. But hell. I was damn pleased with myself. No one in my family had ever gotten a college education."

Back and forth, like a drunk fairy godmother, he waved his cigarette, then stared at its burning tip, speaking with effort.

"I lost that job. I got a sentence, one to twenty, Iowa State Penitentiary. The Dean didn't appreciate that kind of sabbatical. I served 18 months." A dry smile slid up one side of his face. "I was convicted of being a *sexual psychopath*."

This was an idea even my shaky sense of reality could resist. "No way Ricardo," I squeaked. Amazement filled me with a blazing light. . . Yet it was only history to me, his moving face. I squatted and fished through all the whipped cream cans, looking for another empty. Fuck, out of luck. I'd have to empty out a full can to get another buzz. There'd be soft heaps of cream in the sink which I'd have to wash down with the sprayer. How would I explain that to Ricardo? *Not to go there.* I stood up wearily.

"Yes," he said. "A tearoom bust. Who could know they'd hollowed out the wall in the men's room in the student union, and there was a cop holding a camera inside the paper towel dispenser? They had reels and reels of fag dick. Forty of us were arrested. Do ya want to know something else? Candid camera showed that every single one of us tearoom queens washed his hands. You think this is a joke, but it is absolute truth." He sighed. "My career was over. Kaput, just like that. No one even remembers that I had one."

"And Dr. Wittig, the iron maiden, went on to become famous. Even though her butch butt was queer as a three-dollar bill, I always thought, and I wasn't the only one. It was the fifties. Almost every gay man at the institute got sacked. How do you gay gals do it?"

"How do we do what, Ricardo?"

"Oh, I don't know. Live such sexless lives, I guess."

"I don't know what you're talking about, Ricardo."

"Do you have sex?"

"No."

"Ta da. You prove my point. Have you ever had sex?"

"Yeah. Some of it I remember. The early years. I don't know what happened. One gruesome adventure after another I guess."

He sighed. "God you're only twenty-one."

"Almost twenty-one," I corrected him.

"Well, I don't have sex either," he said, disconsolately. "The plumbing seems to work, but nobody's interested."

"You'd do fine Ricardo if you didn't drink so much." It was Sly. She'd come up on us without a sound. It was her way. Tall and thin and hunched about the shoulders, Sly cut the air like a rubber knife. She was followed by a girl in a black silk blouse. The girl didn't bother to introduce herself, or even look at us. Her grey blue eyes reminded me of lake water.

Sly leaned towards me and lay a hand across my wrist. "Time was, there wasn't a fag in town Ricardo didn't screw."

I took my wrist back. "How long ago was that?"

"So young and so cruel," hummed Ricardo. "Sly, this young thing needs a date. She doesn't have sex anymore."

The girl in the black blouse whispered to Sly that she was tired and needed to sit at a table. We watched her choose one by the window, in the corner. Then Sly murmured to me, "I know someone, Camille."

"I'm sure you do." I poured her the usual, a gin and tonic. "But why for me?"

There was a faint whistle through the gap in her front teeth. "I've got Cippoline."

"Camille, did you hear that our Sly has finally been tamed, by a woman named after a mild Italian onion. . ."

"It's her real name. I'm crazy about it," Sly declared.

This, from a mistress of secrets. Sly was a shit and a slut. Unchangeable. Cippoline must really have aspects of the incredible, perhaps the whirling arms of a Hindu goddess, or the equivalent in tits.

"She must be a wildcat," said Ricardo.

"A Brooklyn girl," said Sly, as though that sealed it. "With the slim ankles of Sophia Loren. She grew up nearly on the streets and when she hit thirteen. . .it was. . .it was. . . the return of Rita Hayworth."

"I can't believe anyone could make an honest woman of you Sly."

"It's nothing like that. Cippoline tells me what she wants. Then I manage to do it. It simplifies things. It's emptier. I guess I like that. . ."

Sly spoke quietly and brought her hands up to the edge of the bar. She folded them and looked down, a penitent, and we looked down too, at her long fingers, fastened in the position of prayer. The hands of a lockpicker.

Sly had peculiar fame. In thirteen years, she'd seduced thirteen deeply heterosexual co-workers, most of them married. She told each woman they were her first and only "lesbian relationship," and each proudly guarded the secret of their relationship, while working and lunching with all of the others. Sly was so indistinct this prowess was almost inconceivable. You had to peer through some sort of cloud to even see her: brown eyes, her plainness, her pallid skin.

Perhaps that was her secret. Any conversation with Sly felt private. Her husky lilt snagged a listener but disappeared after you leaned towards it. Not into silence. It sank into my ear like some sort of burr.

"But you have someone for Camille."

"Oh yes." The hands fluttered up. Sly indicated the girl in the black blouse with a tilt of her head. "Married. She's nervous. You'll need to tie her up."

Ricardo's grin flashed. "Are you up for that Camille?"

"Nicole is her name," she went on, her voice very quiet. "Look at her—the bone structure of an Arab and skin the color of grayish milk. In fact, she's part Egyptian and part French. When she was thirteen, she had an affair with one of her Egyptian aunts, so she won't be completely inexperienced. . ."

"Married?" I asked weakly.

"See how supple she is, but somehow fragile. She has that lovely reddish hair. . ."

My mind spun down some sort of tunnel to a little heap at the end. To that girl, Nicole. It wasn't impossible. She could be waiting for me. It was so clear somehow. She'd turn towards the sound of steps and look up, and I'd know that what streamed across her grey blue eyes looked like clouds, but it was her mind, coming together. Silence anyhow. Then that familiar moment of sitting down next to someone and knowing it was just not going to work. Making a move anyway because that comes next, sliding past the eyeball of sex is what comes next. Cream to the blade to the bone as juices explode from the roots of my teeth.

"It sounds like a hassle," I said at last.

"You're young," Ricardo said firmly. "You're supposed to get hassled. It's the price you pay for beautiful skin."

"She'd be so grateful." Sly's tone was melancholy and her mood was carefully, clinically, tender. She lifted up one slender forearm and, as she framed the problems in the marriage, the empty space that a worm like she or I could occupy, she ticked her fingers down, one by one. I'd never noticed before that a fist has a bite-sized piece of darkness inside. Behind Sly, in the corner, I could see the dark silhouette of Nicole washed by yellow light. She was smoking.

"Her husband is named Bertrand. He showers her with presents: silk underwear from France, a thin gold chain she always wears around her waist. But they barely speak. He has the charisma of a toad. It's not that he's an ugly guy. Bertrand is tall, slim, very acceptable. He's just always chilly. It's impossible to connect the gifts to the man.

"Nicole can do anything she wants but leave him. That seems to be their agreement. He's been following her around since high school. He was her English teacher, and when she came here to go to school, he left teaching altogether and found a job working in a bank. I think their relationship began when she was fifteen.

"Nicole needs to prove she's not trapped, that she's not missing anything. She's twenty-eight and she's only had her husband Bertrand, and briefly, that aunt. Sex with Bertrand is pretty sour: he fucks her, rolls off, she gets herself off before he even goes to sleep.

"I like her. She's intelligent, in a small way. She wants something better but she's not serious about it. Nicole lives in fear. The reasons are obscure. She could be almost anyone's captive; it's just that Bertrand's already got her. She'll never leave him, even though she thinks she might. . ."

Sly shrugged and looked me over carefully. "But there's room for you."

"What do you think I should do?"

"I don't care. Do what you like. We'll be at the cafe later. Stop by and hang out with us."

"I have to work. I have another job right after this one."

"Camille works at the massage parlor." This from Ricardo. He liked to make trouble.

"As receptionist," I snapped.

Sly's eyes widened. She stared at me, sympathetically, I think.

"You should take the night off," said Sly.

I thought about it, after they all left, and the bar was empty. There was nothing else to do except polish glasses and memorize a few more drinks in the Playboy bartenders' guide. But I didn't make a decision. My thoughts simply ambled along and I followed them.

Why had I taken this job in the massage parlor? Maybe I just wanted to know what it was really like. There was that whorehouse reputation, spiky and difficult: girls weeping into their pills, everybody drowning.

Wait for me, girlfriend. Speak to me before you crumble like soggy cake.

On the other hand, cut someone's gut, you could try that. You never knew what might happen. Laughs might spill out.

In truth, I never knew why I did a single thing. Any job, any event, was just transportation music, sliding by as I continued my trek to the truth of the story. But somehow it got late. Even the century was drying up; with every tick it took a beating. What had happened to its tiny charm?

As I stumbled away from the bar, through the mini-mall parking lot, my thoughts soared towards the irresistible Dr. Wittig. *She's squalid as a pig, squealing and rooting in her little pen*—suddenly I could see that. It was what she had. My heart lifted and broke. I was so glad to be working for her.

The building that held the parlor was right at the corner. I lunged towards the building door and it gave with the usual squeak. You won't believe this, but I heard her voice. It was Dr. Wittig, whispering to me from the privacy of her home office:

> *What I thought was a forest was really a cluster of violins.*
> *When I walked through that forest their bluster burst*
> *overhead: works of fire.*

Plod plod plod. The parlor was on the third floor and there was no elevator. I watched my shoes as I climbed the dusty stairs, past streaks of moth powder on the walls. Moths fumbled in clouds at the landings, where the light bulbs were. They fell into my face, droppings from a bad dream.

No blame. Some things are so deranged they can't be avoided. And I was only doing what anyone does, waiting for my mistakes. I knew they'd slither up to me like my own personal language. I just hoped I'd recognize them.

I reached the top landing and there was the parlor door. It had a pink frame around a panel of frosted glass.

Behind it was a small lobby with a yellow couch, coated with girls. I could hear them from the hallway. Just as summer ticks across a hot beach, the parlor was a place for girls—to talk or squawk or fall into magazines, bored. The first time I walked in, they just grinned and someone offered me a job.

I opened the door to smells of disinfectant and air freshener. "Hello Camille," Lima trilled. On this particular night, she was the only one on the couch, wearing a pink halter top. Up here tits had sugary resting spots. All the halter tops were bright pink, yellow, turquoise, or electric green. They came from a bin in the back. Girls came in and fished around, exchanging their flannel work shirts for eye candy. However, I wore a black turtle neck because I was the receptionist.

I leered at Lima; my face felt like a billboard.

"You're a Pink Lima tonight," I told her. "Where's everybody?"

"I'm working. So is Dusty, she's somewhere in the back."

That was Trixie talking; she was sitting cross-legged on the floor. Her legs were so long and angular they looked like construction equipment—she was a Lego whore, with flower decals on her blue jeans. Trixie was scowling at a book, while Steve, the day shift receptionist, looked over her shoulder.

"A whole book on itching!" he exclaimed. "You girls are sure into your cats."

"It's the I-CHING," she shouted. "An ancient Chinese oracle!"

Trixie threw her coins. Steve's head sunk as he read aloud:

"The arousing, thunder.

The abysmal, water.

Whoa, Trixie. That's pretty deep."

I settled into my desk. It was my favorite part of this job, being hidden from the waist down. *Hiding your privates: A better way to live.* The desk sat squarely in front of the entrance like a fort.

Clump clump clump. Someone was coming up the stairs. "Dusty! Business!" Trixie brayed, then got to her feet and heaved herself on the couch.

"Yikes, a customer," said Steve. "Gotta go. Bye y'all. Have a good night."

He darted out and we heard him scamper down the stairs. Trixie sighed. "How could such a rabbity fag be so dumb?"

More stamping. Loud enough to flatten the building into threads. Then silence at the door. We stared at the long black overcoat through the filmy glass. It was such a noir moment, and so improbable—one of the moths had finally made it all the way up the stairs. It was surprisingly difficult for them. They had to save their pennies, and they did. They saved and they lied. But, sometimes, all that was not as hard as getting in the door.

The door opened and an old man lurched across the threshold. He stopped, dazed. A muscle fluttered in his throat. He took every one of us in with his good eye; his other ticked back and forth like a metronome.

"Good evening!" I said heartily. He was drab but not poor, and that gave me confidence. I slapped my palms down on the desktop and knocked a few wild tilts out of my desk chair.

"These are our models tonight: Pink Lima, Trixie, and Dusty Bean."

This was a line I said two or three times in four hours. The place didn't do much business. But I always twisted the names a bit. Gave them a little sparkle in the headlights. . .

The old man picked Trixie, who grunted assent. Trixie was a grim girl, and funny looking, but blond. She teased her hair for work, so it sat on top of her head like a yellow muff. The old man took her hand, and she dropped it. "Follow me," she commanded. They took the hallway back to the series of little rooms; someone told me this used to be a dentist's office. Then a door clicked shut.

So, the old guy was about to tumble off his ledge; he was sick of being stuck up there, wherever he was. I got that part; I was filled with understanding with regards to that particular part. But what kept him stuck?

I turned the page back to the beginning of Trixie's oracle. It turned out to be Deliverance:

> *The hindrance is past; deliverance has come. The superior man recuperates in peace and keeps still. . .*

"So, you must be the new girl." I looked up to see Dusty Bean. She had made it to the couch for my call and now she was looking at me. Her bright blue eyes came at me like fists. But they were friendly. It fit her reputation: a big mouth who was generous with fights. She was the color of Goldie Hawn. Thin, yet muscular. Her halter top was black strings crocheted into spider webs that covered each small tit.

After I nodded, Dusty's questions came quickly. Did I like it here? Why was I working here?

I just made something up. I told her I had vague but uncompromising plans to blackmail any professor who had a role in flunking me out, should I happen to spot one here.

Pink Lima cracked a giggle. "Well," she said, her voice all syrupy, "You have your chance. The fellow in there with Trixie is Professor Hemorrhoids."

Silence fell, until Dusty broke it. "Not too much business but what we got is well-behaved. So, we return the favor." She sounded disgusted. "Anyhow Professor H retired years ago, from the biology department. You were in physics, right?"

"Yeah," I said. "Never saw the guy in there with Trixie," I said. I felt a shot of relief which let me know I wasn't up to blackmailing anyone. "It occurs to me," I mumbled, "doing biology your whole life is enough punishment. All those fluids." Then I told Dusty that I was probably too disorganized to carry it off.

"Get organized, baby," said Dusty Bean. "That's the only way. That's how we got this parlor. We struck the old parlor. The owner was a jerk, an asshole. A prick. He thought he could come in anytime and harass the girls. Well, we struck his ass and boy was he surprised. They wrote about us in the paper. Our picture was on Page One. Whores picketing!"

"No way," I said.

"Way," she said. "It gave us the idea of starting our own parlor. Everyone here works as little as possible."

Pink Lima leaned towards Dusty like the Tower of Pisa. "Dusty is such a cool girl. Plus, the best softball player."

"Softball," said Dusty Bean, patiently.

Pink Lima boomed, "*Dusty to the rescue! Dusty to the rescue!* That's what everybody chants when Dusty Bean hits one out of the park. Plus, she's got a great arm. Whether she's throwing rocks or baseballs, she gets it where she wants it to go. BLAST that Bank of America window. . . It shimmered before it shattered. Before a big window breaks, it bends. It was so cool. Do that again, Dusty Bean."

"I don't break windows for no reason, Lima." Dusty gave me a look which seemed to say, *these girls drive me crazy.*

Then she snapped up Trixie's coins. "Let me do your oracle, Camille." I was watching her big scarred hands shake the coins when Professor Hemorrhoids stumbled back into the lobby.

"Goodnight, Professor," Lima trilled.

"Bye bye," he mumbled. And was gone.

Dusty Bean threw the coins nine times, making marks on a paper after every throw. It was pleasantly mysterious. A bit of suspense got spanked every time the coins hit the floor—that was the future, telling me to back off.

"Hey, your oracle came up as Revolution (Molting)," Dusty announced. I leaned over and read from the yellow book—Wrapped in the hide of a yellow cow? That seemed pretty strange. But there were parts that Dusty read aloud:

> *Not every demand for change in the existing order should be heeded. On the other hand, repeated and well-founded complaints should not fail of a hearing. When one's own day comes, one may create revolution. Starting brings good fortune. Remorse disappears. No blame.*

"I like your oracle," said Dusty Bean, her eyes sparking. "I am motivated. I have the revolutionary motivation."

Something began to chug. Blood spirits. I sort of liked this girl. She clapped her arm around my back and I stumbled, almost fell to my knees under her sunny shine.

But I waved it off. "Well, you take the damn oracle. You threw it. I don't like it. I've been flunking and flailing all over the place. Now I just want to rest for the fucking rest of my life."

"You're not failing," she said firmly. "You're relaxing. Don't think of it as taking a hit. Tumble like Alice down your little hole. Falling is relaxing. . ." Then she looked at me as though her eyes were rolling down my gullet. I mean, it was intimate. "You're floating really. So, spend that time looking around. It's good, what you're doing. You're here, with us."

"What happened to my oracle?" It was Trixie, sounding pissed. She'd come back in and was leaning against the door jam.

"It's Camille's oracle now," bubbled out of Pink Lima's mouth. "Dusty Bean threw her oracle and it's better than yours was anyhow. She got revolution!"

Trixie's look was bottomless.

Dusty tapped my knee with a finger. "Listen, you can do anything you want. You want to make some money, go ahead. It can be easy. But that depends on you. It's not for everybody. You have to be trained."

Trixie said, sort of glumly, "It's like cleaning toilets for a hundred an hour."

"Take Chad, for instance. He's mine, but if you want him, take him. He's very very easy. Chad is like this. . ."

"One of my regulars gave me a car," chirped Lima. "When was the last time someone gave you a car?"

Dusty Bean described this guy Chad. It was hard to pay attention. Such an old story and I couldn't care about it. Rejection, shame. Boy, did he try not to go to the whore house, but he could never make it through the month.

Dusty, she was interesting. So sinew. A girl that muscular in barely any clothes, it seemed an exception to every rule. I wanted to lift the silly webs off her little titties. She looked at me with hot blue eyes, her big hands grinning.

Maybe, I thought, I took this job because I was supposed to find a girl with a heart. My whore with a heart, big and warm. I could spend awhile staggering through her chambers. . .

"Chad," said Dusty Bean, "is mostly a head case. His wife won't touch him, and he won't touch you. He just needs to look at pussy."

"Well," I said doubtfully, "it doesn't sound like a big deal." It was just another thing I couldn't think about. Choices. Dusty said I had some. What came up was sitting on Dusty's hips, twisting her nugget. If I could, I'd choose to be her little sex witch. . . Better believe I would.

You can drag a hook but HOW to make it catch.

I said in a panic, "Dusty when is your next softball game?"

"Uhh," was all she said. She looked confused. Trixie gathered up her coins and gave me the game date, then began tossing another oracle. I shot a quick glance at Dusty. We connected as if our eyeballs were attached. Awkwardness rippled through our every nerve. Something happened. It felt sort of like blood pushing into damaged tissue. Sort of ugly. One of those love moments. I relished it. I felt sick.
I knew it would be ages before Dusty and I calmed down enough to carry on a conversation.

ARTIFICIAL

My imagination is a private museum, but some people just move in. They get swallowed. Then deformity starts. My histories have no accuracy to them, but they are crammed with facts.

When I first met Barb, she lived in a Victorian flat which had cherubs carved into the doorway arches. It was Christmas, and strings of colored lights decorated the hard white tree and the pinball machine, rescued by Barb from a dumpster. Barb had a job in a massage parlor, as the receptionist. It was her job to say, "These are our models tonight," which was a signal for all the women on the couch to stand in a half circle around the customer who'd just climbed the stairs. My lover was one of those women, and her whore outfits were carelessly butch halter tops and drawstring pants.

I show my girlfriend the above section and she protests sharply, as she always does when she encounters my version of the facts. She says they just made eye contact with the customers. They didn't stand up. She sounds insulted by the idea of standing up. I vaguely remember that the image of prostitutes in a half circle around a new arrival comes from a book of photographs.

It's odd to think of my sexual imagination as starting out empty, a blank that drew a body along behind it. Then bits of other people fell in. I remember Barb at a party when we were both in our teens, her eyebrows, long strokes of black, her swiveling wit. She was the kind of cute tomboy butch I wish I could carry in my pocket. She came up to me and, without a word, ran her finger along the neckline of my t-shirt, which had a deep round neck.

Nothing else happened. But after that party I couldn't wear the shirt. Whenever I put it on, I was distracted by the moment when Barb ran her finger along the neckline. In fact, I was distracted whenever I just thought of the t-shirt. When I did put it on, I had to stare at myself in the mirror and try to imagine what Barb had seen. This always frustrated me, although the charged feeling returns faithfully, at moments associated with the t-shirt and on other occasions—mystified arousal.

Once every few years I'd try again. I'd pull it over my head and stare in the mirror at the long sleeves, the pinkish red—a rose color, with a peculiar bloodiness. The neck was narrow but low-cut. The swells of my breasts at the neckline looked like tree roots, just where they turn and bulge before going into the earth. I yanked the shirt off. My breasts were drained and white.

It ended up in the basement, and I finally threw it out a couple of years ago, after I held it up to the light and noticed it was lacerated by tiny holes. Eaten by some insect. I suddenly felt disgusted by its age and my hoarding. Instead of taking photographs, I avoid throwing out clothes. I keep them stuffed into old suitcases in the basement, where they get dusty as mummy cloth and smell of mildew. I'm all packed—ready to take a trip backwards in time, with every version of my body.

I walk into the bar where Barb is now a bartender. It's a small place and sparsely decorated, but it has a reputation for interesting music. Mostly men patronize it. Barb comes out from behind the bar and gives me a ferocious hug. "It's so great to see someone I've known for 20 years, who isn't dead," she says.

Elise is in the bar. She pecks my cheek, then turns away with a husky laugh. She's piled her hair on top of her head, leaving drizzly long strings around her neck. When I first met Barb, Elise was her roommate, and here they are, still friends. Barb has good hair, really thick, and long black brows that are wicked and sexy. She cultivates a butch melancholy, and Elise is her buddy, the femme part of gender's artificial flower.

I've never been able to write about Elise. Her stubborn silences coupled with an extraordinary and very feminine fluency resist description. Today, she is savory and plush—with her padded pink satin kimono and pink shoes, her dry husky laugh. She smells like cigarettes. When she's sad or just thinking about something, her eyes narrow and she draws her thumb along her lower lip.

No matter what I write, I believe I will make her angry. I decide I'll change her name and her physical appearance, which immediately gives me a feeling of relief.

I remember waiting with her at a bus stop. The bars had just closed, and we were going home after a night at the clubs. Elise's metallic leggings gleamed neon pink under the streetlight. Her long hair blew back and forth in the wind, and she was smoking a cigarette. Elise was fearless in the dark.

I'd dressed for her that night—a black lace camisole under my long & tangled hair, big paste jewels, something red. Clothes as a stream of erotic gestures. It was my pleasure to be in a sphere dominated by her style, though she unnerved me. We danced separately, with the cute ones who said yes. It felt like working the crowd. All I really wanted to do was observe Elise from the corner of my eye. Of course, she came home with several phone numbers, and I watched—the cool edge to the way she could jot down a phone number or take one, and then slide it somewhere interesting, like the top of her stocking or her bra.

The girlfriends Elise acquired this way were bright funny stories, if also a pain in the ass. The one I remember at the moment was the Swedish countess, a sugary-looking blond named Ingrid. What good is Eurotrash when it's hasn't got any money? She was unbelievably rude. Anyone in her way got a wicked shove, and no matter how many times we were introduced, she never recognized me.

One day Elise told me about Ingrid's childhood, and reality popped, like cracking a knuckle. That shimmer of delirium is the best thing about a story that is both funny and true. Elise had a phrase for those moments: *It's the Funkadelics. They've reincarnated and entered our lives in a new form.*

It seemed that the Count, Ingrid's father, invested all the family's money in rubber boots—not a wise move, as they were living in a country where it never rained. All through Ingrid's childhood that money lay in the basement, in the form of thousands of pairs of red and yellow galoshes. Eventually they disappeared into the dump.

Elise's femininity is permanent (I'm tempted to say eternal). For her fourth birthday, she demanded white go-go boots. When I try to tell the same story as someone like her, I can feel myself falling apart. Parts slide off, chunks of hair and skin—the ones I've rummaged, acquired on the sly. I've assembled a sexual identity that's like another body—my personal Frankenstein. Bony and full of nerves & suffering. It includes me but is detached, like the mirror's alienating resemblance to myself.

There's no question about my sexual tastes. *Bottom's up.* I prefer desires that lacerate and spread, like cracks through porcelain. But the feeling persists, that just around the corner is the room where I started, and it's empty.

Now I live in a house with my fetishes. Like that rosy t-shirt, which sometimes still preoccupies me, even though I threw it out ages ago. It's really my body, multiplying itself, arousals migrating around the tufted living room set and the home entertainment center. Then, like dust bunnies, they float out the window, bouncing slowly, driven by a breeze across my broad suburban lawn.

(I've never lived in the suburbs, but their peculiar melancholy is everywhere.)

Think about it. Your female body. Focus on the young flesh. It has a kind of radiance that other people believe in. You discover, to your surprise, that belief can be aimed at you without being personal. Like that night in the bar, when you glimpse Elise's red thumbnail crushing a phone number. Ink smudges on a wet cocktail napkin—someone's private message disappears between the hem of her stocking and her thigh. With Elise, I imagine the perfect coincidence of inside and outside, although I've never asked her about it.

UNDER GRID: An Obscure Manifesto

Ghost Story

One day about a year ago, a book came in the mail. It was called *When Ghosts Speak* and it arrived by mistake. No one had ordered it. The author, a devout Catholic, was on relaxed terms with that part of the spirit world which had not 'transitioned' by entering 'the white light' (her terminology). Her attitude towards ghosts was offhand and extremely assured. I scanned the book for a few moments before tossing it into the recycling bin.

It turned out to be preparation for an odd incident which occurred a few days later. I was driving on 8th towards Potrero Hill when suddenly a dead friend was sitting next to me in the car, his familiar presence resonant in the empty space. You might say it made a *ghostly noise* (although he didn't speak). Just then a rotary phone loudly rang.

What to make of this? I reflected on my friend's life, which had been rich in unfortunate experiences. In fact, these were the kind of experiences which become lurid and deformed by representation. It's as though a voyeuristic appetite gets released in language and then preys upon the subject—my subject. As a consequence, I feel attracted by the manifold protections of silence. But I will give one example, because the image it creates is, for me, so weirdly Christ-like. While sleeping in Golden Gate Park, my friend was once woken up by rats licking the blood that seeped from scabs on his arms. Such stories burst from him in language that had so much vividness and energy it possessed its own uncanny life. When he died, I had to mourn the death of his language as something distinct from his physical death—a separate loss.

Today I think that the presence of death in life characterizes language. That is the most true part of the story I've just told. Like any native speaker, I handle English with a sense of ease, but over time its uncanny aspect has become more present. Words are the oldest human objects which enter my daily life. Yesterday I was reading some of the riddles of the Exeter book and this word shone forth unchanged:

swaþu swiþe blacu *swift wæs on fore* **swift!**

I'm not construing death as an abstract barrier. It's more of a thin curtain drawn over the churning mass of former times—always present, always invisible. As a joke, I once told a student that language was a zombie—acting alive but composed of dead parts. We both found the idea oddly satisfying.

What does it mean to be close to a person's language? My friend who died had a way with it which meant anything could happen: many startling fabrications. Once he was going to Canada to attend a festival for skateboarders. Probably it was one of those extreme sports events. At the border, they pulled him into a room and showed him a printout from an American law enforcement agency that went on for pages and pages. It contained the details of all his thirty-one aliases.

I'm hesitant to characterize my experience of my friend's ghost as a delusion. This is not because I think that ghosts are real, or, at least, they are not exactly real. It is this: the obscurity of language makes the real quiver.

A speck reads its future from its path through the shock corridor

that place which resides
in the ghost. Similarly, I make my pants
from drought
leather.
Just so. In the manner.

Furl.

An Obscure Text

+ One which is difficult, self-indulgent, private, exclusive.

+ Or, a text which is characterized by the use of codes or slang terms of marginal communities. It is (by intent) incomprehensible, fractured, distracting, irrational, or illegible to outsiders.

+ Or, a text which contains unregulated and confusing erotic elements. In this case, it may be also thought of as an *adult game.* Such private codes have the communicative density of erotic coupling.

+ Or, in the occult vein: a text which is mysterious, cryptic, enigmatic.

The writing I prefer is packed with sensation, relation, insight, but it has a very small audience. In the wider cultural marketplace, such writing is regarded dismissively and the specific basis of this dismissal is its obscurity. This skew troubles the perceptions even of those who resist it.

What I find curious is that obscurity has powers of attraction in cultural fields outside of literature, particularly in popular music. The book *Infidel Poetics* by Daniel Tiffany is an exhilarating exploration of lyric obscurity and it begins with this paradox:

> In popular music today, there is a flourishing market in poetic obscurity—in lyrics composed in various kinds of slang, jargon, or patois, which make little or no sense to most listeners. Animated by the inscrutable or garbled refrain, eclectic communities take root in the urban chatter of hip-hop, the Haitian creole of Wyclef Jean, the cockney slang of British punk, the Jamaican argot of reggae... The practice of including song lyrics and occasionally even glossaries in liner notes appears to have fallen from favor, precisely because the task of deciphering lyrics defies the latest poetic and cultural ethos of obscurity. At the same time, lyric obscurity in this context appears to function as a potent ingredient of publicity and celebrity, as the inevitable condition (and the indelible object) of exposure. (1)

In popular music, lyric obscurity is an efflorescence that arises in response to a need for concealment (criminality, stigmatized community) or under conditions of social disorder. The sense of risk that is communicated is risk of and to the body. The communities which are represented have failed to assimilate—that failure is what is present—and this, fundamentally, is a failure of communicability, and perhaps, too, a failure of legitimacy. The paradox being that this is the locus of powerful expression.

I suspect that the fundamental cause of the disconnect between social undergrounds and poetic communities is class, specifically the academic context for contemporary poetry. In other words, it isn't logically necessary. Of course, observing that class is a barrier does not yield insight into crossing it. Perhaps, as non-academic contexts for poetry proliferate, poetry as a project will mutate wildly on either side of this barrier.

Some of the most interesting material in *Infidel Poetics* relates lyric obscurity to a history of communities of dissidence. Tiffany describes, as a genealogy of modern nightlife, erotic and artistic undergrounds and their 'infidel songs.' He discovers roots of poetry in the canting songs of beggars as well as the broadsheets of radicals. There is also an amazing section on manic rewrites of Mother Goose developed as schoolroom exercises by Stéphane Mallarmé. It was an exciting book to encounter, especially as I spent much of my life in one underground community or another. The rich nexus of lyric obscurity and secret experience has baffled and compelled me for years.

The Obscure Community

Before I was an experimental writer, I was a lesbian. I still am, but as time has passed, my sort of lesbian—who came of age in an underground community—is passing away. I have the odd sense of being out of phase with any image of lesbian identity in part because my beginnings were (or felt like they were) outside the representational boundary.

The community I entered in Ann Arbor, Michigan in the mid-1970s was undergoing a decade of extremity. That meant it was a convergence of collectives, prostitutes, union organizers, drag shows, radicals with history in violent parts of the Weather Movement, and bar life. These components combined and re-combined across all boundaries to produce an ongoing show with propulsive elements of both shock and hilarity. The larger feeling was of having slipped into an exhilarating social life that I could not describe. We had collective existence (and a political rhetoric) but our substance was invisible. This was partly a collective ruse for safety in a violently hostile society—but it was also structural and linguistic.

The coming out narrative is supposed to make experience legible, but I have never been able to write about this period. I still cannot create sentences about the circumstances and time in which I came out. There are many conflicts and contradictions that stymie the project: much of what happened cannot be discussed openly despite the fact that decades have passed. Also, there were so many reversals of expectation in play that representation becomes confusing. Finally, there is the issue of how to navigate the extraordinary gap between private life—a secret community—and what is sloppily termed "the world." Where was I living, if not "the world"?

When I have tried to explore this period, I have ended up circling around the very issues that constrain my writing about it. This passage below is both a description and an enactment of this failure. It's a narrative of a past love affair during this period of extremity. In the excerpt, an effort at representation has failed and, in response, I end up examining taboo as a distortionary field even as the writing shifts away from realism:

> *One could say that my attempt at realistic narrative is a surrender to nostalgia, for the representational failure of realism is well-known. I will not disagree with that. However, nostalgia is the vehicle through which my past has survived.*
>
> *. . .and I want to touch the past lightly, so as not to disturb it. Especially its dewish Utopian qualities. Although it was instability which made it secret and fresh.*
>
> *If light waves can be bent by gravity, scattered by reflectors, sucked up by the bottomless gravity of a black hole. If light can stretch or shrink time.*
>
> *Language is bent. A taboo is a place where language deteriorates, becoming both supple and truncated.*
>
> *Camille's fall for Dusty sent her hurtling through the doors: butch, whore, incest survivor.*
>
> *Into the sturdy, enigmatic presence of taboo.*
>
> *A taboo as presence is both everywhere and nowhere. Language bends around it. One experiences moments of hysteria as recognition seems to be slipping away.* I can't believe you've been a prostitute, *Dusty's mother wails into the phone.*
>
> *The powerful attraction of taboo is anti-linguistic; it stops meaning at the boundary. Privacy and insanity have this in common: shared meaning drops away.*

So, love thrust Camille inside an enigma. I write this, of course, out of nostalgia, to affirm whore as enigma and abstraction.

She is the one who inhabits me and who familiarizes me with the universe.[1]

Her hands probe the sheer tunnel of flesh.

She sheds the weightless freedom of the abstract.

To clarify this line:

"The powerful attraction of taboo is anti-linguistic; it stops meaning at the boundary."

. . .the boundary I'm referring to is not individual but communal. The ability of a community to seal itself is mysterious and powerful (even if temporary). All revolutions (in values as well as governments) begin in these underground and secret spaces.

This recalls a professional colleague of twenty years ago. Working on a yearlong software project, it eventually emerged that our parents had been Communists. Mine left the party after Khrushchev's condemnation of Stalin at the 20th Congress in 1956. His parents never left the party and they also maintained their political involvement in a secret cell for decades, until their death. They never admitted this to their son. He found out by spying on them.

Light and shadow: meaning and the secret cell. As a young man, my colleague protested fiercely against the Vietnam War but was never otherwise politically associated.

---

1. Nicole Brossard, *Picture Theory*.

I also grew up with the silences of former Communists, but it came with an enveloping community. Down the block from my home, there was a house built of pale brick and tall blades of light (windows). Every week, the fathers gathered there, to talk politics, drink whiskey, and play poker. They were all ex-Communists. Several of these men were engaged in civil rights lawsuits related to their period of Communist affiliation that ran for many years. To me, these were infinite lawsuits, stretching from before my birth until after my death. I experienced them as markers of the edge of value; beyond them was nothingness. I wandered around the house fingering the blown glass eggs collected by our host's wife. They were heavy and glistened in my palm. I picked up one after another and peered into their depths: all floating veils and orbs of bright colors. I barely listened to the men, but it was enough.

Intimate Disorder

The terms that would describe us were lurid. . . so distance fell away. We were inside, touching, without perspective. . .

. . .even as we were *outside of society*, ghostly, hidden.

My confusion was not a mistake—it was intimate disorder, or self-in-relation. Confusion is a necessary property of entering a social space (including a text) without a system of defenses in place.

As a young lesbian, the obscurity of my person became a comfortable condition. I didn't think it would ever be disturbed. Now it has disappeared, and I have arrived at a world of objects (persons) presented as recognizable. It seems to me this transformation rests on some basic faults in understanding and perception. Here are a few alternative views:

+ Recognition is extractive. It removes what is recognized from its constitutive relations. Thus, an instant of recognition creates an alien deformity which is experienced as clarity.

+ Recognition imposes a coercive order, whereas obscurity is packed with relation: communal, sexual, political. Obscurity marks an interstice where social relations slip from public to private and understanding becomes tacit (and tactile). It is a space of social darkness which functions opposite to a black hole: it throws out slang, ideas, reconfigured relations, new possibilities for dissent and disorder. This is why in popular music the coolest slang is unfamiliar: underground slang signals authentic social relations.

+ Obscurity is a property of inwardness; language as a substance is imbued with it.

+ Consciousness is like a canoe on an ocean of raw unfiltered perception. We learn the skills of navigation, but moment to moment 'know' almost nothing of what constitutes our 'experience.' The billions of nerve signals that are filtered and processed every second before reaching the level of consciousness constitute a stream of raw data that is antithetical to being, meaning, personhood. But moment to moment, without awareness, we are created from it—from an obscurity which is by condition unknowable.

\+ Not knowing my ancestors does not remove their intimate grasp. Language, likewise, arrives from the past and expresses conditions through me and upon me of which I will never be aware.

\+ Meaning is organized looting of the mind's infrastructure.

The Monad's Tiny Pants

I prefer to use language that carries relation in its texture. While a text may be difficult, relation does not fall away due to difficulty. *Obscurity is a social substance.* Recognition can ripple through the text as sequences of tiny transformations, one question into another, so that a poem riddles itself. Alternatively, the poem may unfold as a sort of suspense novel. Rigid understandings undermined from below.

One aspect of Tiffany's *Infidel Poetics* which I found especially rewarding is his development of an ontology of lyric obscurity. For this, he uses Leibniz's model of the monad, first described in *Monadology*. This model "posits a mode of obscurity integral to the nature of Being itself, a foundational obscurity replicated in our understanding of the phenomenal world, in forms of sociability, and (of course) in language" (Tiffany 11).

A monad is similar to early conceptions of the atom, a thing that is "simple, without parts" (Leibniz 213). Nothing exists other than simple monads and aggregates of monads. Unlike atoms, monads model metaphysical substance, not physical reality. They are characterized by perception (and correspondence), even though they do not communicate. A fundamental paradox is that this is perception without consciousness or sensory properties—the perceptions of a doorknob. This characterization of perception straddles the divide between the material world and consciousness. The perceptions of a doorknob are what precipitate its responses to all the forces of the universe.

Rather than consciousness having sole possession of perception, according to Leibniz's view, the perception associated with consciousness (which he calls apperception) is a small and transient variation: "It is good to distinguish between *perception*, which is the internal state of the monad representing external things, and *apperception*, which is consciousness, or the reflective knowledge of this internal state, something not given to all souls, nor at all times to a given soul" (Tiffany 114).

According to Leibniz, each monad is a mirror which "represents the universe from its own point of view and which is ordered as the universe itself" (Leibniz 278). What the monad perceives in its mirror is the entire universe, but this perception is dappled with obscurity as its point of view is infinitesimal. Thus, its perception is both "clear" and "confused": "Monads all go confusedly to infinity, to the whole, but they are limited and differentiated by the degrees of their distinct perceptions" (Leibniz 221). Because monadic perception combines "infinity and confusion, omniscience and obscurity" (Tiffany 114), opposites not only combine, they have constitutive relations. Obscurity is fundamental to each part and inseparable from the whole, at scales ranging from the infinitesimal to the infinite.

Monadic perception is solipsistic. Monads have "no windows through which something else can enter or leave" (Leibniz 214). The monads know the world by what passes within them. This is similar to a reader who knows the world only through reading a text. Leibniz suggests that a monad may be compared to a crypt whose interior is engraved with inscriptions invoking an external world. Nonetheless, via correspondence, aggregation and harmony, monads produce phenomenological reality.

In Tiffany's use of this model, monadic correspondence can be found in undergrounds, criminal or radical communities, nightclubs. These are sealed but expressive communities which possess and create the secrecy of vernacular speech. They provide a negative sociability which defies the instant and shallow continuities of the internet era.

Tiffany uses this model to ground poetry itself with the negative capability of monadic expression: "Lyric obscurity may trigger a variation of the sublime associated with the abject: a vernacular sublime" (Tiffany 8). Difficulty in poetry is thus connected to the "dangerous speech of various underworlds" (Tiffany 8). In elite culture, this connection is suppressed but a study of etymology reveals it. For example, "slang" and "slum" originate in canting speech, and the OED records that "slum" is a cant word which means "nonsensical talk or writing."

I find this thrilling because it connects my lived experience of subcultures and undergrounds to a model of lyricism that is faithful to darkness and confusion. The monadic expression of a poetic community has a secret harmony with the criminal and the suppressed. Lyric obscurity communicates these secrets without revealing them: "Lyrical knowledge of the sensory world, like monadic perception, is 'miraculous' because it is senseless, because it does not rely on a causal relation to the object" (Tiffany 115). The world is encrypted by language. This doesn't cancel social relations but is expressed by them, as a form of monadic correspondence.

One interesting aspect of the monad is that it is a model of perception generally. Thus, it is applicable to elite perception as well. Tiffany's book led me to read Leibniz and, after this immersion, I had a new understanding of a minor incident that occurred decades earlier. After growing up on the South Side of Chicago in what was then Chicago's only integrated neighborhood, I spent years in a state of cognitive dissonance. I was not able to process the sudden disappearance of Black people and Black culture from almost everywhere I went. A huge and vital complexity had vanished, and this was accompanied by the strange invisibility of the disappearance itself. Of course, this was normal for a white person, but I had grown up in a community stubbornly resistant to white flight and, thus, with different tools and understandings. Sometimes I would sink into a stunned (wordless) spectatorship—for example, when paging through the *New Yorker*. What felt wrong? What was reality? Where was I? I stared at the ads and the cartoons in a state of mystification. One day (in the proverbial flash) it hit me. I realized there were never any Black people in the cartoons. But there were Black people in the streets of New York! And so many cartoons showed the streets of New York! The cartoonists did not see the Black people. They were physically present, but unseen—by every single cartoonist, in hundreds or thousands of cartoons. The cartoonists were drawing the street but were unable to see the street, because their vision had been blocked. In that instant, I grasped the bodily nature and magnitude of the deformity constructed deep inside each cartoonist. I looked away, ashamed for them.

This blindness of the cartoonists is monadic perception: solipsistic to the core. Recall that monads have no windows. They know the world indirectly, like readers of a text. Understandings created by such perception cannot be corrected by experience of the outside as *there is no such experience.* This is a useful corrective to dealing with ideological dominance, whether it be neoliberal economics, psychoanalysis, or prejudice of any kind.

Obscuring Narrative

In my reflections upon these issues, there is a line from an essay by Robert Glück which I have returned to many times. He is describing the questions he and Bruce Boone were exploring in the early days of New Narrative.

"What kind of representation least deforms its subject? Can language be aware of itself (as object, as system, as commodity, as abstraction) yet take part in the forces that generate the present? Where in writing does engagement become authentic?"

I love this quote for reasons which change as I contemplate it from different perspectives. Recently, I have been drawn to its acknowledgement of the deformed subject: deformed by representation, by language itself. This being a starting point of struggle which has both personal and social aspects (dialog). New Narrative has always been attractive to me because it placed this struggle at the center of the project. In fact, this acknowledgment is for me the beginning of authenticity as a possibility.

I am also drawn to this problematizing of narrative precisely because it engages failure. Representation is a failed project. (Acknowledging the failure is not the same as authenticity but it overlaps.)

Giving obscurity its place as a central aspect of social relations (including political revolt) gives writing the freedom to manifest its own obscure condition. It allows a story to disappear—and to appear again.

Once I tutored a student who, over the course of our work together, became psychotic. This happened before my eyes and yet presented itself as a deep mystery. It was, among other things, a mystery in language. After the break, the sentences in his essay paragraphs made no sense but they had great rhythm and were very interesting. They possessed a leaping energy which seemed to be liberated as if language were a demon which had been suffering under constraint.

One day, he asked me if characters chose their author. I sat for a moment silently, transfixed by the prospect of characters floating through the ether as they searched for the right 'host.' What should I say? Where did characters come from?

The silence lengthened and began to feel weird. I came up with something calm and rational, mostly because I didn't want my peculiar behavior to impact a vulnerable student. But I'd like to leave that question open. Of course, there are many answers. But of all of them, it seems to me, the one we most overlook is silence. That is, we overlook the obscurity of the conditions of our invention. We speak into the silence and write likewise. What would it mean to listen to it?

AFTERWORD

Camille & Angie, 1978

It's vexing to use words, particularly when their meaning has changed. It requires such a high level of care. But I am setting forth; why? Not long after my partner, Angie, died of cancer, a friend wondered out loud to me whether it was rough, that the butch-femme subculture which seeded our relationship "had become obsolete." Angie and I had lived together for thirty-six years. The startling question caused a flush of pure grief for the rich intimacy we had shared; after some time, I realized that the grief was strong enough to spur a desire to represent that context.

Sometimes I feel that the truest respect one can show towards the past is to allow it to be something other than a predecessor of the present. Perhaps its alien and most forbidden nature did not reproduce. Exploring the deep lostness of what has died out is a freedom I didn't have when I was young.

1977. Fast stride. Headed down the street. Rollicking, with cowlick and leather motorcycle jacket. In my new Doc Martens, I was going someplace, for sure.

The day changed with the shadow. I am tall but he had to lean down to get in my face. It was a strange feeling, that face of contorted rage plunging towards me, blocking out the sky. His shrieks hummed with malice and hysteria. "You fucking dyke!!" he yelled, over and over. I suspect what set him off was that I existed, and I clearly felt good. There was a long moment when I thought he'd pound me into the pavement.

But suddenly he was gone, mysteriously redirected.

Almost immediately I ran into my friend Meredith. She led me into the nearest bar where she listened without saying a word and bought me a couple of whiskies. Meredith had an encompassing presence and big '70s rock star blond hair. She was a singer in a successful local band. But even when she wasn't singing, she had an internal vibration like a barely audible tuning fork. I think her eyes quivered a tiny bit, deep within that large nest of hair. Whatever it was, it really relaxed me.

Being a lesbian meant living at the edge of a disastrous and threatening form of visibility. Recognition could turn to violence in an instant, although mostly there was erasure and absolute zero cultural capital.

Yet social life constructs itself even when there is intense desire that it not exist. The way we were erased made us hyper visible—to each other. This felt like a form of molecular liveliness: tiny, insouciant, and sharp enough to cut. It gave me a zone of freedom that was intoxicating.

> The terms that would describe us were lurid. . .
> so distance fell away. We were inside, touching,
> without perspective. . .
> . . .even as we were *outside of society,* ghostly, hidden.
> (Under Grid: An Obscure Manifesto)

Living under such conditions changes a person's relation to time. The present is magnified; intensified. Night after night we displayed ourselves at the bar. We could mimic and disrupt the social codes of eroticism and gender. We played with butch and femme with more expressive freedom because we got to be meaningless: a freedom which can't be bought. We were at the intersection of nothing and gender.

> Ink smudges on a wet cocktail napkin—someone's
> private message disappears between the hem of
> her stocking and her thigh.
>
> (Artificial)

Meaninglessness can be infused with relation and feeling. Invisibility is a risk but also a shelter; it can proffer freedom if it becomes a location of community. *All revolutions (in values as well as governments) begin in these underground and secret spaces.* Such places, even when contingent and fragile, are where the stifling rigidities of the historical moment can mutate into something new.

> As a young lesbian, the obscurity of my person
> became a comfortable condition. I didn't think it
> would ever be disturbed.
>
> (Under Grid: An Obscure Manifesto)

It was lovely to be ignored by the dominant culture—a major symptom of the chronic infection that is misogyny is pervasive and remorseless judginess of women. The ridiculous messages that aimed to control and infest women with insecurities and self-hate were too far away to be heard distinctly. This was particularly useful for me because, in my adolescence, I experienced what might now be called gender dysphoria. I simply could not relate to femaleness, at least my own. Being a lesbian at that time was a fantastic shield from the sexism of the dominant culture. Our

FOSTERS

Still from ROSEBUD, a film by Cheryl Farthing 1991, photograph by Della Grace.

Camille & Angie, 1985

oppression and the feminism we invented made the barrier so effective it eased our relationship to our bodies. This was a sweet accident of my youth.

I remember when the lesbian sex magazine *On Our Backs* got its first big-brand ad: Absolut Vodka. It was stunning and even a little uncanny that they were so enlightened they saw us as a market. It became a regular thing, an Absolut Vodka ad on the back cover. Capitalism?

What do you do, when you give yourself the freedom to play with gender and not be suffocated by its images? For us, spoof was an integral element. We were gender shoplifters. Using gender this way put us in the wrong, and that suited me. This was the context the femme in me needed to strut. The moment has passed and so has my interest.

But Angie used to say I wasn't a femme, I just liked power, whereas she was really a butch from childhood.

She was good at fistfights, for example. Headlocks. Add in baseball, tennis, football, basketball. Tennis lessons were available in her working-class neighborhood for twenty-five cents and these led to newspaper stories about a budding prodigy. It didn't happen because her family didn't have the money.

Angie had straight male friends who loved her as much as it is possible to love a friend. She moved among people with disarming frankness and warmth.

My father described her as a realist, a deep compliment and a true one.

A gay male friend recently joked that no matter who was in the room, Angie was the butchest one there. This was partly about social class and then also what we thought of as butch skills, honed with years of dedication: auto mechanics, home repair. She could throw a baseball like nobody's business.

I had a video made of Angie's memorial. It was expensive but worth every penny. There is a haze around violations of the gender contract. People who live that rebellion successfully, with grace and courage, must be seen to be believed. Their disappearance is more profound because the rules they broke in life reformulate in their absence, as if they never lived. But the memorial disrupted that. Angie blazed. The stories about her and her life, the witnessing performed by dear and longtime friends, made a kind of historical document.

I was asked recently whether Angie's gender identity was *he*. It's odd for me to field such a question for Angie. Hers was a working-class butch feminism which took pleasure in violating gender norms, in concert with other butches—emphatically and rebelliously as women. The question has the side effect of obscuring an important part of her life's work. As I explained to my friend, *Angie was a badass super athlete butch dyke who spent at least a decade hauling the word* ***butch*** *out of the trash, so that she and younger lesbians could feel comfortable with it.* Part of this work was being a role model of survival skills: social, physical, political. Survival is a collective accomplishment.

I don't believe my answer to the question about my lover's gender identity can be understood as it stands. It's referencing community experience which is largely unrepresented and invisible. A story that our friend Sally shared at Angie's memorial gives it some context. I've included it below with her permission.

I'm going to share a brief story about something I learned from my friend Angie, something that I use often in my work and when I'm out in the world. First a bit of background: Angie and I became friends in about 1982—I was in my early '20s—and before long we were going off on camping trips together mostly to Big Sur and then later up to the Eel River in Humboldt County. Angie was a great breath of fresh air. She was comfortable with sexuality and really savvy about sexual politics. She was butch and completely unapologetic. She was wild, she loved to laugh, she had a million friends, and she was as in love with the magic of the natural world as much as I was. We could easily spend a day meandering along a stream or a trail looking at everything—plants, rocks, frogs, newts, lizards, snakes, birds. She was eight years my elder and, at that time, I thought of her as a kind of guide to the ways of the world.

. . .On one of our camping trips, Angie and I decided we'd spend the entire day swimming down the Eel River. And so, one morning, we got in the water near our camp at Standish-Hickey and had an unforgettable day, just floating along, watching ospreys overhead, lying around on warm sand banks, examining rocks, and talking. At the end of a long, wonderful day, we climbed out for the last time, dried off in the sun, and hiked up to the highway to hitchhike back to camp. We were hungry and sunburned, and so first we decided to get something to eat at a scruffy looking little bar nearby. I was a little reluctant, but Angie wanted to go in, so we did.

We were shoulder-to-shoulder as we opened the door. It took a couple of seconds for my eyes to adjust to the dark, and for me to realize that we were in what I considered dangerous and hostile territory. There were about a dozen men inside sitting at the bar and they all turned their heads and stared at us. I hesitated and took a step backward. Angie grabbed my elbow and whispered in my ear, 'COME ON. DON'T YOU THINK THEY'VE EVER SEEN A COUPLE OF BUTCHES BEFORE?' And so, we walked in.

Angie immediately started working the room, pointing to the little tv up in the corner above the bar and asking who was winning the baseball game—the Giants or the Dodgers? She asked what they thought about the new shortstop and whether he'd make it in the majors or be sent back down to Triple A. She wanted to know what was on the menu, whether it was homemade, what everyone did for a living, who owned farms, who had herding dogs, what kind of dog was the best herder, whether llamas were better guards than dogs, whether the winter would be rainy, had anyone seen any river otters nearby, offered to show them around San Francisco next time they visited, and promised that she knew all the best restaurants. I was mostly quiet that evening, watching her in action. I'm

> sure you can all picture this in your minds—Angie loosening everyone up, turning the focus of attention from us to them, changing the equation with her enthusiasm, her laugh, her curiosity and her good will. Late that evening, one of the guys gave us a ride all the way to our camp in the back of his flatbed—I remember sitting with Angie, a blue-eyed dog and a couple of bales of sweet alfalfa. The cooling summer air smelled so good.
>
> Later I became an engineer—thanks in part to the encouragement I received from Angie—and I use what I think of as *Angie techniques* when I'm at construction sites dealing with the same kind of flinty, skeptical dudes we encountered at the bar. It's a friendly but firm and unapologetic judo. I picked it up from Angie and I use it all the time.

Is this little story surprising in an afterword? I discovered my need to include it only in the process of composing the text. The discovery accompanied the realization that the more difficult comments I've encountered since Angie's death can be interpreted as acts of lesbian erasure.

The afterword, I came to understand, could be used to create safety for myself. Via the afterword, I can set boundaries on what people feel free to say to me. Because I am a widow—a lesbian widow, with thirty-six years of history in that relationship and embedded in that community—the erasure is intolerable—too deeply painful to be endured. I am unwilling.

My intent is to create silence around myself on these matters, not discourse. I think this creates a nourishing emptiness which is a part of how I want to live now.

Meanwhile, there is the language of the book, which is the meeting place of the living and the dead. It is open for business. I hope that it can be entered by anyone, and feasted upon, like the washed-up carcass of a whale. It reminds me of the last lines of Elizabeth Bishop's poem, "At The Fishhouses."

> If you tasted it, it would first taste bitter,
> then briny, then surely burn your tongue.
> It is like what we imagine knowledge to be:
> dark, salt, clear, moving, utterly free,
> drawn from the cold hard mouth
> of the world, derived from the rocky breasts
> forever, flowing and drawn, and since
> our knowledge is historical, flowing, and flown.

Goodbye, beloveds.

NOTES

Notes

Lynette #1

Bernstein, Charles. "Socialist Realism or Real Socialism?" *Soup*. No. 4. 1985.

Debord, Guy. *Society of the Spectacle*. Detroit, IL: Black & Red, 1977.

Dyer, Richard. "Male Gay Porn." *Jumpcut*. No. 30. March 1985.

Goldstein, Richard. "Kramer's Complaint." *Village Voice*. 2 July 1985.

Weene, Seph. "Venus." *Heresies #12*. Vol. 3, No. 4. 1981.

Under Grid

Brossard, Nicole. *Picture Theory*. Barbara Godard, trans. Toronto, ON: Guernica Editions Inc., 2009.

Glück, Robert. "Long Note on New Narrative." *Biting the Error*. Mary Burger, Robert Glück, Camille Roy, Gail Scott, eds. Toronto, ON: Coach House Books, 2004.

Leibniz, Gottfried Wilhelm. "The Principles of Philosophy, or The Monadology." *Philosophical Essays by G.W. Leibniz*. Roger Ariew and David Garber, eds. and trans. Indianapolis, IN: Hackett, 1989.

Tiffany, Daniel. *Infidel Poetics*. Chicago, IL: University of Chicago Press, 2009.

Acknowledgements

My influences include the New Narrative group (Bob Glück, Bruce Boone, Kevin Killian, Dodie Bellamy, Steve Abbott, Sam D'Allesandro, Mike Amnasan, among others) and fellow travelers such as Eileen Myles, Gail Scott, Carla Harryman, Jocelyn Saidenberg, Rachel Levitsky, Kathy Acker, kari edwards, Renee Gladman, Lawrence Braithwaite, and Abigail Child. If I allow myself to follow the ripples as they expand outwards there are more: Samuel Ace. Michelle Tea. Mary Burger. Dia Felix. Amanda Davidson. Leslie Scalapino. Tisa Bryant. Pam Lu. And still more: early on, I was electrified by feminist poetics, especially as exemplified in Kathleen Fraser's work. And earlier still, Gloria Anzaldúa was a formative writing exemplar and teacher, my first in San Francisco. (This was through the workshop "El Mundo Surdo.")

As a list reduces its contents to items, so this list is a reduction of extraordinary experiences. The cumulative effect was a deep and generous permission that has fueled decades of work. Thank you, everyone! We've been companions of the imagination, spurring one another on. Because of you, my writing has taken risks—erotic, personal, intellectual—in a process which has wavered between delighted confusion and flashes of debasement.

Thanks to the editors, publishers, and friends who have supported this work over the years in the following magazines and anthologies: *Amerarcana*, *Biting the Error*, *Dear World*, *From Our Hearts to Yours*, *Mirage/Period(ical)*, and

Writers Who Love Too Much. Thanks to Abigail Child for permission to reprint "Sex Talk," which also appeared in her collection *This Is Called Moving*. "The Faggot" and "Perils" were originally published as *Swarm* by Bruce Boone and Robert Glück's Black Star Editions. *Craquer* was published as a chapbook by Mary Burger's 2nd Story Books. Thanks to Kelsey Street Press for their permission to reprint several pieces from *The Rosy Medallions*: "BABY," "Fetish," "My X Story," and "Sex Life."

This book would not exist without the dedication of the editors Lauren Levin and Eric Sneathen. *Honey Mine* was originally their idea. At every step they were inspiring co-conspirators with invaluable advice. They have made the book better. I am more grateful than I can say.

My deepest thanks to Nightboat. The press has done amazing work, especially with New Narrative writers. *Honey Mine* being included on their list truly feels like home. I appreciate Lindsey Boldt's support and understanding throughout.

My mother always had a fierce identification with my writing, and I am deeply grateful for the permission this gave me. Her lifelong rule-breaking example has been a great legacy and another source of freedom.

Lastly, I would like to dedicate the book to my dearly beloved partner and wife, Angela Margaret Romagnoli. **You are with me always.**

Camille Roy's most recent book is *Sherwood Forest*. Other books include *Cheap Speech*, a play, *Craquer*, a fictional autobiography, *Swarm, The Rosy Medallions,* and *Cold Heaven*. She co-edited *Biting The Error: Writers Explore Narrative*. Recent work has been published in *Amerarcana* and *Open Space*, the SFMoma blog. She lives in San Francisco, California.

Lauren Levin is a poet and mixed-genre writer, author of the poetry collections *The Braid*, *Justice Piece // Transmission*, and *Nightwork*. They live in Richmond, California.

Eric Sneathen is the author of *Snail Poems* and *Minor Work*. With Daniel Benjamin, he edited *The Bigness of Things: New Narrative and Visual Culture*. His next poetry collection, *Don't Leave Me This Way*, is forthcoming from Nightboat Books.

NIGHTBOAT BOOKS

Nightboat Books, a nonprofit organization, seeks to develop audiences for writers whose work resists convention and transcends boundaries. We publish books rich with poignancy, intelligence, and risk. Please visit nightboat.org to learn about our titles and how you can support our future publications.

The following individuals have supported the publication of this book. We thank them for their generosity and commitment to the mission of Nightboat Books:

Kazim Ali
Anonymous (4)
Abraham Avnisan
Jean C. Ballantyne
The Robert C. Brooks Revocable Trust
Amanda Greenberger
Rachel Lithgow
Anne Marie Macari
Elizabeth Madans
Elizabeth Motika
Thomas Shardlow
Benjamin Taylor
Jerrie Whitfield & Richard Motika

This book is made possible by support from the Topanga Fund, which is dedicated to promoting the arts and literature of California.

In addition, this book has been made possible, in part, by grants from the New York City Department of Cultural Affairs in partnership with the City Council and the New York State Council on the Arts Literature Program.

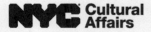

NYC Cultural Affairs

NEW YORK STATE OF OPPORTUNITY. Council on the Arts

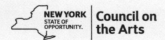